LOST FOR YOU

SIXTH STREET BANDS BOOK FOUR

JAYNE FROST

SIXTH STREET PRESS

Edited by: Patricia D. Eddy — The Novel Fixer
Proofreading: Proofing With Style
Cover Design: Pink Ink Designs
Cover Photo: Wander Aguiar
Cover Model: Tyler Harlow

JOIN THE TOUR

Drop by JayneFrost.com and sign up for the Sixth Street Heat Newsletter for opportunities to receive **Pre-Release Review Copies** of Jayne's newest books, exclusive content, and members only swag.

For Maria
Sometimes you meet someone as weird as you are, and you just click.
That's you :)

PROLOGUE

TARYN
FIVE YEARS AGO

A faint ringtone roused me, echoing off the walls in the loft. Indistinct. Generic. I pulled the blanket to my chin.

Go away ...

"Phone, babe," Beckett grumbled, his voice muffled by the pillow.

Groaning, I patted the nightstand, searching for the source of my annoyance. When I came up empty, I cracked one eye open and spotted my jeans next to the bed, my phone hanging out of the back pocket.

Teetering on the edge of the mattress, I snatched up the device and issued a groggy "Hello."

"May I speak to Taryn Ayers?"

The woman's voice, all business, filtered through the hum of conversation in the background.

As I settled against the pillows, the room spun from too much wine at dinner and too much Beckett for dessert. "This is she."

Beckett draped an arm around my waist, his thumb skimming my ribs. Smiling, I rolled over and brushed a thick lock of hair from his face. His lips quirked but he didn't move.

"Miss Ayers, this is the Travis County Sheriff's department dispatch calling."

The thick fog of sleep receded, leaving me fully awake. "Who?"

"Miss Ayers ... I'm a dispatcher with the Travis County Sheriff's Department."

Slowly, I rose to my elbow. "Yeah ... okay. What is it?"

Beckett's lids fluttered open and his cobalt eyes found mine.

"Miss Ayers, we got your name from Preferred Motor Coach. There's been an accident outside Fredericksburg involving a tour bus. Your name was listed as the point of contact."

Disentangling myself from the sheet, I sat up and scooted to the edge of the bed, my legs dangling over the side. "I'm sorry ... an accident? What kind of accident?"

"A semi-truck crossed the median and hit the bus at a high rate of speed. The survi ... the injured parties are being transported to Brackenridge Hospital via Care Flight."

Beckett's fingers brushed the base of my spine. "What is it, babe?"

When I didn't answer, his footfalls sounded on the hardwood. And then he was in front of me, moonlight from the floor to ceiling window framing his broad shoulders and illuminating the tips of his dark locks.

He needs a haircut.

Shifting my attention back to the faceless woman on the other end of the line, I cleared my throat. "But everyone's all right, though?"

After an eternity, she started to speak, but I couldn't process what she said. Everything after "I'm sorry" faded to white noise. And then, like a crash of thunder, her last words exploded in my head.

"... officers' on the scene reported two survivors and three fatalities at the crash site."

In front of me, Beckett crouched, his lips moving soundlessly as a tiny fissure formed in my chest. And then something shattered deep inside and the phone slipped from my numb fingers.

Beckett scooped up the device and began to speak, but I couldn't hear anything but the four-word refrain echoing in my head.

Two survivors ... three fatalities.

Beckett cupped my cheek. "Taryn ...baby ..."

"Hmmm?"

When I didn't look up, he slid his fingers into my hair and gently tipped my chin, forcing me to meet his gaze. "Baby ... you've got to get dressed now."

Tears rolled down his cheeks, and I tracked a tiny rivulet with my finger. "Why?"

Catching my hand, the crease in his brow deepened. "Why ... I don't ..." Clumsy fingers circled my biceps. "Here ... let me help you."

Wobbling to my feet, I yanked free from his hold. *"Why?"*

Beckett scrubbed a hand over his face. "Babe, I don't know why." He snagged my jeans from the floor and shoved them at me. "Please, just get dressed. We have to go to the hospital."

Two survivors and three fatalities.

A calm washed over me. Sweet relief. "It's a mistake."

"Taryn—"

"Listen to me!" Clutching his arm, my nails sank deep into his skin. "Don't you see? Rhenn, Tori, Paige, and Miles." Holding up a finger for every name I ticked off, I wiggled my digits. "That's four. It's a mistake."

Beckett crushed me to his chest. "Babe, it's not a mistake. We have to go now. Please."

Confused, I peered up at him, the placid smile wobbling on my lips. "But I just told you ..."

Taking my face between his palms, he rested his forehead against mine, anchoring us together. "Taryn, listen to me. There were five people on the bus. You didn't count the driver."

Chapter 1

TARYN

PRESENT DAY

*P*aige used to talk about fate. She believed in that shit.

"Everything happens for a reason," she'd say.

Of course, she didn't say anything now. Except to me. Don't get me wrong, I knew it wasn't her. But when I talked to myself, the voice in my head that answered was hers.

Sipping my drink, I stared out the window of the plane into the pitch-dark Texas sky.

This is where I felt closest to Paige, in that space between heaven and earth.

When you were careening through the air at five hundred miles per hour, defying the laws of nature, anything seemed possible. Even a conversation with your dead best friend.

"I signed an all-girl act today," I murmured into my next sip of vodka and cranberry.

Light bells of laughter that I'd know anywhere echoed in my head, and then that voice. *"Not as good as we were."*

Paige's memory always brought up the Austin Dolls, the all-girl group that Tori, Paige, and I formed *before* Damaged.

I snagged a couple of pretzels from the foil packet on the tray table. "They don't have to be good. They just have to be passable."

Like me.

While Tori and Paige were born with music in their blood, I had to work for every note. And hard work only got you so far when you were standing shoulder-to-shoulder with two powerhouse talents.

So, I'd stepped aside. It had saved everyone the awkwardness of asking me to leave. Tori had already hooked up with Rhenn, and the music they were working on ... well, it was magic. Paige was the only one who protested the demise of the Dolls. She would've been content to play the dive bars on Sixth Street with Tori and me forever.

Forever, as it turned out, only lasted twenty-four years. And if I had known how it was going to end, maybe I wouldn't have slipped into the background. At least Paige and Rhenn would still be alive.

"Quit thinking like that," I chided myself.

And in that moment, I had to wonder if that was the reason the voice in my head sounded like Paige. To assuage my guilt. Because if Paige forgave me, then maybe I could forgive myself.

The fasten seat belt sign illuminated, and the captain came over the intercom to announce our descent into Austin.

I tossed back the last of my drink. And the voice was quiet for the rest of the flight.

My phone vibrated as the Google Alerts continued to pour in.

A secret wedding for Beckett and Maddy?

Beckett parties in Vegas with supermodel, but where's Taryn?

Beckett leaves Taryn high and dry as settlement in Damaged case looms.

"Taryn?"

Dazed, I looked up and found Ethan, my driver, eyeing me in the rearview mirror. "Huh?"

Concern creased his brow. "Um ... we're here. Did you need me to take your bag upstairs?"

Glancing around, I realized that we were, indeed, parked in front of Bluebonnet Towers. I'd lost a good thirty minutes scrolling through the avalanche of stories that hit my phone before we left the airport.

"Um ... no." I shook my head. "I got it. Thanks."

As I moved for the door, Ethan twisted in his seat. "Listen, Taryn ... I'm sure there's nothing to any of those stories."

Ethan could barely look at me as he forced out the lie. He knew Beckett. What he'd become since the accident.

Schooling my features into a practiced smile, I pushed open the door. "No worries. We're not together. Haven't been for a long time."

It was the truth. I broke up with Beckett seven months ago after he moved to Los Angeles to record the latest Leveraged album—and hooked up with Maddy Silva. The funny part? Except for the sex, nothing much had changed. I was still his manager. Still the person he trusted most in the world.

Becks claimed Maddy was just a friend, but the photos of them in Vegas more or less blew that lie out of the water.

Waiting on the curb for Ethan to fish my suitcase out of the trunk, I scrolled through my messages, zeroing in on the one from Beckett. Expecting one of his long-winded excuses, I stared at the two words in the little box.

I'm sorry.

Ethan dropped my rollaway on the pavement. "Are you sure you don't need any help?"

Apparently, I needed a shit ton of help. Because I was fighting to hold myself together.

I'm sorry.

"No." I smiled that fraudulent smile. "I'm good, thanks."

Before I broke down right in the middle of Sixth Street, I waved, spun on my heel, and headed for the glass doors.

It wasn't until I was tucked inside my sixth-floor loft that I allowed the first tear to fall. Sniffling, I kicked off my shoes and wandered to the kitchen for some wine.

Propped against the counter with the glass in my hand, I finally opened Tori's message.

I'm up if you need to talk.

Of course she was. The girl rarely slept. And like me, she monitored the social media coverage of the bands we managed.

Well, some of them.

Twins Souls, the company we'd formed after Tori had recovered from the accident that almost took her life, was now the premier management company in the business with over a hundred acts on our roster. But only three mattered. Leveraged, Revenged Theory, and Drafthouse. The bands I'd handpicked and then propelled to the top of the industry to preserve the legacy Damaged left behind.

Reluctantly, I swiped my finger over Tori's name.

"He's an asshole," she blurted, not bothering to say hello. When I didn't respond, she added, "You know he didn't mean to ..."

Her thought trailed off as she grappled for words.

Swallowing my tears, I climbed the stairs. "To what? Get photographed? He's not cheating on me, you know?"

"Whatever," she grumbled. "He should be more discreet."

After wiggling out of my skirt, I dropped onto the unmade bed and closed my eyes. "Why? So he won't hurt my feelings? He's allowed to have a relationship."

"Relationship?" Tori scoffed. "Beckett's never had a relationship with anyone in his life except you."

The invisible string that tied me to my lost love tightened around my heart, and I wondered if Beckett still felt it. "Well that's not the case anymore." Sighing, I rubbed my tired eyes. "You're going to have to face facts sooner or later. We're not getting back together."

"Maybe not right *now*," Tori protested. "But he loves you."

My mouth dropped open, but instead of offering another rebuttal, I said, "I know. I love him too."

I brushed my thumb over the infinity tattoo on my ring finger, identical to Beckett's. We'd gotten them when we were eighteen. The ink was faded now, with small hairline cracks. But the symbol endured. Kind of like Becks and me.

Mollified by my confession, Tori said, "We should hang out tomorrow night. Grab some dinner and—"

Her sentenced died when she hissed.

Anxiety stiffened my spine, and I sat up. "What is it? Are you in pain?"

She managed a labored breath. "No. I'm all right."

The strain in her voice sent a fresh wave of panic crashing over me. Digging my iPad from my tote, I flipped to my calendar and, sifting through Tori's schedule, my heart squeezed.

"You saw Andrews on Tuesday?"

It sounded more like an accusation than a question.

"As a matter of fact, I did," Tori snapped. "Would you like to see the report?"

She knew I wanted to see the report. Which is the reason she waited until I was out of town to go to the doctor.

"I'm not trying to get up in your business," I said quietly. "I'm just, you know ..."

So many adjectives sprung to mind, I couldn't finish the thought. The two weeks Tori had lingered in the coma had been the worst in my life. I'd already lost Paige. And now, every time Tori's pain flared from the injuries that would never fully heal, I panicked. I couldn't lose her too.

"Yeah, I know," she finally replied, her tone considerably softer. "It's been a bad couple of days."

I should've cancelled my trip. Sent one of the junior managers traipsing across the continent.

Glancing at the clock, I chewed my bottom lip. "You should get some sleep. Maybe take a pain pill and—"

My heart leapt in my throat when Rhenn's voice, crooning "Down to You," echoed in the background. And then silence. Picturing Tori on her bedroom floor, sorting through all the old photos and memories, it broke me in places that had no bones.

Wobbling to my feet, I grabbed a pair of jeans from the floor. "I'm coming over."

"No," Tori said, emphatic. "I'm fine. I don't want you driving all the way out here in the middle of the night."

For the millionth time, I cursed Rhenn and his decision to build a house on the northern shore of Lake Travis. For years I'd begged Tori to leave the place. It wasn't even a home, more like a mausoleum. A monument to the life she'd never have.

Stepping onto the balcony, I breathed in the humid air and leaned against the railing. On the street below, people congregated, and I could almost hear the music.

After a long moment, Tori cleared her throat and then said softly, "I miss him so much, T. Sometimes I just want ..."

The anguish in her voice cut through the miles, and I could feel her pain so deeply it stole my breath.

"I know, Belle. Me too."

Her pet name slipped out, the one Rhenn bestowed on her when we were just kids. Lost in another place, we drifted like that for a long time.

When my lids got heavy, I went inside and crawled into bed.

"You want me to stay on the line?" I murmured.

Tori sighed contentedly, so I rolled onto my side, the phone still pressed to my ear. "Night, Belle."

Chapter 2

CHASE

*M*y fingers curled around the edge of my seat, thumbs digging into the marred wood. Anxiety slithered beneath my skin as I stared at the lectern in the front of the old church. Shifting my gaze to the cross behind the altar, I inclined my head, hoping for once that I'd feel ... *something*. Not that I didn't believe in God. But I'd never subscribed to the theory of ceding control to a higher power. At least in terms of my disease.

Disease.

I suppose it was. Thousands of twelve steppers couldn't be wrong, could they? But inside, I knew what I was. An addict. Recovering. Clean. A success by any stretch of the imagination. Still, I had a hard time believing that God, or whatever higher power existed, had a hand in my sobriety.

Eleven years ago, when I'd pulled myself from the pit of addiction, I did it on my own. Well, not completely. Vaughn had helped. Along with the counselors at the rehab.

I shifted my attention to the front row where all the newbies sat, looking around with wide, fearful eyes. I knew what they wanted. A cure. But there wasn't one. They'd always feel it. The itch.

At least they had family here. Most of them anyway. In the six months I'd spent in rehab my old man never showed his face. Not until the day I was released.

"They get you fixed up, boy? I hope so, 'cause the labels got a gig lined up."

And then Tyler Noble, standup father that he was, pressed a flask into my hand and told me to get over myself.

Jerking from my daydream when I felt a firm hand on my shoulder, I met Vaughn's liquid brown eyes. He leaned a hip against the pew. "It's been a while since I've seen you here," he said, surprise coloring his tone. "Glad you remembered the address."

Vaughn was one of the few people who could make me feel like a disobedient child. He saw past what I was now—the most successful land developer in the state, owner of two music venues and a handful of buildings and restaurants—and straight to the kid he'd found shaking under the blankets my second day in rehab. That was my rock bottom. I'd done some fucked up shit when I was using, but truth be told, I didn't care. After the age of twelve, I hadn't been sober long enough to care. I cared that day though. The fog had lifted just enough to reveal one truth—selfish as it was—I didn't want to die.

Adopting a relaxed posture, I slung my arm over the back of the pew. "Nice to see you too." I tipped my chin to the window in the sanctuary where three faces peered out from behind the curtain. "How's she doing?"

The she in question, Logan Cage's sister Laurel, had just finished a thirty-day stint in rehab. Today, she'd graduate. Which meant nothing, really.

Vaughn stroked his graying beard, thoughtful. "As well as can be expected. She didn't exactly come to the program of her own free will."

I chuckled. It had taken both Logan and me to drag Laurel to the facility, kicking and screaming. The bite mark on my arm had faded, but since Laurel had broken the skin, I'd always have a little memento.

When Vaughn shifted his feet, my smile withered. "What is it?"

He sighed. "Logan."

I'd known my brother's bandmate since he was a kid. Back then, I'd been too wrapped up in my addiction to pay much attention. And as soon as I got clean, I took off to California for three years to attend school and free myself from my dad's influence.

We were close now though.

Close enough that when Logan found Laurel in Nashville, strung out and swinging from a pole at a seedy strip club, he'd come to me for help. Begrudgingly.

"What about him?" I asked, studying Vaughn's face.

The aging counselor liked to put a positive spin on everything. But if you peeled back the layers, the old man had a shit ton of tells.

"He nixed the idea of sober living."

My brows shot to my hairline. "What?"

In the grand scheme of things, thirty days clean was nothing. It took months to get into the habit. To strengthen your mind enough to push aside the impulses.

"I'm not saying she can't do it," Vaughn was quick to interject. "Because she can."

There it was, that undying optimism.

Glancing around at all the faces, I did a mental tally. Of the forty or so addicts in the room, all but eight would relapse. And soon.

"The odds are against her."

Vaughn nodded, rubbing some imaginary crick out of his neck. "That's what I wanted to talk to you about. Is that loft in your building still empty?"

Crossing my arms over my chest, I cocked my head. "You mean the one above mine?" A smile curved Vaughn's lips, but I wasn't amused. I lived above a bar, for fuck's sake. "Do you really think that's a good idea?"

"Honestly, no. But it beats the alternative."

One look at Vaughn's face and I knew the other option on the table was worse. "Logan, right?"

My stomach sank when Vaughn offered a weak nod.

Logan didn't have any clue about the pitfalls facing his sister. He actually believed that rehab was the cure. But it was a first step, nothing more. A Band-Aid over a bullet wound.

"I'm not a babysitter."

Vaughn held up his hands in surrender. "It was just an idea. Let me go talk to Logan."

When Vaughn turned to leave, I pushed to my feet. "I'll go."

I checked my phone as I headed for the parking lot. We still had a half hour before Laurel would address the crowd. Plenty of time for me to convince Logan to get his head out of his ass. Sober living was the only thing that made sense.

Logan hopped to his feet when I entered the small courtyard. "Is it time?"

"Sit your ass down," I growled, closing the gap between us.

Talking to Logan usually required finesse. The kid was batshit crazy. But I didn't have the time or the patience. And something told me he knew that deep inside, I harbored a brand of insanity that matched his own.

Logan dropped onto the stone bench, a smile curving his lips. "What's up your ass?"

Resting a hip on the table, I crossed my arms over my chest. "Are you trying to fuck up Laurel's recovery?"

The smile faded, and hairline cracks formed in the frozen ponds of Logan's pale blue eyes. "Why would you say that?"

My focus shifted to his hands, balled into fists at his sides. But it wasn't rage I detected. It was fear. And as shitty as it was, I could work with that.

"What has Laurel told you about her addiction?"

Hoisting myself onto the table, I clasped my hands in front of me, and waited for Logan to reply.

He lifted his chin, trying and failing at indifference. "Doesn't matter. I know it was awful."

Tipping forward, I locked our gazes. "If it was so damn awful, baby sis wouldn't have been doing lap dances at twenty bucks a pop to feed her habit. And she wouldn't be thinking, right this very minute, that she'd rather be high."

"You don't know that," Logan snarled through clenched teeth, his top lip trembling from the effort.

I blew out a breath. "I do know that, bro. Because when I got out, I spent about fifty-five minutes out of every hour thinking about using."

Logan's shoulders sagged and his eyes drifted to the church. To Laurel. "What stopped you?"

"Those five minutes of clarity. Eventually they turn into ten. And then an hour. Pretty soon, a day."

"A day?" Defeat colored his tone, but I smiled at that.

Because it proved my point. Logan had no idea what the hell he was dealing with.

"You're seeing it all wrong. We just got to get her to ten."

Logan turned back to me, anguish coating his features. "How?"

"Well, Vaughn runs a really good sober living facility and—"

"*No.*" Logan bolted off the bench, shaking his head. "She's my sister. I'll take care of her. I'm not abandoning her again. Never again."

Whatever guilt had taken residency in Logan's head was not about to listen to reason. All he could see was the little girl who lived in his mind's eye. The one who got swept away.

With a sigh, I eased off the table. "Okay. It was just a suggestion. There's something else we can try."

Laurel wandered around the Starbucks, her fingers skimming every item on the shelves. In her free hand, she clutched her thirty-day chip like the piece of plastic could ward off every evil in the world.

A headache brewed behind my eyes as I moved forward in the slow ass line. Every caffeine junkie, wanna-be poet, and out of work musician on Sixth Street was here.

Laurel sidled up while I was checking my phone, a bag of chocolate covered espresso beans pressed to her chest.

"Can I have these?" she asked in a breathy tone, peering up at me
through her lashes.

Her smile wobbled when I pinned her with a blank stare. She
knew what I was—an addict, just like her. Gaming me was out of the
question. But I guess she wanted to test the boundaries.

I took the beans. "Anything else?"

"Can I have a caramel macchiato?"

I saw the faint hope in her eyes as she waited for me to reply, like
maybe I wasn't some douchebag who wanted a piece of her soul in
exchange for a lousy cup of coffee.

"Sure."

A flush rose on her pale skin as she pointed toward the patio.
"Thanks ... I'm going to go find Logan."

Shaking my head, I stepped up to the register and came face to
face with Shana.

Well, shit.

"Hey, Chase."

Forcing my lips to bend, I set the beans on the counter. "Hey
darlin'. Can I get two of the usuals and a caramel macchiato."

Pulling three cups from the stack next to the register, she fluttered
her eyelashes at me. "If you want the usual, you're going to have to
wait until my shift ends at three." Her voice dropped to a conspirato-
rial whisper. "And we can definitely do two."

I handed over my Starbucks card. "I'm busy today. Just the coffee
and the beans."

Shana pouted as she rang me up. A month ago that pout was cute.
She'd used it on me the night we'd hooked up at Nite Owl, the
smaller of the two bars I owned on Sixth.

Scribbling my name across the waffled sleeves, she arched a brow.
"I can always come by the bar tonight."

I shoved my hands into my pockets. "Sorry, I've got plans."

I'd told Shana that I didn't do the girlfriend thing before I bent her over the couch in my office. From the look on her face, that conversation had conveniently slipped her mind.

She didn't even pretend to hide her contempt when she shoved the card into my hand.

I dropped a ten in her tip jar and then strolled to the end of the counter. As I waited for my order, I wondered why I continued to hook up with women I met at the bar. But I knew the answer. At Nite Owl I was anonymous. Just a bartender who occasionally performed a set on the weekends. Women didn't expect much from *that* guy. On the other hand, if they knew I owned the Phoenix Group and was Cameron Knight's brother, things would get more complicated.

Tipping my chin to the dude who dropped off the coffees, I grabbed the tray and then headed for the patio to deal with the real issues.

Logan met my gaze when I dropped into my chair, his blue eyes beseeching.

Passing him a cup of coffee, I said to Laurel, "I forgot the Danish. You mind grabbing me one?"

Rolling her eyes, she pushed away from the table. "Sure. What kind?"

Since I wasn't going to eat it, I didn't give a fuck. "Surprise me."

Visibly relaxed, Logan reached into his pocket. "Hey, get me a pecan roll. Extra gooey."

Brushing away his hand when he held out a one-hundred-dollar bill, I offered Laurel my Starbucks card instead. "Use this. They probably don't have change."

She stared at the piece of plastic for a long moment, then looked me dead in the eyes. When I didn't waver, she chuffed out a breath and snatched the card from my hand. "Can I get one too, warden?"

Smiling, I eased back into my chair. "You can get anything you want. As long as you can buy it with that card."

Logan's lips parted, but I nudged his foot and he kept his mouth shut.

Once Laurel was out of earshot, he leaned forward and hissed, "What was that all about? You just made her feel like—"

"She's two hours out of rehab. Did you forget that?"

"What's that got to do with it?"

That part of Logan that wanted so badly to believe that Laurel was cured was clearly in command, so I took the opportunity to bring him back to reality.

"One time," I chuckled, shaking my head, "my mom gave me her last twenty bucks to go get something at the store. She didn't see me again for two days."

Logan sobered, shifting his focus to the plate glass window.

"It's too much temptation," I said quietly. "Trust me on that."

The anguish was back, etched into the lines on Logan's forehead. "I do trust you. It's just ... She thinks she's coming home with me. Maybe I could bring her over to your place in a couple of days."

Forty-eight hours at Logan's, and we'd be back at square one. "You've always got some Betty hanging around your loft. And more than a few of those chicks share Laurel's former vocation."

Logan frowned. "I don't date strippers anymore." A group of girls walked by our table, and Logan's attention drifted for a moment. "Unless they're working their way through college. Then I'm just doing my part for higher education."

He waggled his brows, and I snorted.

"You don't date at all. That's why it's better if Laurel doesn't see random chicks doing the walk of shame out of your bedroom."

Logan assessed me over his cup as he took a drink. "What about you? Aren't your little friends going to be put off having my sister one floor up."

I shrugged. "I don't invite women to my loft. So as long as Laurel stays out of my office, we don't need to worry about her running into anybody."

I'd tried the whole relationship thing a couple of years ago. One month into it and I was climbing the walls, but I gutted it out with Alyssa for another month to see if it would stick. The only thing that stuck was the impression I was being strangled with monotonous sex and endless chatter about our "future."

I blew out a breath and went on, "Look, it's not permanent. I've got plans for that space. It's just until Laurel gets on her feet."

Logan laughed. "So Cameron got to you, huh? Convinced you to spend a million bucks on a recording studio so he doesn't have to leave Lily to jet off to LA to lay down tracks?"

"My brother has fuck all to do with it. It's about Willow."

Surprise lifted Logan's brows, and I was a little shocked myself. When Sean, the band's drummer, first brought his little girl around, I kept my distance. Kids weren't my thing. But the little beauty stole my heart. And her daddy's too. Sean made it clear that he wouldn't do anything that kept him away from Willow and her mother for too long. And if spending a couple of bucks to build a studio helped ease everyone's load, I'd do it. Music was a gift. And no one should have to choose.

Expecting Logan to scoff, I lifted my chin. Instead he smiled thoughtfully. "That's cool. If anyone's worth that kind of scratch, it's Willow-baby."

I chuckled into my next sip of coffee. "Let's not get crazy. The studio's a good investment."

"What studio?" Laurel interjected as she reclaimed her seat.

Waving off the Starbucks card when she tried to return it, I replied. "The one I'm building above Nite Owl. But for the time being I've decided to clear out the space and let you stay up there."

Laurel snapped her gaze to Logan's. "I thought I was moving in with you?"

Sliding his chair next to his sister's, Logan leaned in close enough for their heads to touch when he spoke. "Don't be afraid. You're not doing this alone. I'll come over every day."

"It's not that." Laurel twisted her hands in her lap. "It's just ... I don't even have a TV. I don't mind sleeping on the floor, but ..."

Laurel's subtle manipulation worked like a charm, and Logan jumped to his feet.

"Best Buy first or Ikea?" he said, offering Laurel his hand.

Bolting from her seat, she threw her arms around her brother's neck. "Oh, Logan! Thank you!"

He hugged her tight as she peppered his cheeks with kisses, contentment supplanting the guilt for a moment. But Logan was sadly mistaken if he thought Laurel's problems could be fixed with a little cash. He'd learn that lesson soon enough, so for now, I wouldn't burst his bubble.

"You want to come with us?" Logan asked me as he fished his keys from his pocket.

"Nah." I rose from the chair and stretched. "I'm going to get a refill and head to the office."

Laurel glanced over her shoulder as Logan led her away, giving me a little wave.

What did you get yourself into?

Lost in thought, I wove through the maze of tables and past the knots of people standing around sipping their coffees. Thankfully, Shana was too busy chatting with a coworker to notice me placing my order.

At the pickup station, I slid a hip onto one of the stools and checked my email while I waited for my coffee. I smiled at the barista when she pushed the venti cup in front of me.

As I rose to my feet, warm fingers brushed my arm. "Excuse me, I think that's mine."

When I swung my distracted gaze to the voice, beautiful blue eyes the color of the hill country sky locked onto mine.

"The drink?" the girl said, tipping her chin to my coffee. "I think it's mine."

"Shit ... sorry." I tightened my grip reflexively when her fingers curled around the cup. "Have we met?"

Her smile evaporated. "I don't think so."

She was probably right. Because if we'd met, I'd remember.

Still holding firm to her cup, I brushed aside the déjà vu. "That's a shame."

An irritated sigh. "Can I have my drink please?"

The scowl was kind of adorable, though I don't think cute was what she was going for. Still, I was up for the challenge, so I offered her my free hand and said, "I'm Chase."

"Good for you."

Astounded by her ability to remain straight faced, I let go of her cup. "You know ... It's always nice to meet someone from out of town. Around here when someone gives you their name, it's customary to return the favor."

I had no doubt the girl was pure Texas. The drawl was a dead giveaway, along with the crimson staining her cheeks when she realized she'd forgotten her manners.

Tucking a strand of rich, brown hair behind her ear, she tried for a smile, but only managed the faintest curve of her lips. "Sorry. I'm just really tired. Jet lag."

Hoisting her backpack on her shoulder, she made to leave.

"You still didn't tell me your name." Holding up a hand when she narrowed her gaze, I pulled a card from my back pocket. "Okay, how about this ... you can tell me tonight when we meet for drinks."

Curiosity sparked in her eyes as she read the card. "Where's Nite Owl?"

I leaned against the counter, smiling. "Just down the road a piece. Are you familiar with Sixth?"

She choked on her sip of coffee, but quickly recovered. "Yeah, I'm pretty familiar."

She was familiar all right. Hauntingly. Maybe we could figure it out after the drinks. *Naked.*

I inched a little closer. "So, what time do you want to meet?"

As she pondered, I zeroed in on the name scrawled in black Sharpie on the waffled sleeve encasing her drink.

Taryn ...

Blinking, I searched her face for a long moment. "You're Taryn Ayers."

When she flinched, I realized it sounded like an accusation. Still, I waited to see if she'd correct me. But all I got was a forced smile. It was the saddest thing, those beautiful lips bending against their will.

Before I could respond, Taryn turned on her heel and headed for the door.

It should've ended there. Because it wasn't about me. It was about my brother. Cameron already had to overcome being Tyler Noble's son. But even my father never burned the bridges that I did in the industry. There was no unfulfilled six-figure contract with Tyler's name attached to it. And Tyler didn't overdose backstage at a concert venue.

But I wasn't thinking about Cameron when I followed Taryn out of the coffee shop. And my brother was the last thing on my mind when I caught up with her at the light on Congress.

"Taryn."

I wasn't aware that I'd said her name out loud until she swung her stormy blue eyes in my direction. And for a moment I thought fate would intervene and save me from myself. One word. That's all it would take. And I'd go.

But then she smiled, and the clouds receded from her gaze. "Yes?"

That wasn't the word I was looking for. "Yes" held all kinds of possibilities. None of them good.

Adrenaline coursed through me and I felt it. That rush I got when I crossed the line. Any line.

"So ... are we on for drinks at seven?"

Chapter 3

TARYN

TARYN

I glanced down at the card still clutched in my hand. Chase Noble. I wanted to get the guy's name right when I told him to go to hell. Of course, smiling would probably take some of the bite out of the nasty retort. And I *was* smiling.

Why was I smiling?

Pressing my lips into a firm line, I jabbed the button for the crosswalk. "I don't think so, Chase."

He took his place at my side as I waited for traffic to clear. "Maybe that's the problem."

I slanted my gaze to his. "Excuse me?"

He shrugged. "You think too much."

A response coiled around my tongue, but my phone vibrated in my hand, distracting me. I scanned the dozen new messages cluttering my screen. And if I wasn't in the middle of downtown, I'd swear I lost reception. Because I didn't remember hearing my phone go off once. Ever since I walked into the coffee shop, my thoughts had been occupied with other things. Like the guy next to me.

The light turned green, and I took a step, only to have Chase tug me back to his side. "Careful."

My response sailed away on a breeze when a bike whizzed by, crunching the leaves where I'd been standing.

Heat rose in my cheeks. "He was going the wrong way," I grumbled, watching the cyclist's spandex-encased backside weaving through traffic.

Chase had yet to let go of my arm so I gently tugged it free. "Well, thanks," I said, and after glancing both ways, I ventured onto the busy street only to have Chase fall into step beside me.

I gave him the side eye. "What are you doing?"

He shrugged. "Waiting the appropriate amount of time to ask you out again."

Biting down a smile, I asked, "And what's the appropriate amount of time?"

When we were safe on the sidewalk, he faced me. "I guess around five minutes if I hold true to form."

This time I couldn't hold back a laugh, but to my horror, it came out more like a snort. Shaking my head, I fished my keys from my pocket. "Well, this is me."

Chase took out his phone and glimpsed the screen. "I've still got one minute."

Amused, I leaned a hip against the trunk of my car. "I can save you the trouble and say no right now."

Breaching the small gap that separated us, he swept a lock of hair out of my face. "But you're not going to say no, are you?"

Recalling the way the light seeped from his eyes at the coffee shop when he found out who I was, my stomach tumbled. Whatever gave him pause, he'd merely overlooked it for the moment.

There was no smile, no humor, just sincerity when Chase said softly, "It's just a drink, Taryn."

A refusal formed on my lips. Because there was no good reason to say yes. But that's exactly what I said. I had to forcibly keep my hand from covering my mouth to hide my surprise.

Chase smiled like he knew it all along. "Great. I'll see you at seven."

Scampering for the safety of my car, I cursed my shaking hands and pounding heart. Adjusting the rearview mirror, I watched as Chase headed in the opposite direction, wondering why in the hell I'd just agreed to have drinks with a stranger. As soon as he was out of view, I realized that my phone was vibrating against my palm.

One look at the screen and my good mood evaporated. Ash Devonshire.

I considered sending the call straight to voicemail, but in a moment of white-hot anger, I swiped my finger over his name.

"What do you want, Ash? Haven't you caused enough trouble?"

A long sigh. "Taryn, if you'd just let me explain."

Shifting my focus to the crumpled copy of the *Austin Statesman* on the passenger seat, I hissed, "Explain? You were supposed to write a memorial series. A tribute."

"I agreed to write a series on the Damaged legacy," Ash replied calmly. "Like it or not, Beckett is a part of that."

"Did Maddy Silva join the group when I wasn't looking? Because most of this article is related to her. You fucking *interviewed* her." Sagging against the seat, my heart squeezed with the betrayal. "And you brought me into it. Why?"

"You're part of it, Taryn," he said quietly with zero conviction. "The legacy. Your relationship with Beckett."

"Don't play dumb, Ash. You're not some out-of-the-loop paparazzo."

Ash cut his teeth writing freelance articles for the underground newspapers covering the Sixth Street Music beat. After Damaged hit the scene, I gave him all the exclusives. Ash made a nice chunk of change selling articles to *Time*, *Newsweek*, and *Rolling Stone*. But Ash's real break came after the accident. I gave him the first interview. The hardest interview of my life.

Ash received an award for that piece and landed a cushy job as the Arts and Entertainment editor for the *Austin Statesman*.

"Listen to me," Ash growled, exasperated. "There are some things you don't know. If we could just talk."

"What things?"

I heard a door slam, and then the hum of the newsroom in the background. "Just meet me. We can't do this over the phone."

His plea touched a chord. A place inside that I reserved for a select few. Years of history, and I knew if we met in person, I'd soften to Ash's plight.

"I don't want to see you," I said, resolute. "It's not just about me. What about Tori? You know there's a media ban when it comes to talking about a Damaged reunion. And what did you do? You devoted three paragraphs to that shit! She's not going to get a moment's peace now."

"The story is out there!" he roared. "You're signing talent like a madwoman! I can't just avoid the topic. With the five-year anniversary of the accident coming up, everyone's speculating about a Damaged reunion."

A lump formed in my throat, hard and unyielding. "Don't you think a reunion might be a little difficult with Rhenn and Paige pushing up daisies at Oakwood Cemetery?"

Paige—the string that bound us. She loved Ash, far more than anyone ever knew. Their longstanding affair was another reason he had my trust and unfettered access to the bands I managed.

Ash sucked in a harsh breath. "Christ, Taryn. That was low."

Any small amount of guilt I felt for causing the obvious pain evaporated when my focus shifted to Maddy Silva's quote next to Ash's byline.

I found my soul mate.

Reflexively, my thumb skated over the infinity tattoo on my ring finger. "Lower than giving Beckett's new girlfriend three fucking pages of prime real estate in the *Statesman*?"

Ash cursed under his breath. "You don't know everything. You think you do, but you don't. There are still two more pieces in the series."

More? My stomach pitched at the thought of two more weeks of this.

"I don't suppose either of those stories includes an interview with Dylan—you know, the lead singer of the band? Have you forgotten about him? When he finds out you threw Tori out there, he's going to tune you up."

"No, he won't," Ash said wearily. "You'll feel differently once you see how it ends."

Resting my head against the side window, I gazed at the clouds gathering to the west. Storms always came in from the west, rolling through the small Texas towns bordering the hill country with their two-lane, undivided roads. Dangerous roads. Lightning struck in the distance, so faint it was merely a flash, lost in the gray morning sky.

"I already know how it ends," I said thickly.

Rhenn and Paige were gone. Tori was broken. I hadn't seen Miles in months. As for Beckett and me? Our love was the last casualty of the accident. Maybe it was only fitting that Ash cataloged our public demise.

Straightening in my seat, I let out a staggered breath. "Fine, Ash. You win. When and where? And don't even think about coming to Twin Souls."

A tension headache throbbed at the base of my skull when I thought of how Tori would handle this. The reunion show meant everything to her. To us.

Paper rustled in the background, and I rolled my eyes. Ash was the only person I knew who still used a Day Planner.

"Uh ... how about four thirty at the Driscoll?"

I was about to reply with a standard yes when I thought of Chase and our date. "Make it four."

Ending the call before Ash could reply, I slid my car into drive and then headed west toward Twin Souls. And the storm.

Chapter 4

CHASE

I skimmed the lyrics for the song I'd just composed. Not a song—a *ballad*. Written about a woman I'd spent less than ten minutes with. And not just any woman. Taryn Ayers.

Out of the corner of my eye, my laptop called to me. Reluctantly, I answered, hauling the device onto my lap. I stared at the Google search box with Taryn's name, and in a moment of weakness, I hit enter.

A neat row of Taryn's pictures populated the screen. Foregoing the gallery, I opened her wiki page. Easing back against the cushions, I scrolled through the article, astonished at her accomplishments.

When I got to the bottom of the page, my fingers hovered over the touch pad.

"Damaged Accident and Aftermath."

Blowing past the photos of the wreckage from the crash, I went straight to the aftermath.

Clicking the first link, a photo of Taryn and Beckett Brennin on the roof of Breckenridge hospital with the Care Flight helicopter in the background appeared. It was like peering in on the worst day of someone's life, frame by frame. Beckett looked shocked. But Taryn?

The way her legs were bent slightly and oddly angled, just a little off, it was apparent she wasn't standing of her volition.

How the fuck did someone have the insensitivity to take these pictures?

Disgusted, I moved onto to the next photo. Taryn in a black dress at the double funeral service at St. Mary's Cathedral. Kneeling at the altar with her small hand flat on Paige's white casket, she gazed upward, tears streaming down her face. She looked like a shattered angel.

"Jesus ..."

Unable to stomach another photo of Taryn with vacant eyes and pale skin, I skipped to the article that delved into the inquiry of the accident. The National Transportation and Safety Board found Xtreme Modifications solely at fault. But in the court of public opinion, Taryn was hung out to dry.

I did another quick search but didn't find one statement from Taryn defending herself.

"Hey, bro," Cameron said as he entered the room. "What are you doing here?"

I blinked at him. "Uh ..."

He flopped down next to me and leaned in to catch a peek at my screen

"Porn?" He smirked.

Rolling my eyes, I slammed the lid. "I prefer my women three dimensional. And I *am* working. I had a crew here all day cleaning out Laurel's new digs."

He pulled a face. "You're really going to let her live here?"

"You make it sound like she's going to be sleeping in my bed. She's living upstairs."

Hopping to my feet to shake off the images of Taryn with vacant eyes and pale skin, I headed to the fridge. Pushing aside the six-pack of beer, I opted for water. At twenty-nine, with eleven years clean, I knew my kink. *Drugs*. Any and all. Still, when I first got out of rehab, I didn't drink for years, and even now I didn't drink often.

Since I wasn't sure of what weapons Laurel used to fight the big monsters, I'd need to lock up the alcohol for the time being. Keep it out of her reach.

"What are you doing here so early?" I asked, holding out a can of Dr. Pepper for my brother.

Confusion lined his brow. "It's three o'clock. Band practice?"

Shit ... I'd wasted hours writing the song and obsessing about Taryn. I was good at obsessing. Not that it hurt me any. I made it through Stanford in three years instead of four and then I built the Phoenix Group from nothing to a thriving enterprise in seven years.

Still, it unnerved me, the way I couldn't stop thinking about Taryn.

I reclaimed my seat. "Guess I lost track of time. Where's the rest of the crew?"

"Christian's running late. And Sean had to pick up Willow from speech class or something. He'll be here any minute." Cameron took a drink as he peered at his phone. "I saw Logan unloading all the shit he bought for Laurel."

When I saw the concern darkening my brother's hazel eyes, I sat forward. "What kind of stuff?"

He glanced at my wall of electronics. "The kind that are easily pawned. Xbox. Flat screen. Stuff like that."

Cameron had seen me at my worst, when I was willing to sell the coat off my back, or his, for a fix.

I took a sip of water to wash away the sour taste of guilt. "Keep your views to yourself until there's something to worry about," I warned. "I've already talked to Logan. Don't get between him and Laurel. I'll handle it."

Cameron pressed his lips into a firm line when Logan exited the freight elevator, wiping sweat from his brow. "It's fucking boiling out there." Looking between Cam and me, he narrowed his eyes. "What?"

"Nothing," I replied. "Where's Laurel?"

"Upstairs trying to figure out her new TV."

I scowled when Logan plopped onto the white sofa with his dusty jeans and dirty hands. Unfazed, he snatched my water bottle from the table and downed half the contents before offering it back to me with a smug smile.

"Dude, I have no idea where that mouth has been."

Grinning wider, he waggled his brows. "Well ... if you really want to know ... there was this Betty I met last night at the—"

"Spare me," I grumbled, my focus on the notepad of unfinished lyrics. "I meant to ask, are y'all making any headway getting your audition with Twin Souls?"

Totally self-serving dick move, and I was all about it. Which was a little concerning since blatant manipulation was something I'd left behind a long time ago.

Logan's face fell. "Hell no. You remember when I told you about that memorial concert, the one that Twin Souls is planning for the fifth anniversary of the ... um ... thing?" When I nodded, he continued, "Well Sean read an article in the paper yesterday, and it's definitely on. I guess Taryn is focusing all her energy on that."

A prickle of awareness danced over my skin. "Taryn? I thought you were trying to get a meeting with Tori."

Cameron snorted a laugh. "Seems Tori doesn't handle the talent. Logan over here has been working the wrong partner."

Logan lobbed his empty bottle at Cameron's head, and when my brother threatened to respond by dousing his friend with Dr. Pepper, I didn't even flinch. I was too busy thinking about what wooing Taryn entailed.

Ambling to the kitchen and opening the fridge, my hand hovered over the water, but the beer beckoned, so I grabbed a bottle. Loitering near the island, I took a long sip and then asked Logan, "Have you talked to Taryn?"

Invited her out for a date? Dinner and a night of sweaty sex?

Who was I kidding? This was Logan. Dinner was a stretch.

He shrugged noncommittally. "Not yet."

Since I was only half listening when Logan told me about the concert, I scratched my head. "Where exactly is the show taking place?"

"Zilker Park, if you believe the rumor mill. So it won't be any time in the next few months. Not with Austin City Limits in September."

Months ...

If I planned it right, I could scratch the itch with Taryn and be nothing but a memory in "months." It's not like I ever got involved with the band's management. Cameron understood my reasons for never mixing with the music industry folks. The pain it caused. And the risks.

Christian walked into the room, Sean a step behind. With a smile, I grabbed a Starburst from the table and wandered over to Willow, curled in her daddy's arms. Pressing the candy into her tiny hand, I earned a giggle from the little princess and a glare from her father.

My brother hopped to his feet and stretched. "Want to go jam with us?"

I patted Cameron on the back on my way to the couch. "You go ahead. I wouldn't want to show you up."

The guys crowed, but Cam merely shrugged, an easygoing smile tilting his lips.

Grabbing my laptop, I waited until I heard the faint footsteps two levels above before opening the lid. I chided myself for my itchy fingers as I clicked on another photo of Taryn.

Sad blue eyes filled the screen. And those lips, struggling to maintain a fake smile. A lyric popped into my head, so I paused to jot it down.

You wear the summer in soft blue eyes. A bittersweet sky, tainted with lies. Let me end your season of pain. Dry the tears that fall like rain.

Satisfied with the sappy sentiment, I closed my browser.

Taryn would be here in three hours. Anxiety and excitement warred at the prospect of seeing her. I sucked down the rest of the beer and forced myself to answer some emails.

Chapter 5

TARYN

A little before one o'clock, I stepped off the elevator on the third floor of the Driscoll Hotel. Tugging at my pencil skirt, I made the trek down the long hallway, cursing the sky-high Louboutins pinching my toes.

On the off chance that Ash invited a staff photographer to memorialize our meeting, I wanted to look professional. Which was a joke, really, since I'd negotiated some of the most lucrative deals in the music industry wearing jeans and a T-shirt.

Arriving at the double doors, I tucked an unruly strand of hair behind my ear and then rang the bell.

Ash greeted me with his usual lopsided grin. "Thanks for coming, Taryn."

Despite what he'd done, I fought the urge to return the smile. Ash wore the same sadness in his eyes that I saw when I looked in the mirror. And I knew it was because of Paige.

"Let's get this over with," I said, brushing past him. "I've got to get back to the office."

I hadn't told Tori where I was going. With the press camped out like vultures at Twin Souls, she had enough on her plate.

Pausing in the living room, I looked around. A single Tiffany lamp in the corner provided sparse light, and the drapes were secured tightly over the windows.

Whirling around, I glared at Ash. "Are you trying to set a mood? We're not on a date."

"Stand down, T-Rex," came a gruff voice from the shadows. "The suite was my idea."

My heart stuttered as I turned to the sound.

"Dylan ... ?" In answer to my question, the table lamp next to the couch flicked on, and Dylan's gray eyes found mine. "What are you doing here?"

My voice was small. Reed-thin. Because I didn't want to know what Beckett's bandmate was doing in a room with a reporter from the *Statesman*. All signs pointed to one thing: damage control.

"Come here," Dylan said.

My feet obeyed the command without question. Because it was Dylan. We'd known each other since my first day of junior high when he'd followed Beckett and Rhenn to our table in the lunchroom. That was Dylan's way. Not exactly shy, but unobtrusive. Even after Rhenn died, leaving Dylan to step up and lead the band I'd positioned to take the spot Damaged left behind, he'd never truly embraced the fame. He'd hung back, like always, allowing Beckett to claim the lion's share of the spotlight.

When I made it to the couch, the lump in my throat doubled in size. Shadows occupied the space under Dylan's eyes, and worry lines bracketed his mouth.

He pushed to his feet, and then strong arms banded around me. "Jesus, it's good to see you."

Nodding against his chest, I mumbled, "Does Tori know you're here?"

"Not yet." With a final squeeze he pulled away and, taking my hand, he dropped onto the cushions. "Sit down. I need your help with something."

Recalling the last time Dylan had asked for my help, I froze. And then I was back there, in that room inside the funeral home with all the empty caskets, holding Dylan's hand with numb fingers.

"I'm thinking the black for Rhenn." Dylan had turned to me then, tears spilling onto his cheeks. *"But I need your help picking one out for Paige."*

The memory slipped back into that shadowy place, and I did as Dylan asked, easing onto the cushion next to him.

Dylan blew out a breath and then said to Ash, "Go ahead."

With a grim nod, the reporter walked to the flat screen and inserted a thumb drive. After handing Dylan the remote, he sank into a wing chair and clasped his hands, his gaze fixed on the floor.

I wanted to run, but when I tried to do just that, Dylan's palm came down just above my knee.

"It's okay," he said, sounding anything but sure. "Just watch."

Grainy footage flickered to life on the screen, and a throaty female voice boomed from the speaker.

Yes ... baby ... fuck me.

When the girl's face came into view, my mouth went dry. Harper Rush, the singer I'd scouted in Biloxi three months ago. Her long, dark hair spilled over her shoulders as she bounced up and down, and I almost believed she didn't know she was being taped. But then she looked straight into the camera and smiled.

So far, I'd avoided looking at her partner. The face wasn't visible. But the thick, wavy brown hair on the pillow was familiar.

My heart slammed against my ribs, knocking the wind out of me.

Beckett and Harper? On tape?

This isn't happening.

Jerking my gaze to Dylan, I pleaded, "Turn it off! Please ... Dylan ... turn it off."

Gaze locked on the screen and an iron grip on my leg, he shook his head.

And then Harper's companion spoke.

"I'll fuck you all right. Turn over."

My head whipped to the screen in time to see the couple reverse positions. And it was Dylan's gray eyes shining in the low-resolution light. Muttering a string of curses, he pounded into Harper, twisting a hand into her hair. The camera got a nice shot of her face when he yanked the long strands, and her head snapped up. Just when I thought it couldn't get worse, Dylan squeezed his eyes shut and tipped forward, releasing Tori's name on a groan.

Dylan hit a button, and the image froze. For a long moment, he didn't say anything, his gaze fixed on the screen.

"There's more," he finally said. "But you get the gist of it."

Questions filled my head, but I didn't know where to start. As bad as the sex tape was, it could be weathered. Dylan was single, and a rock star. But a tape of him whispering the name of his dead best friend's wife? That bell could never be un-rung.

"Were you two ... you and Harper," my voice cracked, and I cleared my throat, "involved? I mean ... the tape, did y'all ... ?"

"I was drunk," Dylan roughed out. "I only slept with her once, and I didn't know she was taping it. I didn't ... I didn't know what I was saying."

He let out a staggered breath and then hung his head, likely to hide his eyes. But there was no need. Dylan's unrequited love for Tori was the worst kept secret in our group. Everyone knew it. Even Rhenn.

Rubbing my arms to ward off the chill that came out of nowhere, I turned to Ash, confused. "Where do you fit in?"

He cocked his head, regarding me with wounded eyes. "Harper contacted me, and I met with her. She showed me the footage. And then I called Dylan."

"Who else has seen this?" I asked, a sudden panic rising in my throat. "Who else besides—"

"Just us," Dylan replied. "Harper wants momentum for her new album. So she thought she'd get the tape out there. But after Ash told me, I threatened her—"

"You what?" I screeched, hopping to my feet.

"Legally," Dylan growled. "I'm not that fucking stupid. I told her ... I offered ... *fuck* ..."

He tipped forward, braced his elbows on his knees, and then buried his head in his hands. Reclaiming my seat, I rubbed small circles on his back. "What did you offer?"

"I said that you'd manage her. That you'd do for her what you did for us. She agreed to turn over the tape if she gets a contract with Twin Souls and her album takes off."

Stunned, my hand fell to my side. "Dylan ... it's not ... it's not that easy."

With all the moving parts, the chances of pulling this off without someone finding out were pretty slim. If the label got a hold of the tape, they'd release it for the publicity alone.

"Are you sure she hasn't shown it to anyone else?" I asked. "Someone at the label?"

Dylan shook his head. "No, I convinced her that Metro wouldn't release the album if she put the tape out."

"It's only a matter of time, though," Ash chimed in. "Harper's not the sharpest tool in the shed. But she knew what she was doing, coming to me. She expected me to release the tape. And I told her I would."

Incredulous, my mouth dropped open. "You what? How could you?"

Ash fixed me with a glare. "Did you want her to go to somebody else? I told Harper I had something more salacious in the pipe. Then I threw together that bullshit story with Maddy and all the stuff about the reunion show. I was only trying to buy us some time."

Sitting back, I absorbed the magnitude of what Ash said. It made sense. Any story about Beckett and me would draw the public's attention long enough to do whatever needed to be done with Harper Rush.

As if he could read my thoughts, Ash said, "There was no time to get your input. I finished writing the story two hours before it went to print, after we agreed that there wasn't another play."

We?

"Who's we?" I asked thickly.

Dylan released a slow, controlled breath. "I told Beckett about the tape after Ash did the interview with Maddy. He didn't know beforehand. But then he agreed that it was the best way."

While I sat reeling at the thought of my best friends tossing me to the wolves, Ash plucked a folder from his briefcase. "Beckett had a couple of conditions, though."

With a shaky hand, I took the file, spilling part of its contents onto the floor. When I reached down and picked up a handful of photos, my heart squeezed. Melting into the cushions, I sifted through the pictures of Beckett and me from the Sadie Hawkins Dance in the eighth grade. And the ones from the trailer that Beckett and I moved into when I was seventeen. Tears stung my eyes when I came across an image of us in front of the Welcome to Las Vegas sign.

Clutching the long-forgotten memories, I opened the file and glanced over the neatly typed notes.

Taryn is my heart.

Infinity and beyond.

My one true love.

Phrases jumped from the page, each one clawing at the door to my soul I'd closed on Beckett. I kept reading, even after the lines blurred together.

Shoving the past back into the folder, I turned to Ash. "What is this?"

"It's the rebuttal Beckett insisted on for Maddy's interview. Look it over so I can get your response. He wants it out there as soon as possible."

My response? I swallowed hard, smoothing my hand over the file. Sweet words and pretty lies about a future we'd never have and a painful past I wanted to forget. "One thing at a time, Ash. Let me concentrate on setting up a meeting with Harper first."

Dylan shoved to his feet, visibly relaxed. I guess transferring the burden to my shoulders lightened his load.

As if he'd just noticed my outfit, he smirked. "Guess we're gonna have to pick someplace fancier than a barbecue joint for dinner tonight."

"Dinner?" I asked, confused.

"Yeah, I figured I'd go by the office and surprise Tori. You know she's going to want to do dinner." He ambled to the mirror, combing a hand through his long hair. "We should rent out a back room somewhere and get everyone together. You can arrange that, right, T-Rex? Who all's in town?"

I blinked at Dylan. It was one thing to assume that Tori had no plans. She spent her free time with me and her memories. But I wasn't her.

Dylan spun around when I didn't reply. "T-Rex?"

"Oh ... um ... let me think." I rattled off the schedules of all twelve members of the Big Three. Because, of course, I knew them. When I was finished, I grabbed my purse and pushed to my feet. "Let me know where y'all want to go, and I'll make the reservation. But I'll have to pass."

Dylan slung his arm around me and brushed a kiss to the top of my head. "You can take a night off. You're the boss, remember?"

I peered up at him and forced a smile. "It's not work. I've got a date."

Chapter 6

CHASE

Eyeing the crowd at the door of the bar, I placed five beers on the tray for Megan, the waitress working the floor.

Garnishing the Corona's with limes, she mused, "I can't believe it's so busy. It's only seven, and I haven't even had time to take a pee."

Bridgette, my bar manager, looked up from her paperwork and said, "Are you complaining, Megs? You're working the prime station tonight. But if it's too much, Lainey can pick up some slack."

Megan's cheeks flushed pink. "No, of course not. I'm just not used to being this busy when Chase isn't playing a set."

She smiled at me, her liquid brown gaze lingering on mine for a moment longer than necessary. Sure, I was the boss, but in this industry, that didn't preclude a little after-hours fun. And Megan had made it abundantly clear she was down for it.

I glanced pointedly at her tray. "Nobody likes warm beer. Better get those delivered."

"Oh … yeah. I'll just …Yeah." Cheeks flaming, she turned on her heel and scampered away.

Bridgette sighed and tied on an apron. "If you weren't playing undercover CEO, the waitresses might leave you alone."

Bridgette was one of the only staff members at Nite Owl who

knew I owned the place. I'd hired my brother's high school girlfriend years ago when I bought my first restaurant on Sixth, and now she ran most of the day-to-day administrative operations for both my bars.

I wiped my hands on the towel draped over my shoulder. "I'm more worried about them following me upstairs."

"Because you're so damned irresistible?" Bridgette scoffed. "Give me a break. You and your brother both think women are only after one thing."

Raising a brow, I leaned a hip against the bar.

"Jesus, Chase. I meant a *commitment*." Bridgette drew out the last word and watched me flinch. Satisfied with my reaction, she continued, "Most of these girls are just in it for a quick and dirty. And that's all good. Telling them you own the place probably wouldn't change that. Believe it or not, these," she pointed to her tits, "don't automatically lower our IQ. Women have goals beyond finding some dude to take care of them."

Maybe all the zeros in my bank account did play into my overall fear of motive. But one look at my mother was proof that money wasn't the deciding factor. Callie had followed my father around like a puppy since they were teenagers, giving him two sons and all the love he could ask for. And Tyler never returned the favor. I couldn't stand him, but deep in my heart, I feared we were alike in more ways than one.

I brushed a kiss to Bridgette's temple as she poured a draft beer from the tap. "Thanks for the advice. I'll take it into consideration."

She placed the pilsners of Miller Lite on the tray, shaking her head. "No, you won't. Do you want to deliver these, or should I?"

Following her gaze to the other end of the bar, I forced my lips to bend, returning Tiffany's finger wave with a curt nod.

"Fuck," I muttered. "I didn't see her down there."

"Looks like she brought a friend to sweeten the pot," Bridgette chortled. But when I busied myself wiping a spot off the clean bar like it was my sole purpose in life, she cocked her head. "I'm guessing the Doublemint twins aren't on the agenda tonight."

My eyes drifted to the clock, then the door, scanning the small crowd huddled around the bouncer. "No. I have a ... thing."

Bridgette hoisted the tray. "You really need a wingman. I'm tired of being a traitor to my own kind, running interference for your many admirers. You don't pay me enough for that."

I barked out a laugh. "I pay you plenty, Bridge. And I'm not asking you to run interference. I'm honest with every chick I ..." A sardonic smile curved her mouth as I struggled for the word. "Date," I finally managed to choke out.

"Taking a woman to your office to rattle the walls is dating?" She flounced away, calling over her shoulder, "Good to know."

My focus returned to the front door, and my heart jumped into my throat when I spotted Taryn offering her ID to Seth, my bouncer. I ogled her unabashedly, from the skinny jeans hugging her curves to the silky ivory blouse to the strappy sandals.

God, she had a great ass.

And then I noticed the gorilla beside her snaking an arm around her waist. Even from this distance, which I cut substantially when I slid out from behind the bar, I could see the leer on the dude's face and Taryn's elbow against his stomach. I called to Seth, who seemed more interested in examining Taryn's ID than dealing with the asshole dry humping her leg, but the bouncer didn't hear me over the steady beat of the music pouring from the speakers.

Bridgette's hand shot out, grabbing my arm as I passed. "Chase, what's going on?" Her gaze followed mine to the skirmish. "Let Seth handle it."

I shook off her grip and pushed forward.

"That's really sweet of you," I heard Taryn tell the gorilla as I neared. "But I'm meeting someone."

A laugh rumbled from low in the guy's chest. "That's okay. The more the merrier. We'll find your friend and make it a party."

Catching the guy's wrist, I wrenched his arm behind his back. "What if her friend isn't interested in partying?"

The kid shrieked, "Ouch! Let me go. I didn't do nothing."

I shoved the kid in Seth's direction, scowling. My bouncer was lucky I had my hands full, or his arm would've been the one I was about to break.

"What's your name?" I asked the kid wiggling to free himself from my hold. "Calm the fuck down and tell me your name."

The kid quit squirming long enough to wheeze, "Jake."

"Well, I'd say manhandling a lady qualifies as something, Jake," I growled. "Ask Seth here for your cover charge back and then use it for a cab to carry your ass home."

"He's got a friend, boss," Seth advised as he retrieved some cash from the lockbox.

Jake nodded vigorously. "Yeah, a friend. I've got a friend."

The kid had a pleading tone as if he were trying to convince me there was someone inside the club that would report this incident if he did, indeed, go missing.

Releasing Jake's arm in favor of a strong hold on his neck, I nudged him toward the door. "Wait outside, and someone will send your friend right out."

"Yes, sir. I mean ... thank you ... sir," Jake stammered.

And then he was off, lumbering toward the exit with a couple backward glances to make sure I wasn't following. When I turned my attention back to Taryn she was biting her lip to keep from laughing.

I wasn't amused. "Are you okay?" I tilted her chin so I could examine her face. "Did he do something to you? Touch you?"

"No. It's fine. He was just drunk." A nervous bubble of laughter tripped from her pretty lips. "It's my fault. I forgot my cash, and I couldn't get in without paying the cover."

My gaze snapped to Seth. "What?"

He held up his hands. "She wasn't on the list, boss."

"I'm not talking about the cover," I growled. "That dude was pawing her, or didn't you notice?"

Warm fingers trailed down my arm. "Are you under the impression I can't take care of myself?" Taryn asked.

I blew out a breath and returned my attention to Seth. "We'll talk later. Put her name on the list."

"Got it. Karen, right?"

Taryn shifted her feet. "No, it's, um ... Taryn."

I could see the exact moment when Seth put it together. His eyes widened, and his shoulders straightened. He no longer registered my presence because all of his focus was on Taryn. "Shit ... I didn't recognize you." He slid off the stool to get a better look. "You're her ... You're Taryn Ayers."

The small crowd waiting to turn over their cover charges went quiet, and Taryn dropped her gaze to the floor. "I ... um ... *Yeah*."

At the subtle shift in energy, I pulled Taryn to my side. She kept her head down as I spun us toward the main floor. When we emerged on the other side of the bar, I ushered her through the door marked No Admittance and into the hallway that led to my loft.

"I shouldn't have come," she said, her breath uneven. "Do you have a back entrance?"

I rounded on her, and when I caught sight of those eyes, impossibly large as she blinked up at me, I couldn't help myself.

My mouth crashed into hers, my tongue demanding entry as I maneuvered her against the wall. Her lips parted on a gasp. But then her hands were in my hair, and it was all hot breath and soft moans. And fuck, the taste. Like strawberries fresh from the vine.

"Fuck, you're sweet." My palms glided up her sides, inching towards her breasts. "I knew you'd be sweet."

Her little pants warmed the hollow of my neck. "So are you."

I stroked her jaw with the pad of my thumb, and even in the dim light, I saw the flush color her cheeks.

"One more taste."

It wasn't a question. More like a vow. One more taste and I'd peel her off the wall. One more taste and we'd go get that drink I'd promised. One more taste and I'd be able to control myself.

My lips ghosted over hers. But this time it wasn't my restraint in question. Taryn levered up on her toes, and twining her fingers into my hair, she pulled my mouth to hers. Frustration poured off of her as she fumbled to find her rhythm.

Cupping her cheek, I broke our connection. "Easy, Taryn ... I'm right here."

When our lips met again, our tongues tangled in perfect sync. As we fell deeper into the kiss, one thought rolled around in my head. I wanted Taryn in my loft. In the one place she shouldn't be. The craving won out, like I knew it would. "Come upstairs with me?"

Smiling, she whispered, "What's upstairs?" as if it were a secret. And maybe it was. Because I sure as fuck couldn't tell anyone.

"My loft."

She inclined her head, a funny smile curving her lips. "You sleep here?"

"And shower." Twirling a lock of her hair around my finger, I grinned. "And watch TV. Cook, on occasion."

Taryn's gaze shifted unknowingly to the door to my loft. To the place where I wanted her.

I dipped low and whispered in her ear, "Say yes."

And to my amazement, she did.

Chapter 7

TARYN

*C*hase held my hand as he led me up the narrow staircase. Despite our hot and heavy make-out session in the hallway, my stomach churned with apprehension.

Are you really doing this?

A one-night stand.

Throughout my career, I'd seen more walks of shame from hotel rooms, tour buses, and broom closets than anyone should witness in three lifetimes.

But I'd never had one. I was a *relationship* girl.

My already queasy stomach dropped when I thought about where that had gotten me. All the years I'd wasted with Beckett.

You think too much ...

Chase was right. Very wise for a guy who lived above a bar.

I glimpsed his ass as we climbed. With a body and a face like his, he could afford to be a free spirit. He didn't have to spend much time in his loft with a room full of women downstairs who'd give their eye teeth to take him home.

We topped the stairs, and Chase flicked a switch, flooding the space with light. "You hungry? I could call the kitchen and order some appetizers."

He let go of my hand, and I swayed in my spot as I gazed around. I'd expected a dank space with empty cases of liquor and a mattress on the floor. But *this* was not that. Three white, overstuffed couches in the living area cupped a theater-sized flat screen. A formal dining table with hand carved clawed feet that seated ... twelve? My breath hitched when I spotted the alcove lined with bookcases that went up, and up, all the way to the twenty-five-foot ceiling.

And in the gourmet kitchen with all the gleaming stainless-steel appliances stood Chase, hands in his pockets, watching me.

"You hungry?" he repeated.

His features were schooled into a mask, and I couldn't tell what he was thinking.

"I ... uh ... yeah, I guess."

I guess?

I sounded like a teenager. Biting my lip, I twisted the strap on the wallet attached to my wrist.

Chase inhaled a controlled breath and then slid around the island, his boots echoing like thunderclaps off the high ceiling as he closed the gap between us.

"What's the matter?" he asked.

Five minutes ago, I was ready to jump Chase in the hallway, but I flinched when he took my hand. If he noticed, he didn't show it, placing a feather light kiss to each of my knuckles.

"Talk to me," he urged as he laced our fingers and pulled me toward one of the sofas. I sank down next to him, and he slipped my wallet off my wrist and tossed it onto the table. "Now, what's up?"

"Nothing." I stared down at our joined hands. His were large. Not rough exactly, but not smooth. Capable. "I'm just ... this is a really nice place."

"Thank you."

A nervous laugh bubbled up. "It's not what I expected."

Chase dipped his head, searching for my eyes. Reluctantly, I lifted my gaze.

"What did you expect?" he asked, a small smile tugging his lips.

God, those lips.

"I don't know. You're a bar manager."

It was his turn to avoid eye contact. Wrapping a strand of my hair around his finger, he examined the curl. "Actually ..." He looked at me then, searching my face, "I own the place. The bar and the building."

I felt my brows rise. "Oh ..."

He tugged the wisp of hair coiling his finger, smiling. "You got something against bars?"

"No. Not at all."

"Bar owners?" he persisted, inching forward. I shook my head, too enthralled by his voice and his eyes to form a verbal response. "Guys with tattoos?"

That startled an honest-to-goodness laugh out of me. "No."

But then he knew that. Chase knew everything about me, or at least he could without much effort. A Google search would yield anything from my kindergarten picture to a photo of me cussing out a photographer in the middle of Whole Foods.

I frowned, and Chase tipped my chin with his index finger. "There's that look. You thinkin' again, Sweet Taryn?"

My shoulders slumped, and I wondered how he did that—read me so well. "Yeah, I guess I am."

A victory smile curved his lips, and he moved in slowly. "We can't have that."

His hand molded to my waist as he dropped a kiss to my lips. I opened for him, and our tongues tangled and twined. And then I was on my back, against the most comfortable heap of pillows I'd ever felt, with Chase on top of me.

"Fuck, you are sweet," he rasped as he worked the buttons on my blouse. Not all of them. Just enough to expose my bra.

Chase scored his teeth down my neck to the tender flesh overflowing the sheer, lace cups. And then lower. When his mouth clamped around my nipple, I sunk my fingers into his hair, and he groaned in appreciation.

Heat pooled in my belly, and I rocked against him. "Chase ..."

My brows dove together when I heard the echo. It wasn't my voice though, but definitely female.

Chase heard it too because he cursed and propped up on his palms.

"Bridgette!" he roughed out through clenched teeth. "Don't take another fucking step!"

"Sorry," he said to me as he pulled me upright and then began to fumble with my buttons.

I brushed his hands away, my cheeks on fire. "I got it."

Cursing, he pushed to his feet and stomped toward the stairs. Hushed voices drifted up as I stood on wobbly legs to smooth my jeans and tuck in my blouse. If there were another exit, I would've used it. My focus shifted from the floor to the ceiling, to the windows, and I briefly considered jumping.

Chase reentered the room, and to my horror, a redhead trailed behind.

Oh my God. *He's married.*

But the woman didn't seem angry. She was smiling. At me.

I blinked up at Chase, startled when his hand slid to my nape. "I'm so sorry. I've got a thing ... downstairs. Can I get a raincheck?"

My gaze shifted back to the smiling redhead. His *thing,* I assumed. "Of course."

Before I could bolt, he brushed a feather light kiss to my lips. "So fucking sweet."

"Boss?" came a small voice, and Red smiled when we both looked her way. "I'm going to go downstairs. I can't leave Megan in charge of the bar."

"Yeah, go," Chase replied, barely able to contain his agitation. "I'll be there in a few."

"She works for you?" I asked when we were alone. "She's not ..." Inclining his head, he narrowed his gaze and waited for me to finish. "Your girlfriend?"

"I don't have a girlfriend, Taryn. I don't really ..." I held my ground while he fumbled for the words to let me down easy. "I'm not good at relationships."

"Neither am I."

A beat of silence, and then Chase pulled me close. "One more taste."

He wasn't really asking. But it didn't matter. I gladly reciprocated, opening for him when his lips touched mine. Because I knew what this was. Not quite a brushoff. But a missed opportunity.

My chances of seeing Chase Noble again were slim. So I took the little bit he offered and tucked it away with the other could've beens.

Sitting in my car in the underground parking garage in my building, I frantically searched for my clutch wallet. After one final sweep of the floorboards and the backseat, I came to the inevitable conclusion that I'd left the damn thing in Chase's loft.

Shit.

I dug my phone from my back pocket, then realized that I didn't have Chase's number.

With a frustrated sigh, I headed the three blocks to Nite Owl. Miracle of miracles, I found a space out front. Since I still didn't have any cash, I hoped Seth the bouncer hadn't gone home for the evening.

To my relief, he was still at his post. When the big bruiser saw me marching up, he was all smiles. "Back so soon?"

Unfortunately.

I gave him a little shrug as I passed.

The bar was packed four-people deep, but I spotted the redhead from the loft a mile away.

Inching between two occupied barstools, I waited to get her attention. Her eyes widened when she saw me.

"Taryn." She gulped. Visibly.

She was doing that deer in the headlights thing, so I took the opportunity to glance at her name tag.

"Hi, Bridgette." I smiled, willing her to focus. "I left something in Chase's loft. I know he's busy, but can you get him for me? Just for a second."

Bridgette's head tilted in a peculiar way, her brows drawn so close together they formed one red slash above her confused green eyes. "Um ... I can't right now. You know ... he's ..." She pointed her finger at the ceiling.

I looked up, as if Chase might be hovering above the bar Mission Impossible style. Then I heard it. His smooth voice pouring through the speakers mounted to the rafters.

The fuck?

I swung my gaze to the small stage, and there he was, under a single spotlight, crooning into the microphone. His fingers moved effortlessly across the fretboard as he strummed the worn six string, a perfect marriage between the wood and the flesh. Few people found that balance. Beckett. Paige. A handful of others that everyone knew by name.

And that voice. Mesmerizing. Pitch perfect.

I vaguely registered Bridgette calling my name as I pushed through the crowd, then managed to secure a spot in the shadows at the corner of the stage. Regardless of where I stood, I knew I'd be anonymous. Nothing was visible to Chase beyond the borders of the single spotlight.

The small crowd cheered enthusiastically when he finished his song.

A woman in the audience shouted, "I love you, Chase!" and like someone well accustomed to living in the light of the darkness the stage provided, he smiled in the general direction of the voice, and said, "I love you back, darlin'."

Applause rose up, and Chase adjusted the strap on his guitar, grinning wider.

"I've been working on some new stuff recently. Let's see what y'all think."

As he plucked the opening chords, my focus shifted to the guitar.

A Fender Concert Series. The instrument was at least fifteen years old and as seasoned as the man playing it.

Maybe our chance meeting wasn't chance at all?

As the truth sank in, I committed each feature of Chase's face to memory. Even if he offered nothing more than a good time, I wouldn't see him again.

Back at the bar, I flagged Bridgette down. "Could you do me a favor?" I picked up a pen abandoned next to someone's credit card receipt and then jotted down the address for Twin Souls on a cocktail napkin. "Can you tell Chase I left my wallet in his loft and have him mail it here?"

She looked down at the napkin, confused. "Sure, but he'll be finished in like fifteen minutes. If you want to wait, have a drink, I'm sure he wants to see you."

I'm sure he does too.

My nails dug into my palms as I balled my hands into fists. "No. That's okay. Just have him mail it. Thanks."

As I spun to leave, I ran straight into the guy behind me. Cold beer breached the rim of his cup, dousing my shoulder before trickling down the front of what used to be my favorite blouse.

And ... it was official; the night couldn't get any worse.

Mumbling an apology, I headed for the door, leaving Chase's velvety smooth voice and handsome face in my rearview mirror.

Chapter 8

CHASE

*S*weat from the performance trickled down my back.

"I don't understand." I blinked at the address on the napkin, then up at Bridget. "Taryn was here?" Bridgette chewed her lip, staring at the scrap of paper in my hand. "Just tell me what the fuck she said."

Bridgette was still salty about the way I'd talked to her before the show. But, shit, she was the one who barged into my fucking living room.

Lifting her gaze, Bridgette peered at me with glacial green eyes. "She came in for her wallet. I guess she left it in your loft. But then she saw you on stage and got pissed off and left."

I rolled my head to get out the kinks in my neck, and when that didn't work, I swiped a bottle of Gentleman Jack from the top shelf.

As I poured three fingers into a rocks glass, Bridgette propped her hip against the bar and said, "When I saw Taryn in your loft, I thought maybe Logan and Cam finally wore you down—convinced you to use some of your connections to get them that introduction at Twin Souls they've been angling for. But after I saw you kiss her, I got the feeling it wasn't business."

Scanning the crowd over the rim of the glass, I ignored her question for as long as I could. But the girl was relentless. I finished my drink, and she still hadn't moved an inch.

Pouring a second shot, I sighed. "Nope, not business."

Bridgette sucked air through her teeth, shaking her head. "Then I'm assuming you fed her the standard 'I'm only a bar manager' line?"

Bridgette walked the razor's edge of insubordination on a regular basis. Usually I didn't mind. But I wasn't about to stand here and let her dress me down in my own bar. On the clock, no less.

"Let it go, Bridge."

Since I was the one that needed to let it go, I crumbled up the napkin and stuffed the wadded paper in my pocket. Whatever was between Taryn and me—crazy attraction, fascination, lust—it was over now.

"You should've known that wouldn't work on her," Bridgette mumbled.

Blowing off my glare, she flounced off, taking the expensive bottle of bourbon.

Fuck this.

I ducked out from behind the bar, heading for my loft at a good clip, but my phone buzzed, slowing my steps. A message from Calista, the sober companion I'd enlisted to help with Laurel. Logan may not have agreed with transitional living, but this was non-negotiable. And since I trusted Calista with my life, she was the natural choice.

Dropping Laurel off. The kid is a handful. Refused to go to a meeting.

"Fuck," I growled and then nearly tripped over the leg blocking my path. Glancing from the shapely calf to the bronzed thigh, I drank in the ample cleavage spilling from her body-hugging tank top.

Tiffany.

"Hey, darlin'," I said.

Her lips curved into a welcoming smile around the straw of her cocktail. "Great set." She nudged the empty chair with her foot. "Have a drink with me?"

I'd always enjoyed the cat and mouse with Tiffany. Even pictured her mouth wrapped around my dick on a couple occasions. But tonight, nothing stirred below the belt.

I flopped onto the wooden chair and looked around, hopeful. "Where's your friend?"

If Tiffany couldn't get the job done, maybe a double shot was what I needed.

"She's around." Her foot brushed the back of my denim-clad calf. "Did you want me to find her?"

Bridgette picked that very moment to stroll up to the table. She slammed a rocks glass in front of me. More Jack I assumed from the color of the liquid.

"Figured you might need this."

I met her furious gaze with a smile. "Thanks, darlin'."

Exasperated, she flounced off.

"Friend of yours?" Tiffany asked with a smirk.

I picked up my drink, my gaze roaming over Tiffany's tits. I could clearly see the outline of two pebbled nipples straining the thin fabric of her camisole.

Well, fuck me. Why not?

"I have friends," I slipped my free hand over hers, "and I have *friends*. Bridgette's not that kind of friend. Know what I mean?"

Tiffany licked her lips. "I know exactly what you mean. Why don't you finish your drink and we'll go find Amber?"

A night with Tiffany and Amber sounded like the kind of distraction I needed. She shivered as my palm skimmed up her arm.

I tipped forward, and we were eye-to-eye. "You read my mind."

What the actual fuck are you doing?

Less than fifteen minutes ago, I was headed out to the parking lot at Nite Owl with two very willing women. Then, inexplicably, I waved down a cab and hustled them into the back seat.

Now, here I was in the lobby of BlueBonnet Towers being scrutinized by the night watchman.

Phone wedged between his ear and shoulder, he fanned himself with Taryn's license, smirking.

Blowing out an exasperated breath, I glanced at his name tag while I drummed my fingers on the marble desk.

Murphy.

"Sorry to bother you, Mr. Morales," Murphy said to the head of building security. "I've got a Chase Noble trying to access the mainframe to speak to a tenant. Says he works at the Phoenix Group."

Even if I hadn't heard Javier's roar, I could pinpoint the exact second my head of security delivered the news. Murphy's face went ghostly white, the smile dropping from his lips.

Pulling the receiver from his ear like the plastic was burning his skin, Murphy held it out for me. "He wants to s-speak to you, Mr. Noble."

Mr. Noble? Ten seconds ago, I was pond scum. If I were a betting man, I'd place a hefty wager that the security guard now knew he was standing in front of the owner of the whole damn building.

Murphy swallowed hard, his gaze darting to the tattoo on my forearm. A phoenix rising from the ashes. The same insignia etched on the door of the building. And engraved on the brass insert between the elevators. And on his paycheck.

Lifting the phone to my ear, I rested my elbows on the marble counter while a string of apologies raced across the line from Morales.

"Javier ..." Ignoring me, my head of security continued to splutter. "Javier, *enough.* Murphy was just doing his job." I pinched the bridge of my nose as the chatter continued. "No need to get all worked up. I don't have my badge. Don't apologize."

I handed the phone back to Murphy while Javier's squawking continued. Murphy stared at the receiver, unsure.

"Just hang up," I said. "He'll be at it for the next five minutes, at least."

Stunned into silence, Murphy followed my order.

"I meant what I said. You were just doing your job." Handing Murphy my Nite Owl business card, I glanced over his red face and no-nonsense crew cut. "But hear me on this: there are plenty of people in Austin that don't look like typical ..." Millionaires? Moguls? Every moniker screamed arrogance. "Businessmen. We have a lot of artist types in this city. So don't judge a book by its cover. You hearing me?"

Murphy nodded, and I was a little afraid the dude might keel over, so I continued, "If Javier gives you any shit, you call me. You didn't do anything wrong."

Murphy ran a hand over his short crop of spiky hair. "Yes, Mr. Noble. I'm sorry. I—"

"No worries. If you can just call Ms. Ayers and announce me, please? Tell her I have her wallet."

Murphy glanced at the screen. "She's in 6F. Just turn right when you get off the elevator. It's the fifth door."

I leaned across the desk. "I don't care if the president walks through that door. You never allow anyone onto that elevator without being announced unless they're on the tenant's approved list. Or I'll fire your ass myself. We crystal on that?"

Speechless again, Murphy nodded.

My bravado melted away as he pressed the button for 6F. After all this trouble, I'd look like a total whack job if Taryn refused to see me.

Gripping the edge of the desk as Murphy explained the situation to Taryn, I waited for the verdict.

He set down the phone with a smile. "She said to go on up."

I didn't let out the breath I was holding until I reached the sixth floor. Pausing in front of 6F, I pulled Taryn's little clutch from my back pocket.

Before I could knock, the door swung open. My greeting caught in my throat as I glanced over the silk robe tied loosely at Taryn's waist. Miles of creamy skin from her neck to her navel begged for my touch. Or my tongue. I was still debating the options when she folded her arms over her chest, blocking my view.

"How did you know where I lived?"

I leaned against the doorframe. "Driver's license."

Zeroing in on the little studded coin purse in my hand, Taryn made a grab for the wallet. "Thank—"

"Hold on." Catching her hand, I slid her arm behind her back. "Why did you walk out of the club that way? You couldn't wait fifteen minutes?"

"If you wanted me there, you would have asked me to stay."

She was right, of course. But as I stared into her stormy eyes, I couldn't figure out why I'd ever wanted her to leave. With her body pressed to mine, everything else seemed inconsequential.

"My bad."

Hurt flashed across her features like a lightning strike. "You don't have to keep up this game anymore, Chase. I get it."

"I have no clue what you're talking about."

She chuffed out a breath. "Just give me your demo. I'll pass it on to one of the junior managers."

Her hand landed on my chest, fisting my shirt. Did she want to let me go or hold on tight?

A whole lot of wishful thinking, and I opted for the latter, pulling her closer. "I'm kind of insulted that you'd pawn me off on a junior anything. But lucky for you, I don't hold a grudge. And I'm not in the market for a manager."

It bothered me more than I'd like to admit that Taryn didn't appreciate my music. Before any of her clients ever dug their way out of the dive bar scene, I had an agent, a manager, *and* a record deal.

She narrowed her eyes. "You expect me to believe someone with your talent has no interest in the music business?"

Taryn flung the words like a javelin. Definitely not a compliment.

Still, I smiled. "I can assure you, I have no interest in the music business. I don't have a demo, and the only deal I'm interested in is whatever will get you out of that robe."

Ghosting my lips over hers, I worked my way to her cheek and then to her ear. Fuck, she felt good. Too good.

"You want me to leave, Taryn? I'll leave." I flicked my tongue over her earlobe. "Tell me to go."

Is that what I wanted—for Taryn to tell me to leave? It's what I needed. The girl was a craving. An all-consuming flame. For me, that was dangerous. If I weren't fairly certain that once I buried myself in her sweet body the hunger would subside, I might've been worried.

Her fingers trailed my jaw, but I tipped my head back. "Not good enough. You gotta say it."

"Don't," she croaked.

Sliding my hand to her thigh, I hoisted her to eye level. "Don't leave? Or don't stay?"

She blinked. "Don't leave."

Something in her tone threw me a little. Vulnerability? Uncertainty?

"Are you sure?"

Quit trying to talk her out of it, you stupid fuck.

Breathy, she whispered, "Yes."

And I couldn't resist any longer. I buried one hand in her hair and tilted her head at just the right angle. A chaste kiss to her lips, and then I moved down and down until my face was buried in the crook of her neck. Rain. She smelled like the rain.

"Just a taste," I murmured.

And when she arched, pressing those perfect tits against me, I stepped inside with her in my arms. Into the storm.

Chapter 9

TARYN

*C*hase kicked the door closed, trapping the rest of the world on the other side. He wasn't part of my past or my future. Only my present. A stitch in time not tainted by everything that came before. And for once, that was enough.

At the foot of the stairs, Chase's hands slid to my ass. "Hold on tight, Taryn. Don't let go." I slanted my gaze to his and found that same hesitation I saw earlier. Or maybe not, because a second later we were climbing.

As he eased me onto the bed, he pressed a kiss to my lips and then rumbled, "Tell me what you want."

I didn't know what I wanted. And why was he asking?

"I ... um ..."

Palming my breast, his thumb circled my nipple until it rose to a painful peak. "You want my mouth here?"

I nodded, sliding my hand into his hair.

His palm skimmed lower to the juncture of my thighs. "How about here?" Chase nudged my legs apart, and then his fingers dipped inside my panties and, ghosting his lips over mine he asked, "What about here?"

I lost the ability to think, let alone speak, when he pushed a finger inside.

"Say it, Taryn. Tell me you want my mouth right here."

He added another finger and began to thrust, his thumb grazing my swollen clit.

"I want ... Oh ... fuck ..."

My response died on a moan when Chase claimed my mouth. His kiss was hungry, possessive, and his tongue kept perfect rhythm with his fingers as he stroked.

Molding my hands to his shoulders, I held on tight when he found a spot inside my body that sent all the blood rushing to my head. "Chase ... I'm going to ..."

He kissed his way to my nipple, and when he scored his teeth along the pebbled peak, I fell to pieces, grinding out my release on his hand.

"Fuck, Taryn," he growled. "I can feel you coming."

Embarrassed, I pressed my head into the pillow. I'd never flown apart like that so easily.

Chase's mouth continued to explore along my ribs and over my stomach. And then he was there.

I peered down with a hammering heart. "Chase ... what are you ...?"

Our eyes locked as he dragged his tongue along my inner thigh. "Tell me to stop, and I will."

His gaze was all intensity and fire and want. He wanted this. *With me.*

"Don't stop."

The groan that ripped from my chest when his tongue flicked over my clit echoed off every wall. And then Chase dove in with wild abandon, one arm coiled around my leg and those talented fingers thrusting deep inside me again. When I started to soar, his teeth joined the party.

"Oh God ... Oh *God* ..."

My back bowed, and I called his name, shattering under his

touch. When the euphoric haze receded, I found Chase watching me, a hint of that victory smile curving his lips.

He pressed a kiss to my hip, and then to each breast, and finally to my mouth. "You ready for me?"

Was I?

Don't think ...

His words from this morning quieted my thoughts, and everything outside this room melted away. Wrapping my legs around his waist, I took what he had to offer.

Oblivion.

Chase rolled onto his back, panting, and I heard the snap of latex as he pulled the condom off. I snorted a laugh when he tossed it into the trash. "Good shot."

I had no filter after sex, and normally that was fine. But I didn't know Chase, and my brand of humor wasn't always on point.

He laughed, though, and tugged my arm, urging me toward him.

Sprawled on his chest, I peered up with heavy lids.

"The calm after the storm," he said as he ran a lazy hand up and down my spine

"What does that mean?"

Though I didn't think there was a universe where Chase could pull off shy, that's just how he looked.

Tucking one arm behind his head, he shrugged. "You remind me of these storms up by where my grandparents used to live. The sky would turn all colors of blue and gray." Tilting my chin, he smiled. "Like your eyes. And then the rain would come. Warm rain. That's what you smell like."

Sifting my fingers through the dusting of baby fine hair on his chest, I sighed. "I guess I can live with that. Where is this magical place?"

"Stonewall. Right off 290. It's outside of—"

A boulder landed on my back, steeling my breath. "I know where it is."

As I fought to untangle our limbs, Chase caught my wrist. "What is it?"

Even with the blood pounding a thunderous beat between my ears, I heard myself say in a calm voice, "Nothing. I just ... I need the bathroom."

His eyes stayed on me as I shrugged into my robe and hurried to the bathroom.

Stumbling to the medicine cabinet, I searched the shelves for the outdated prescription.

I sank onto the side of the tub with the bottle in hand and tried to pry off the safety cap.

"Fuck."

My trembling fingers wouldn't cooperate, and I squeezed my eyes shut.

"Need some help?"

Jerking my gaze to the door where Chase stood propped against the frame, I swallowed hard. "No."

The word came out as a strangled rasp.

Chase contemplated for a moment before slowly pushing off the wall and, crouching in front of me, he curved his hands around my bare thighs. "Let me help you, baby."

Help? He couldn't help. Nobody could.

"You can't," I whispered.

Deft fingers gently pried the bottle from my grasp, and then Chase pushed to his feet and wandered to the sink while I focused on the swirling patters in the tile floor.

He returned with a glass of water. "Here."

I scowled when he popped the cap off the bottle with ease.

"Stupid bottle," I grumbled.

He pressed an orange pill into my palm and knelt in front of me. "I'm sorry," he said, brushing the hair out of my eyes. "I know the accident was on 290. I just ... I wasn't thinking. I forgot."

Swallowing the pill, I nodded. "So did I."

And I had. For a minute, or ten, I'd forgotten the one thing that was always with me. I'd forgotten Paige. And that could never happen.

When I got up the courage, I met Chase's concerned gaze. "It's been a long day. I think I should get some rest."

I waited for him to exercise the out clause, but instead, he started rooting through the bottles of scented bubble bath on the ledge surrounding the garden tub.

"What are you doing?" I asked when he turned on the faucet.

"Drawing you a bath. Warm, hot, or extra hot?"

"Um ... hot, I guess."

After pouring a liberal amount of thick, purple liquid under the stream, Chase shoved to his feet. "Towels?"

The medication calmed my nerves but did nothing for the embarrassment. I didn't want Chase's pity. The sooner I got into that tub, the faster he'd leave.

"I'll get it," I said as I wobbled to my feet.

When I returned from the linen closet, Chase was seated on the edge of the tub, a smile tugging his lips. "Are we going to share that, or are you expecting me to air dry?"

"Huh?"

He stalked toward me. "I guess we'll share."

Slipping an arm around my waist, he urged me toward the tub. Lingering above the sweet smell of gardenia wafting from the frothy bubbles, I could smell Chase all around me.

He smelled new.

New?

Fucking pill, messing with my head.

"Do you need help with that?" Chase asked, dropping his gaze to my fingers coiled tight around the sash on my robe.

"No. I got it."

Fumbling with the tie, I stole glances at Chase's Adonis-like frame when he turned to adjust the water. Mesmerized by the Celtic knot inked on his shoulder, I shuffled forward.

His stilled as I traced my finger over the script woven inside the intricate design.

Soul Bound.

Hope Drowned.

Redemption Found.

"Who said that?" I asked.

He slid his boxers off his hips and then stepped into the tub, sinking into the cloud of bubbles. "I did. Now come here."

I pondered for a moment, staring at his outstretched hand, and then I slipped my robe from my shoulders and joined him.

"Fuck."

The audible groan tumbled out unbidden, and Chase laughed, pulling me flush against him.

"I like your dirty mouth."

I snorted, my head dropping to his shoulder. "You think I'm bad? You should hear Belle."

Soft lips brushed my temple. "I have no idea who that is."

Shocked, I sat up and slanted my gaze to his. "Really?" He shook his head. "Oh … it's uh … Tori."

He nodded, and rather than pepper me with questions, which I kind of expected, he shifted his focus to my shoulder and smiled. "This is beautiful." He ran his palm over the tribute etched on my skin—two birds soaring above a pale gray sky toward a brilliant sun. "Does it mean anything."

It meant everything.

"It's for … *them.*"

I waited the requisite three seconds to see if Chase needed further explanation before slumping into my former spot. The steady rise and fall of his chest loosened the stone over the place where my deepest thoughts resided.

A silent tear slid down my face, falling into a cloud of bubbles.

"Do you think death has a quota?"

"A quota?" Confusion laced his tone. "I don't understand."

"I was supposed to be on the bus that night, did you know that?"

I heard him swallow, absorbing the news, the thing they never published in the papers.

"No," he said quietly.

"So if three people were supposed to die that night," I continued, "maybe if I had been there, Paige would've lived. Or Rhenn."

Chase's arms tightened around me. "There is no quota. It was their time. Their destiny."

Tears clogged my throat, but surprisingly, I controlled the torrent. "Do you believe in heaven?"

Chase blew out a breath. "I suppose I have to. Since I know there's a hell, there's got to be a heaven."

Inclining my head, I looked up at him. "If there is a heaven, do you think they're together?"

He tucked a stand of wet hair behind my ear. "I think so, baby."

Nodding, I rested my cheek on his chest. "Me too."

After a long moment, Chase ran his hands over the goose bumps on my arms. "You cold?"

Numb, that's what I was, thanks to the pill. After a time, I began to drift and Chase brushed his lips over my ear. "Let's get you out of here."

I let him pull me up and then swayed in my spot while he made quick work of patting me down with the fluffy towel.

After my robe was securely in place, I mumbled, "Thank you ... I'm going to go to bed."

Someone really needed to write a manual on the proper way to say goodbye after a one-night stand, because this was awkward as hell.

Tucked under the covers, I waited for Chase to emerge from the bathroom. But my heavy lids had other ideas.

When I finally heard him rooting around for his clothes, I murmured. "Th-thanks for everything, Lock ... lock the door when you leave, okay?"

The mattress dipped, and strong arms banded around me.

"Are you trying to get rid of me?"

No.

But all I could manage was a sigh.

Soft lips brushed my shoulder. "Sleep, pretty girl."

And even though I knew it was probably some sense of misguided chivalry that kept Chase here, that's just what I did.

Chapter 10

CHASE

*B*linded by the sunlight pouring through Taryn's window, I reversed our positions and pulled her on top of me.

When did the sun come up?

The question floated away as she groaned and picked up the pace, riding me into the ground.

"Fuck, slow down, baby," I growled. "I can't ... I can't stop."

Palming her breast, I pinched her nipple to drive her over the edge when I felt her inner walls start to clench around my cock.

She tipped forward, her palms flat on my chest and her eyes screwed shut.

"Yes ... yes ... I'm coming. Chase ..."

Burying my face in the crook of her neck, I breathed in the sex and sweat clinging to her skin. And me. I was all over her.

"Right here, baby."

She shattered, and like the hurricane she was, she took me right along with her. When the storm passed and our breathing was the only sound in the quiet room, the magnitude of my fuck up settled on me like a five-hundred-pound weight.

Staying the night was a mistake. A mistake I could've corrected by leaving before Taryn woke up. But instead, I roused her from her sleep and buried myself in her sweet body like a man possessed.

She rolled off me and then threw her arm over her eyes, groaning, "When did the sun come up?"

Laughing, I pressed a kiss to her pouting lips and then climbed out of bed. "At dawn."

"Hmm," she mused and, rolling onto her stomach, propped herself up on her elbows and looked out the window. Caramel highlights shimmered in her hair, some trick of light I assumed. Either that or the two rounds of epic sex elevated her to sainthood.

Shaking my head, I ducked into the bathroom to dispose of the condom.

When I returned, Taryn was in her robe, that damn phone attached to her ear, pacing. "I don't care what it takes, Harper. You've got the ticket. Get on the damn plane. If you're not here by three, the deal is off. I'm not negotiating."

She ended the call and then tossed the phone onto the bed, glaring at it like it was a venomous snake.

"Everything cool?" I asked as I laced my boots.

She jerked her gaze to mine, a smile curving her lips. "Oh, yeah. Everything's good."

I pushed to my feet. "You've got a great poker face. But these lines right here," cupping her nape, I smoothed the tiny wrinkles around her mouth with my thumb, "they give you away."

"And you're an expert in frown lines?"

"No. But I've negotiated my share of deals."

Since there were no accidents, my slip of the tongue could only be blamed on one thing. I wanted to see Taryn again.

She picked up the breadcrumb I offered and replied, "What kind of deals?"

I blew out a breath and looked around. "This building for one. When I bought it, it was in foreclosure. Just an old warehouse. But the bank didn't want to let it go."

Chancing a peek at Taryn's face, I paused and let it sink in. Likely, she had no earthly idea whose name was behind the corporation who owned BlueBonnet Towers. And even if she decided to check, which she would, there wasn't much to find. A simple LLC in the name of the Phoenix Group, owned by a larger holding company, Nobelesque. Since she knew my name, the pieces would fall into place.

She sank onto the bed, circumspect. "The Phoenix Group owns this building." Her gaze flicked to the tattoo on my forearm, a phoenix rising from the ashes. "You own the Phoenix Group?"

"Yes."

Her brow arched impossibly high. "And you work as a bartender?"

I laughed. "No, darlin'. I tend bar at Nite Owl, the bar I own. I don't freelance."

Her lips wobbled as she tried to keep from smiling. Since I didn't intend on telling her anything else for the moment, I pounced, dropping a kiss to her mouth as I eased her onto the mattress. "You laughing at me? Bartending's honest work."

She twined her fingers into my hair, pressing her lips together. "Not laughing," she said when she got herself under control. "I'm just wondering how many other hidden talents you have. Do you juggle?"

"As a matter of fact ..."

The front door slammed and she jerked to her elbows. "What the hell?"

Thundering footsteps sounded on the stairs. "Taryn! Are you here?"

Shooting to her feet, Taryn fumbled to secure the wrinkled sheet under her arms. "Don't you dare come up here!" she hollered a second before Beckett Brennin stormed into the room.

Skidding to a stop, his gaze floated from Taryn to me and back to her.

"What the fuck is going on?" he roared.

Since I wasn't sure if the asshat was talking to me, I rose to my full height. Brennin wasn't small, over six feet by a hair, but the couple inches I had on him gave him pause.

"What are you doing here?" Taryn asked with enough surprise in her tone to let me know she wasn't expecting him.

"I live here."

Brennin looked straight at me, and it was like fate had stepped in to save me from myself. But if that were the case, why did I have the urge to wring the fucker's neck until he took it back?

In the few seconds that elapsed, the precious time I could've spent hauling ass for the door, Taryn found her voice. It was small, but emphatic, with a warmth around the edges that made me see red.

"You don't live here, Becks. You haven't lived here in months."

Brennin leaned against the doorframe, his cool façade at war with his clenched fists. "I haven't been in town for months, Taryn. But the last time I was here, I slept in *that* bed."

Our eyes met and his cool demeanor crumbled. "Now why don't you get the fuck out of here and let me talk to my girl."

I had a couple of choices: leave or describe the multitude of ways I'd made his girl come in the past few hours. Option two was definitely more appealing, but option one was clearly the way to go.

Taryn must've have sensed it, because she grabbed my arm. "Don't go. Beckett was just leaving."

Brennin barked out a laugh. "I'm not going anywhere, T-Rex. And we both know it."

Taryn cringed. Brennin smiled. And my thoughts drifted back to option one.

I jerked when my phone vibrated. Wrestling the device from my pocket, I hit ignore on Logan's call, then scrolled to a text—also from Logan.

Where are you? Is Laurel with you? That Calista chick just called. She can't find her.

"Shit," I muttered as I tapped out my reply.

She's not with me. I'm on my way.

"Is everything okay?" Taryn asked, all her focus on me.

Clarity took hold, and I raked a hand through my hair, prepared to give Taryn the "it's been nice" speech. "Listen, I gotta go. I think ..."

Beckett snorted, and I met his gaze. One prick to another, I guess he recognized the beginning of a brush off when he heard one.

Before I could stop myself, I took Taryn's hand. "How about dinner tonight?"

What the fuck are you doing?

The answer came when she smiled. Like I'd given her a gift.

"Sure. I mean ... if you want."

I swept a tangled lock behind her ear. "Yeah, I want. How's seven o'clock work for you?"

The sparkle returned to her eyes, driving away the clouds and revealing a clear blue sky filled with possibilities. "Good. Seven's good."

I pulled Taryn in for a quick peck, but she cupped my cheek and her lips parted.

"I'm right fucking here!" Brennin whined as she deepened the kiss.

When my phone rang, I pulled away to check the screen.

I hit ignore, but not before Taryn caught a peek at Laurel's name flashing on the display.

I didn't have time to explain, so I dropped the device into my pocket. "See you at seven, baby." Taryn nodded, questions swimming in her eyes. "And pack a bag. We can stay at my loft." With a pointed look at Brennin, I added, "Nobody will interrupt us there."

I headed down the stairs, and before I reached the bottom, Beckett was whining. As I pulled the front door closed, I tried not to imagine some outlandish scenario where they ended up tangled in our sex sheets.

Bypassing the elevator, I headed for the stairwell.

Cursing under my breath as I flew down the concrete steps, I hit redial on Laurel's number.

"Where are you?"

She rambled incoherently but finally managed to offer a street. I recognized the neighborhood.

"Stay put," I warned. "And I swear to God, if you're any more fucked up when I get there than you are right now, I'm taking you straight back to rehab."

Chapter 11

TARYN

"What the hell are you doing here?" I hissed, pushing Beckett out of the way as I headed for the stairs. "Don't you have a supermodel waiting for you back at your place?"

It only took thirty seconds for my claws to come out. A new record.

Stalking to the kitchen, I yanked open the cupboard while Beckett eased onto a barstool.

He picked up a wooden napkin ring we'd bought in Denmark and twirled it around his finger. "The only girl I have is you. I've been going out of my fucking mind. Why didn't you answer your phone?"

A bag of coffee clutched in my fist, I whirled around. "Do you really want me to answer that?" He dropped his gaze to his clasped hands. "Didn't think so. Now tell me what you're doing here."

I turned my attention to the state-of-the-art coffee pot and glowered at the machine. Usually, I left the brewing to the professionals at Starbucks since my coffee tended to taste like sludge.

Starbucks.

Where I met Chase.

Yesterday ...

Beckett's gruff voice interrupted my self-recrimination over the guy I picked up with my morning coffee. "I came here for you. Didn't you talk to Ash? And what about your little friend? What's his story?"

I ducked into the fridge to grab the cream. "His name is Chase, and he doesn't have a story. He owns ... um, Nite Owl Pub on Sixth Street."

And this building. And a lot of other things. But I left that part out.

I poured cream into two cups, cringing when Beckett's arms slid around my waist. "That's digging into the archives a little, isn't it, babe? A dive bar on Sixth?"

"You got your start on Sixth."

He rocked me slowly, the way he used to. "Is that what the guy wants? A start?"

Spinning around, I glared up at him. "Are you saying the only reason a guy would ask me out is because of who I am?"

Beckett's hands curled around my hips, and he traced small circles on the bones. An intimate gesture he'd perfected when we were fifteen and he was trying to convince me to go all the way. "I didn't say that. I'm only pointing out that it's a little strange that some random guy chats you up in a bar on Sixth without an endgame. You're pretty recognizable." He narrowed his gaze. "What were you doing out by yourself at a bar anyway?

"I didn't meet him at the bar. I met him at Starbucks."

Don't ask. Don't ask.

"When?"

I busied my hands pouring the coffee. "Yesterday."

"So, my girlfriend goes out and picks up some dude the day before I come home." He leaned closer, his accusatory tone a low growl in my ear. "Nothing strange about that."

Blowing right past the point about not knowing he was coming home, I shoved the cup into Beckett's hand. "I'm not your girlfriend. There's no press around, so drop the act."

"What the hell are you talking about?"

"I'm talking about that crap you fed Ash." His mouth dropped open to protest, but I rolled right over him. "I understand why y'all offered up the story. But I read Maddy's quotes. 'Beckett and I are deliriously happy,'" I mocked, ditching my southern twang for a ridiculously high female voice. "'We're so lucky we found each other.' Where is your lucky girl now, Beckett? Waiting dutifully at your hotel until you square things with me? Why? We're not together. And just so you know. Tori's pissed. I'm not the only one who got hurt with this little stunt."

Despite everything, I didn't want to fight. Beckett was my first love, would always be my first love, and love still glowed between us. For a long time, I believed I couldn't love anyone else.

"I'll make it right with Tori. I'll explain and—"

"No, you won't," I said quietly. "I'm moving heaven and earth to make sure that Tori never finds out about any of this. But she's so raw. The producer is calling about your album. The label is pissed. You're over budget and off schedule. That's on me." I tapped my chest. "I couldn't go to LA because of your girlfriend, and now this."

All the things I'd been keeping inside bubbled over, and I let my head fall forward.

Beckett sat down at the dining room table and then buried his head in his hands. "You don't understand."

"Then tell me."

I took a seat beside him and he entwined our fingers, caressing my infinity tattoo. "She's not my girl. You're my girl. And she knew that."

The collar of his shirt gaped just enough to see the edge of the large "T" emblazoned over his heart. As if he could read my mind, he laid my palm flat on his chest. "You're the only one I've ever loved."

"I'm not the only one. I haven't been for a long time."

With a ragged sigh, Beckett raked a hand through his hair, shoved back from the table, and started to pace. I waited, wondering whether I was giving him time to collect his thoughts or rope to hang himself with. Eventually, shoulders slumped, he sank down against the half wall separating the bar from the kitchen. "Maddy Silva means nothing to me. Nothing." He shook his head, as if saying it made it so. "Things got out of hand, but it wasn't—it isn't what you think."

I didn't want to hear any more. With Becket, the cure might be worse than the disease. Still, I joined him on the floor, drawn to his side by the tether that bound us.

"Becks ... What aren't you telling me?"

Sighing, he pulled the smokes from his pocket, holding out the pack. A familiar longing gripped my chest. I'd given up the habit long ago, but the craving remained. Cigarettes and Beckett Brennin, my two strongest weaknesses.

"Take one," he taunted. "You know you want to."

"God, you are a bad influence." Snatching the Marlboro, I leaned in for a light. "Oh, sweet Lord—" I groaned as I inhaled, "—that's so good."

Beckett lit up, then to my dismay, he steered the conversation back onto its previous course. "I miss you, babe." He flicked his ash in the coffee cup he snagged from the table. "I can't ... I just want us to be what we used to be."

I leaned my shoulder against his. "We are what we used to be. You're my best friend. And that'll never change."

"What would Paige and Tori say about that?"

After a couple of beats, I smiled sadly. "Paige wouldn't say anything, but Tori would correct me."

He nodded, entwining our fingers. "I understand why you, um, went out with that guy. But I'm back now."

I frowned. "It's not about another guy. You and I don't fit anymore." *Maybe we never did.* Stopping short of that admission, I added, "We've been on this roller coaster for too long, Becks. I just want to get off."

He reached for the sash on my robe. "I can help you with that. In case your friend wasn't up to the task."

Desperation lit every corner of his face. And judging by the look in his eyes, he'd option the expired marriage license in his safe if I gave him the chance.

But why?

"Are you going to tell me what's got you talking crazy?"

"I'm saner than I've ever been. Just let me prove it." He searched my face, and finding no cracks, his mask of indifference slid into place. "Fine, Taryn. Have it your way."

I dropped my cigarette into the cup alongside Beckett's. Smoke rose from the bottom as the two butts sizzled and then fizzled out altogether. All heat and intensity, followed by the inevitable slow burn, dwindling to nothing.

Just like Beckett and me.

Taking the mug from my hand, Beckett set it on the bar, then helped me up. "I'm not giving up on you. Or us. And if your friend is smart, he'll stay out of my way."

Beckett's ardor would cool the minute he caught sight of a leggy brunette to divert his attention.

"Well, since you showed up here out of the blue, I'm sure your schedule is a mess. Let me grab a shower and we'll head to the office to sort it out. I've got a meeting at five with Harper."

He perked up. "You got her to come here?"

"Of course, I did. Isn't that why y'all got me involved? To clean up your mess."

"Yeah." He scrubbed a hand down his face. "I'm just glad it's almost over. Maybe Dylan can get his head out of his ass, and we can finish the album."

"I thought ..." Inclining my head, I studied him. "Aren't you the one having the problem with the producer?"

"I can handle that dude." He shrugged. "I was just taking some of the heat off Dylan."

Maybe we were more alike than I thought. In his own way, Beckett was picking up the slack. And how long had that been going on?

I climbed the stairs and then paused on the landing to gaze down at Beckett, scratching at the place in my brain where our passion used to reside. It was tempting fate, really, but I needed to find out what was left of us.

Nothing.

It was strange, the hollow feeling. Not quite sad. Just empty.

Disappearing into my room, I locked the door.

On Beckett and our past.

Chapter 12

CHASE

I rolled down the busy street, scanning all the vacant faces hidden in the shadows. Spotting a girl with a mass of blond waves slumped in the corner of a bus stop shelter, I laid on the horn. Laurel lifted her gaze, peering around with narrowed eyes.

"I found her," I said into the phone as I screeched to a halt at the curb. "Call Vaughn. Tell him to meet us at my loft."

Logan let out an audible breath on the other end of the line. "Is she okay?"

"I don't know what she is. We'll be there in twenty. Unless I have to take her to the hospital."

Ending the call, I hopped out of the car.

Laurel lifted her head as I approached, sneering at me with unfocused eyes. Her hair was an unruly mess and makeup and snot smudged her face.

"Laurel ...?"

Shrinking against the metal wall, she took a swing. "Go away!"

"Laurel! It's me!" I barked, catching her wrist and hauling her to her feet. "Look at me."

She stopped struggling, and her face contorted. "Ch-Chase ...?"

Crumbling against me, she fisted my shirt with grimy hands. "I-I didn't use. I d-didn't use."

Ignoring her babbling, I checked for bruises and then scooped her up.

"I didn't use," she insisted as I tucked her into the car. "You gotta b-believe me. I d-didn't."

Laurel's words weren't worth the air she stole to breathe them. That's not to say I didn't want to believe her. But I couldn't. I'd lied too many times myself. Bold-faced lies to people I loved.

Tipping her chin, I examined her pupils. "What did you take? Tell me right now."

Tears spilled from her bloodshot eyes. "N-nothing, I promise. I just d-drank ... a-a lot."

Once I was behind the wheel, I wrestled the seat belt over her lap.

A jeer erupted from the sidewalk, and I turned a heated glare to the guys loitering near the car, brown paper sacks in hand. It was a brown paper sack kind of neighborhood. One of the worst in town. Dealers pushed product in the open, and I counted at least three hookers in the vicinity. Rolling into this hood in a car like mine could only mean three things: supplier, pimp, or John.

While I wasn't cool with any of the titles, John was by far the worst. Not that I gave a fuck if you got your kicks paying for sex, but on this side of town, a John in a fancy car screamed target. Better the brown paper bag bunch thought I was a pimp.

"What?" I mouthed, narrowing my gaze as one of the guys stepped closer to the car.

He paused to glance over my long hair and tattoos, buying me enough time to pull away from the curb before he could reach for whatever was tucked into the waistband of his pants.

Laurel groaned when I jerked to a stop at the light.

"Tell me right fucking now," I growled. "Do you need to go to the hospital?"

She mumbled a garbled response, but "no hospital" was all I could make out. I took her wrist, searching for her pulse. Strong and steady.

Groaning, she tipped forward, spewing vomit all over the seat, the floorboard, and herself.

I lowered the window and, fighting the bile at the back of my throat, I called Logan.

His short, clipped breaths bled through the speaker. "Is she all right?"

I glanced at the crumpled mess beside me as I drove. "As far as I can tell, she's just drunk. Her pupils aren't pinned. She just puked all over my car. I told Vaughn to bring a nurse. He'll piss test her to find out what's floating around in her system."

"Okay," Logan said quietly. "I really ... I don't ..."

Vodka fumes emanated from the yellow puddle at Laurel's feet. "Just get someone to clean my car. Don't worry about the rest."

"Sure, man," he replied, raw emotion tinging his tone. "Whatever you need."

"And, Logan," I glanced at Laurel, vomit dripping from her chin, "if she's dirty, she's going back to rehab. Even if she's just drunk, we gotta deal with it. Whatever Vaughn says, we follow his lead. You got that?"

Vaughn held the small, clear vials up to the light, smiling. What the aging hippie counselor was grinning about I couldn't imagine. Then again, it wasn't his Mercedes in the alley with vomit all over the leather seats.

"She's clean," he announced, cutting his gaze to the sleeping figure bundled under the blanket on the couch in my loft. "She drank a shit ton of booze. But no drugs."

Laurel hadn't regained consciousness until an hour ago. Belligerent, she'd stumbled to the bathroom to take the drug test before falling back into an alcohol-induced slumber.

Logan paced in a circle, rubbing the back of his neck. "What if the drugs are already out of her system?" He turned to us, panic suffusing his tone. "What then?"

Vaughn and I wore identical looks of amusement.

"It doesn't work that way," I replied. "The alcohol will burn off pretty fast. But drugs don't metabolize that quickly."

Logan nodded, and for once I was grateful for his naïveté. He and Cameron experimented with weed in the old days. Maybe some Molly. But, thank God, neither fell victim to the druggie lifestyle. Good or bad, Logan and Cameron liked to "feel" their feelings.

"Water ..." Laurel croaked. "I need water."

I intercepted Logan with a firm hand when he jumped to do his sister's bidding. "Stay back. I got this."

He shoved his hands into his pockets, nodding.

Laurel met my hard glare with one of her own when I slid a bottle of water in front of her. Defiant, she rolled her eyes and then stared at the ceiling.

"Sit up and drink the fucking water," I snapped. "You're dehydrated."

Logan inched his way from the shadows. He'd seen this side of me. Plenty. But this was different.

Laurel lifted her chin, glowering at me like she was the injured party, so I leaned close to her face to make my point. "Get up. Now!"

Her eyes widened, and she pulled herself into a sitting position.

"This is my house," I reminded her as I took a seat beside her. "Don't waste my time with your bullshit. I'm trying to help you. We're all trying to help you."

Guilt etched her features. Unfortunately, guilt and shame ebbed in the face of the next high, so it meant nothing. Lasting remorse only existed in the land of the sober.

But I could tell Logan was falling for it, so when I caught his eye, I shook my head imperceptibly.

"I-I'm not trying to waste your time," Laurel said, her chin quivering as she held back tears. "I'm just ..."

Sick. I got that. And the fact that Laurel was on the verge of admitting it was a good sign.

Phase two began when Vaughn sank into a chair, placing the test kit with all the vials on the table in front of her.

Righteous indignation swept the guilt right off Laurel's face. "I told you I didn't use." She sniffed, crossing her arms over her chest. "I just had one too many."

"No, darlin'," I said. "*One* is too many. And I told you that."

"I'm not a drunk," she bit out, her anxiety escalating quickly. "I can have a few drinks."

I shot Logan a look, my jaw clenching with irritation as he nodded in agreement. *With Laurel.*

"No, you can't. Not one drink," I said, gesturing to the door. "And if you don't like that particular rule, feel free to pack your shit and get out of my building."

"But ..." Laurel turned her attention to Logan, big eyes beseeching, but thank fuck, he looked away.

"No 'buts,'" Vaughn interjected, raking a hand through his long, gray hair. "No 'ifs.' No 'whens.' No booze. *Period.*" He changed seats, sliding onto the couch on the other side of Laurel, and with a gentle hand on her knee, he said, "Why don't you tell us what happened."

Laurel leaned forward to grab her bottle of water with a shaky hand, and once again, I had to keep Logan from helping.

"She's got this, dude," I said, easing back against the cushions. "Li'l sis managed to lift several glasses, or bottles, to her lips in the past twenty-four hours. She doesn't need your help to wash the vomit out of her mouth."

The muscles in Logan's bicep twitched, and anguish lined his brow as he looked down at his sister. "What happened, Laurel?"

Staring at her bottle, she avoided Logan's gaze.

"Answer your brother," I prodded. "Don't you think he deserves it?"

Laurel took a sip of water and then heaved a sigh. "Everything was fine," she said quietly. "I went downstairs to find you. But you were onstage. During the set, some guy offered to buy me a drink. I turned him down. And then ..."

"Then?" I asked calmly.

"When you finished the set and left with those girls, I figured—" she lifted a shoulder, "What the hell? Might as well have some fun too."

Ignoring the part where Laurel tried to lay the blame for her little stunt at my feet, I propped my boots on the coffee table. "Since when does fun involve getting shit-faced drunk and ending up in front of a crack house?"

Tension radiated off Logan in waves. He clasped and unclasped his hands, likely to keep from wringing my neck.

Laurel didn't notice, though. Another sip and she continued. "The guy wanted to take me home ... to ... you know." She looked over at her brother who nodded sympathetically. "And I thought that was fine. But then he said he wanted to get high, and we ended up at the crack house to score." Her brow furrowed as she shook her head. "But I didn't want to. So I got out of there and I called you. Were you still with those girls?"

Ignoring everyone else in the room, I tipped forward, holding Laurel's gaze when I said, "Who I was with doesn't matter. If you'll notice, I hightailed it over there to pick your ass up. And by the way, you need to get out to my car and clean up your mess. You puked all over the front seat."

With the buzz wearing off, Laurel's self-preservation skills kicked in and she replied instantly, "Okay."

I sighed and then began in a softer tone, "No one is telling you not to have a good time. Or to date. But if you can't tell the difference between a dope fiend and a regular guy, you've got some issues to address. And no more booze." I placed a knuckle under Laurel's chin, forcing her to meet my gaze. "That's a hard limit. Are we clear?"

She nodded.

"Go take a shower, you stink." I motioned toward the staircase to her loft. "Let the grown-ups talk about some options for keeping you busy during your free time."

Laurel stood, her eyes sweeping over each of us in turn. "I'm sorry."

Hardening my jaw, I nodded, but kept my expression firm until she was out of the room.

"What the hell, dude?" Logan hissed. "She's trying. Why are you being such a hard-ass?"

Lifting a finger, I waited until I heard footsteps upstairs to focus my attention on Laurel's surly big brother. "What do you think she is, dude? Fragile? A damsel in distress?" I arched a brow. "She's not."

Logan stared at me like I'd just landed here from another planet.

"What Chase is trying to say," Vaughn interjected, "is that Laurel knows what she's doing. We can't indulge her whims or excuse her bad behavior."

Logan slumped in his seat, biting his lip. "She should have called me. I would have—"

"You would have tucked her into bed and given her a bowl of ice cream," I replied. "That's why she called me. Laurel wants to get better. If she starts calling you, and not me or Vaughn, then we got problems."

"But you weren't around," he retorted. "You left the bar with those girls."

"And what Betty did you happen to be spending the evening with?" I asked, shaking my head when he looked away. "Exactly. I can't babysit twenty-four seven, and neither can you."

Turning to Vaughn, I asked the tough question, "Is having Laurel in a loft above the bar going to help her or hurt her? Give me your honest opinion."

Vaughn rubbed his scraggly beard as he contemplated. "Well, we've got an unusual situation. Logan is her brother. Her only family that she'll speak of. She needs that tie, but I agree, she can't live with him."

Logan stiffened, but Vaughn continued without missing a beat. "Having her here, with you right downstairs is a good option for now, despite the drawbacks. Even if we moved her away, got her a place with a sober companion, she could walk out. She's drawn to you, Chase. And in the end, if she doesn't feel the support, she'll fold."

Vaughn let that sink in and then added, "Let's talk rules. No going into the bar alone. And she needs to get a job during the day."

Pinching the bridge of my nose, I said, "I'll line something up for her at The Phoenix Group. But I don't want her in the bar, even if I'm there."

Logan glanced at his phone. "I've got rehearsal and a show to do tonight, but I can cancel." He looked to me for guidance, anxiety coating his features. "I'll cancel if that's what I need to do. Just say the word."

I shook my head. "Nope, you go ahead. Vaughn's got this covered for tonight. He's taking her to a meeting."

Logan's eyes narrowed. "What kind of meeting?"

Vaughn pushed to his feet, wincing as he stretched his back. "NA. Narcotics Anonymous."

"You want her to start hanging out with a bunch of addicts?" Logan scowled. "Good plan."

Somewhat amused, I shook my head. "Dude ... What do you think I am?"

Chapter 13

TARYN

*H*arper crossed her arms over her chest, glowering as I set down my briefcase.

"The Omni?" She looked around the luxury suite with disdain. "Really, Taryn ... you couldn't do any better than the *Omni?*"

When I'd discovered Harper in Biloxi, she was working as a backup singer in a shitty lounge. I'd seen the dilapidated trailer she'd shared with her mother and two siblings. And the threadbare clothes held together with safety pins. Yet now she postured like royalty, looking down her nose as she sat in one of the nicest hotels in Austin.

"Are you under the impression that you have some kind of control over this situation, Harper?" She opened her mouth, but I plowed right over her. *"You don't."*

Harper sat back, crossing her arms over her chest, but said nothing, so I continued. "Have you ever heard of a nuisance claim?" She shook her head. "Yeah ... didn't think so. I don't have time to go over it in detail, but here's the gist: sometimes it's more expedient to make a deal than put in the man hours to clean up the mess. And that's what you are ... a *mess.*"

Fury lit her gaze as she latched onto the only word in my speech that bolstered her hope: *deal.*

Shifting her focus to the cheap laptop on the coffee table, she smiled. "Have you seen what I have?"

Reading people was my superpower, and detecting the hidden desperation in Harper's tone, I tipped forward, smiling. "Have *you*? That tape of yours—it's a gift. I should be thanking you. You've just guaranteed Dylan and Leveraged an insane amount of publicity. If I were just his manager, we wouldn't be speaking."

I waited a few beats for Harper to digest her reversal of fortune, then mused, "I'd have to do a little fancy footwork to explain how the tape came about. It would take a lot of interviews to make sure that every single rag in this country knew the details—how you recorded Dylan without his knowledge—then threatened to release the footage to get traction for your own album. But once that was done? He'd be the victim." I sat back, drumming my fingers on the arm of the sofa. "Then, I'd really bury you. I'd make it my personal mission to ensure that you'd never get paid for singing another note."

When I was certain that every last drop of blood had drained from Harper's face, I let her off the hook.

"The payoff for most managers is well worth the nuisance," I said as I pulled the stack of papers from my briefcase. "But not for me. Dylan's my friend. He might want to have a family someday, and I don't want your little sexcapades hanging over his head. So, as much as it pains me, I'm willing to offer you a deal." I tossed the thick stack onto the table. "A one-time only offer. But know this, if you don't take me up on it, you'd better learn to like making money on your back. Because the only offers you'll be fielding will have the words "threesome" and "girl on girl" attached. You won't be complaining about a suite at the Omni, because the only room anyone will ever pay for again is the Motel 6 where they film your next porno." I looked around. "I don't think they have room service, but you might be able to convince your fluffer to run down to the gas station and pick you up one of those pre-made sandwiches."

Harper gulped, cutting her gaze to the papers. My pulse returned to a somewhat normal beat when she snatched the stack from the table. "How do I know you're not trying to trick me?"

"You don't. But I can assure you the offer is legit. I'll manage you, promote the first album and negotiate a tour in exchange for an iron-clad confidentiality agreement and the tape. Then we part ways. There's no option to renew, but you'll be able to pick up a new manager."

Unable to contain her smile, Harper's leg bobbed as she scanned the documents.

"Look at me, Harper." Distracted, she met my gaze. "That agreement binds both of us. If anything leaks, anything, I'll sue you. And my lawyers are better than any you'll ever hire. All the money you make from the album?" I snapped my fingers. "Gone. Just like your reputation. So save yourself the trouble and tell me right now if anyone else has seen the footage."

My stomach sank as she squirmed. "I showed the reporter from the *Statesman*," she admitted. "But I have the only copy. Me and Dylan."

I discretely let out the breath I'd been holding. "No one else?" She shook her head. "All right then, I'll give you a couple of days to have an attorney look over the deal, if you can find one that doesn't mind dealing in extortion." Grabbing my briefcase, I shoved to my feet. "And another thing—you may be in my stable but consider yourself off limits to my other clients. It's in the paperwork. You don't speak to Dylan or anyone else on the roster. Are we clear?"

Harper's smirk turned my stomach. "Crystal."

I strode to the door with bile rising in my throat. I'd made a lot of deals, but never one this distasteful.

Alone in the elevator, I toasted my new low as I tapped out a message for Dylan.

Mission Accomplished.

Once the text to Dylan was sent, I swiped my finger over the newest name on my contact list—Chase Noble.

I'd done a Google search this afternoon and found out very little about the man. Despite owning a good chunk of the city, Chase had managed to keep himself out of the public eye. Which accounted for the look on his face when we met.

Something came up. I'm going to have cancel. Maybe some other time.

My heart sank just a little when I pressed send. But it was for the best. The farther Chase stayed away from me and my brand of chaos, the better.

Chapter 14

CHASE

I doodled on my notepad while Davis, the project manager for the Arboretum overhaul, droned on about budgets and permits.

Turning in my chair, my focus shifted to the general vicinity of the Twin Souls offices.

Maybe I should text Taryn and try to reschedule our date?

Date ...

Sure, I wanted to fuck the girl stupid, but that didn't make it a date.

Not that it mattered. She was pretty clear in her text.

Something came up. I'm going to have to cancel. Maybe some other time.

"Chase?"

I shook my head to clear the fog and found eight sets of eyes peering at me with concern. Clearing my throat, I focused on my notes. But the only thing I'd written was a bunch of lyrics about sliding doors and missed opportunities.

"So where were we?" I asked, clasping my hands in front of me.

Davis tossed his pen on the table and sighed. "Let's revisit this at another time folks. Our fearless leader is a bit distracted today."

Davis was ten years my senior and well respected in the business, but he didn't run the Phoenix Group. I did.

"I appreciate your concern, bud," I said. "But time is money. *My* money. We've got a crew at the Arboretum waiting on permits. Let's figure this shit out."

Chatter erupted once again, and Violet, my CFO, slid some documents in my direction. "You okay?"

What the fuck was with everyone today?

"Fine." I glanced over the numbers, and none of them sank in, so I shoved the paperwork aside. "Bottom line it for me, Vi. What are we looking at?"

Following along as Violet went over the raw numbers, my gaze flicked to Davis. And since he looked sufficiently chastised, I gave up on the idea of ordering him into the field for the rest of the week to grind it out in the Texas sun.

When the meeting adjourned, I went back to my office and tried to concentrate on the paperwork but all I could think of were Taryn's fingers in my hair and the way the sunlight framed her body when she was above me.

Snatching my phone from the desk, I turned it over and over in my hand.

"One more taste."

The words no sooner left my lips than I was tapping out a message.

Is this an all-night kind of something, darlin'?

Licking my dry lips, I stared at the screen, my pulse racing when dots jumped around the little box.

I'm not sure.

I sat back, smiling. "Me either, baby."

"Who are you talking to?" asked Calista, hovering by the double doors to my office with a look of confusion.

A flush rose from my collar, and I tossed the phone on the desk like she'd just caught me trying to place a call to my dealer. And then I was smiling, because, maybe she did.

"No one. What are you doing here?"

Calista took a seat, twisting her hands in her lap. "It's about Laurel."

A twinge of apprehension corkscrewed in my chest. If Laurel had scared Calista off, my chances of helping her dropped by half.

Grabbing the folder of checks Violet had given me, I picked up a pen. "What about her?"

"I thought maybe you could join us at a meeting tonight."

A meeting.

As in: gut dumping in front of a room full of strangers in a church basement.

I allowed one uncomfortable shift in my chair before replying, "I thought Vaughn was taking her."

A zen-like smile curved Calista's lips. She was a hardcore twelve stepper, saved from falling over the edge by the meetings she attended. "There's always room for one more."

"I'm a little busy," I said with a shrug. "I'm sure y'all have it handled."

Calista's smile faded, and after a long moment she leaned forward. "You wouldn't be under the impression you're cured, would you?"

I wasn't cured. I'd never be cured. And if I had a doubt, the look on Calista's face served as a stark reminder. We'd met in rehab, and sometimes when I looked at her, that's all I saw. The reflection of who I used to be in her eyes.

"Nope," I said flatly. But I've got it handled. It's my program. I'll work it my way."

"And what way is that?"

Averting my gaze, I searched for an answer. In reality, I hadn't worked my program for damn near fourteen months.

"Fine, Calista." I smiled, hoping the mock irritation masked my true emotion: dread. "Where and when?"

She checked her watch, a worn timepiece far past its fashion expiration date. "A half hour." Hopping to her feet, she slid her purse strap over her shoulder. "First Baptist on Trinity."

"I'll see you there."

As soon as she was gone, I picked up my phone to get directions. Because unlike Calista and Vaughn, I didn't make a habit of memorizing the addresses of every NA meeting location in the city.

The box with Taryn's text begged for a reply so I tapped out a message.

I'll be around all night. If you get finished early, or late, come by.

The drive to the church took all of five minutes, not nearly enough time to prepare.

And though I'd never been here before, I trudged down the rose-lined path on the side of the building, the sweet scent invading my nose as I searched for a set of stairs. Meetings like this were always tucked away, perhaps for privacy, but more likely so unsuspecting churchgoers wouldn't stumble upon the ugliness.

I took a seat behind Vaughn and Calista, who had Laurel caged between them. She turned, a surprised smile curving her mouth when she saw me.

I'm as surprised as you are, darlin'.

I smiled back.

Fifteen minutes later when the quasi leader of the group opened the floor for confessions, I couldn't force my lips to bend with a forklift. I hated being here. Loathed everything about the weakness that made it a requirement.

My phone buzzed and, latching onto the reprieve, I fished the device from my pocket, a calm washing over me when I saw Taryn's name. If I were honest, it was like the feeling I used to get before I scored.

I could probably drop by. It may be late though.

That was as good as a yes in my book so I nudged Vaughn's shoulder.

"Gotta go," I whispered when he twisted to look at me. "Business emergency."

Confusion creased his brow, but I didn't stick around to explain. As I headed for my car, I tapped out a text to Taryn.

Good. I really want to see you.

Fuck, Desperate much? I held down the delete button.

I really want to fuck you.

I smiled at that one, because it was true. More than true. But still not the vibe I wanted.

You feel like sharing a pizza?

Satisfied, I hit send, then slid behind the wheel of my car. The air conditioning blasted my face as I pulled onto Trinity Blvd, gunning the engine like someone was chasing me.

Patting the pocket of my T-shirt for the phantom pack of smokes, I tightened my grip on the wheel.

You don't smoke.

As I waited in line at Rudinos for the custom pie, I wondered if my control was an illusion. Did old cravings ever really die, or did they wait for a moment of weakness, rearing their ugly head when you least expected it?

Chapter 15

TARYN

*C*heers thundered outside the conference room door at Twin Souls. Sometime in the last hour, an impromptu game of NERF basketball had started in the fishbowl, the outer office where the junior managers and their staff had their desks.

From the chatter filtering through the door, it sounded like a heated match between Dylan and Beckett, and each of the boys had a cheering section that rivaled that of an NBA basketball team.

Rubbing my temple, I thumbed through the batch of signed contracts from my last trip while Tori sat at the other end of the table scowling at the speaker phone.

"That's not going to bring him to the phone any quicker, Belle," I said wearily. "And please try to hold onto your temper."

She chuffed out a breath and I could almost see the smoke come out of her nose.

"Ms. Grayson." Councilman Harlson's voice blasted through the speaker. "Thanks for your patience. I was just looking through your file."

Cutting through the pleasantries, Tori rushed to say, "Council-man, your office has been in possession of our check for three months. Twin Souls has acted in good faith, securing vendors for this event. Why was our permit denied?"

I gave Tori a small smile of encouragement, rewarding her for her professionalism.

"Well," the councilmen drawled, "it seems there was a clerical error."

Tori's butt rose out of her chair, and I sighed, wondering how much ass I'd need to kiss if she cussed out the man in charge of the City Planning office.

"You rejected our permit due to a clerical error?" she growled, incredulous.

"Ms. Greyson—"

"*Mrs.* Greyson," Tori snapped.

"Of course, Mrs. Greyson." A long sigh. "The clerical error was not solely our fault. A Ms. Ayers from your office proffered a check for two hundred and fifty thousand dollars, and the bank rejected it."

"What?" Tori screeched. "There's got to be some mistake. Our business account has plenty of money to—"

"Oh, no," the councilman chuckled, "it had nothing to do with the funds. According to your bank, Ms. Ayers is not on the corporate charter."

Silence hung thick, and I stared down at my hands.

I'd never pushed Tori to make me a partner and I never would. Twin Souls was her company, built on the legacy of her husband, her twin soul.

"Taryn Ayers has full authority to sign any check on behalf of this company," Tori finally said. "Clearly this is an issue with your bank."

"Yes, well, be that as it may, I don't have any control over the bank the city uses," the councilman said. "But since the funds have been verified, I'm happy to report that our office issued your permit today granting Twin Souls full use of Zilker Park for the Ron Grayson/Paige Dawson Memorial Endowment Concert."

Tori sank into her seat, staring at the phone, her face growing paler by the second.

Sliding out from behind the desk, I made my way to her side. "It's

Rhenn Grayson," I corrected the councilmen. "The Rhenn Grayson/Paige Dawson Memorial Endowment Concert."

Tori blanched when the councilman offered another weak laugh. "Yes, I see ... It's right here. *Rhenn* Grayson."

Bracing a hand on Tori's shoulder, I said, "Thank you for taking the time to clear this up, councilman. We appreciate your help."

I hurried to end the call before the old fool put his foot in his mouth again. Tori swiveled her chair and gazed out the window, but I knew that expression; she was somewhere else.

Resting my butt on the table, I said gently, "Have you ever seen Harlson?" No response, so I nudged her chair. "Huh?"

Tori shook her head, listless.

"The man is pushing seventy-five. Of course he doesn't know who Rhenn is. I'm sure the last musician he could name wore bell bottoms."

A smile ghosted Tori's lips. "I guess."

I took my seat, and after a moment, Tori let out a staggered breath and then returned to sifting through files.

"We have to get this right," she said quietly. And when I looked up, her watery gaze was locked on mine.

"We will, Belle. I promise."

An hour later I stretched my legs. Though the ruckus in the other room had died down, it hadn't diminished completely. As long as Dylan and Becks were here, unpaid interns and hourly employees, long off the clock, remained.

"Drink?" I asked on my way to the break room.

Tori nodded, and when I returned with a Dr. Pepper for each of us, she lifted a confused gaze.

"What is this?"

My mouth went dry when she flipped the file around, revealing a photo of Dylan and Harper. They were at the studio, with Dylan's chest barely grazing Harper's back as he looked over her shoulder, studying an arrangement she had in her hand. All in all, it appeared innocent. Unless you'd seen what I had on that tape.

I cracked open the soda and then took a drink to peel my tongue off the roof of my mouth. "That's Harper, um, Rush. The girl I scouted in Biloxi a few months back."

Tori pulled out a memo and, glancing it over, her frown intensified.

"What is it?" I managed to croak.

"The label wants to know if they're an item." Tori's gaze flicked to mine. "So they can use it to promote the albums."

Joint, as in both albums.

"I'll talk to Dylan," I said as casually as possible.

Tori was quiet for a long moment, then shoved the picture back in the file. "It's probably nothing."

Placing the folder in our "pass" pile, she moved on.

"We're not passing on Rush," I said as I sank back into my chair.

"I don't like her." Tori scribbled notes without looking up, like the subject was closed.

"That doesn't matter, Belle. Harper is talent, *my* domain."

My only piece of the kingdom, and the one thing I'd insisted on from the start. I handled talent acquisition, *period*. And I'd hide behind that privilege now, except, I shouldn't have to.

Irritated, Tori lifted her gaze. "The whole damn company is my domain, Taryn. Since I own it."

Whether she meant to say it or not, it was out there. And rather than back down, I eased farther into my chair. "That's not the way it works."

My dry tone caught her off guard. Hell, it caught *me* off guard.

Tori narrowed her eyes, then shoved to her feet. With deliberate steps, she walked to the door and dumped Harper's file in the trash on her way out.

When Tori returned, a steaming plate of food in her hand, her brows drew together as she watched me tossing stuff into my backpack.

"I warmed up some Thai." She offered me her plate. "Where are you going?"

Seething, I picked up my phone, rereading Chase's message.

Come by anytime.

"I'm tired. I'll figure this stuff out tomorrow."

Leaving Tori with her noodles and her mouth slightly agape, I stormed out.

Beckett jogged over, NERF basketball in hand, as I marched through the office. "Hey, babe. You hungry? Let's go grab some dinner."

I glanced briefly at the group of female interns as I shouldered my way out the door. "I've got plans. There's plenty here to keep you busy."

Waiting for the elevator, I clenched my teeth when heavy footfalls sounded behind me.

And then Beckett's breath fanned over the back of my neck like a warm breeze. "Did you pack a bag?"

Stepping onto the lift, I turned to face him.

"Yes or no?" he persisted, slamming his hand on the closing door.

Jabbing the button, I looked him in the eyes. "Yes."

His hand fell to his side and the door slid shut. "This isn't over," I heard him yell.

Closing my eyes, I slumped against the back wall. "Yes, it is."

I couldn't bring myself to go to Chase's. Instead, I drove for hours. For all my posturing, I wasn't one-night stand material. Even if that one-night stand stretched into a week or even two. In the end, I'd want more.

That voice in my head that belonged to Paige urged me to take a chance.

You don't have enough fun. Live a little.

But I couldn't be like Paige. All fun, no strings. And I didn't inspire lasting love in men the way that Tori did.

I was the in-between girl. The friend you loved for a lifetime, who wasn't the love of your life.

Could I be that for another man? Was that even an option with Chase?

Maybe he had enough friends. But then, so did I.

Chapter 16

CHASE

a knock at the door woke me with a start, and I sat up. *Taryn.* Hauling to my feet, I ripped a hand through my hair as I thundered down the stairs. She blinked up at me when I flung open the door.

"Is it too late?" Cringing, she took a step back. "It is too late. I'm sorry. I'll just ..."

Her face was drawn and shadows bruised her eyes. Whatever she'd done today, the stress of it had taken its toll.

Catching her wrist before she could get away, I pulled her toward me. "It's not too late. Come in."

Taryn chewed her bottom lip, unconvinced. "Are you sure?"

"Of course, I'm sure," I said, lacing our fingers as I urged her up the stairs. "I told you anytime."

Which Taryn obviously took literally since it was almost midnight.

"Are you hungry?" I asked as I guided her to the living room. "I've got pizza."

Sinking onto the sofa, Taryn looked around as if she didn't know how she got here. "Yeah, that sounds good."

She forced a smile when I eased down beside her with a couple of slices. "Thanks."

Digging into the pizza I hadn't fully enjoyed earlier, I asked, "So what had you so busy tonight?"

"Nothing really." She picked at her pepperoni. "I went for a drive and ended up halfway to San Antonio. And when I came back I wasn't sleepy so ..."

With each word, her shoulders curved inward and she got a little smaller. Before she disappeared completely, I took the plate from her lap.

She peered up at me with those stormy eyes, a crease between her brow.

"I'm glad you came by. Regardless of the reason."

I brushed a kiss to her mouth, and her lips curved into the faintest smile. I'd seen so few of Taryn's smiles that I treasured every one.

Deepening the kiss, I maneuvered her onto her back. "I've been thinking about you all day."

Conflict furrowed her brow once again. "Me too."

Sobered by the battle raging in her eyes, I ran my thumb over her bottom lip. "Is that so bad?"

Sliding her arms around my neck, she fiddled with my hair. "That depends. If you want a friend with benefits, I think I can do that. But if you just want the benefits, I'm not built that way."

"So ... what are you saying? You want to be friends?"

She pressed a kiss to my lips, soft as a feather. "Friends, at least. Is that too much to ask?"

Confounded, I shook my head. "No. Why would you think any different?"

"Because you don't have to be friends with someone to fuck them. And if I pass you on the street, I don't want you to treat me like a stranger."

I thought of all the women I'd fucked who were exactly that —*strangers*. People I didn't care to know. Taryn wasn't one of them.

I pushed to my feet, offering my hand. "Okay, let's be friends. We can have a sleep over." She laughed as I hauled her upright. "I could braid your hair." I tugged my T-shirt off as I pulled her toward my bed. "Or we can watch chick flicks."

Smiling, she took off her blouse. "You can braid my hair some other time."

I eased onto the bed and reclined on my elbows, watching as Taryn wiggled out of her jeans. When she was down to her panties and her bra, she climbed on top of me.

"Friends?" she asked, her fingers poised on my belt buckle.

Gripping her waist, I held her in place, grinding my hard length against her center. "Sure, baby." She relaxed for the first time, and I flipped her onto her back. "Now, answer me one question."

She nodded, and I kissed my way to her ear. "How many ways do you want me to make you come, friend?"

Chapter 17

TARYN

*D*ylan paced the length of my office while I stared out the window. I could just glimpse the top of the cluster of buildings on Sixth where Nite Owl was located. Where I'd left Chase this morning with only a swift kiss and a mumbled goodbye.

I didn't even really know why I went to his loft last night. Except that he made me feel ... special. And not for what I did or who my friends were or what I could do for him. Just because.

"Did you hear me, T-Rex?" Dylan asked as he hovered in front of my desk.

Abandoning my daydream, I spun my chair around and then opened my laptop.

"No," I said as I opened my email. "But I can guess. And just like I told you the last ten times, Harper will sign. Now sit down, you're making me crazy."

Falling into the chair, Dylan raked a hand through his hair. "How do you know?"

Irritated, I typed in my password. "I just do. Harper wants to be a rock star not a porn star."

My conviction never wavered, even as I cleared my schedule in case I needed to get ahead of this thing. Opening a message from Metro Music, I cursed.

Dylan leaned forward, hands clasped like he was bracing for bad news. "What is it? What did she say?"

Glaring, I peered at him over my screen. "It's about the album. Why didn't you tell me that none of the tracks were salvageable? Trent is threatening to bail on the project if you don't get your head out of your ass."

I glanced over the lengthy list of grievances from Trent, the famed producer it took me months to woo.

Dylan hung his head. "The tracks aren't that bad," he insisted with zero conviction. "I played one for Tori yesterday and she—"

"Tori isn't producing your album!" I slammed my head back against the chair, squeezing my eyes shut. "The only reason Leveraged isn't harnessed to a three-album deal like everyone else is because of the contract I negotiated. If the band defaults on this album, the label has first right of refusal on the next one. Do you understand what that means? They could put a stop to your next album. Either that or we pay Metro a shit ton for all the studio time they gave you."

"What do you want me to do?" Dylan jumped to his feet. "As soon as this shit is squared with Harper, I'll re-record the whole fucking thing! I'll get it done in two weeks!"

"You better. Because the PR department already wants to kick this shit into overdrive. They sent over a picture they have of you and Harper in the studio. You looked pretty cozy."

Dylan pressed his palms flat on my desk, glaring. "I never said I didn't know the girl, T-Rex. I don't just fuck women without a conversation. I'm not Beckett."

The words ripped through me like a bullet, leaving a gaping hole in their wake.

Falling into the chair, Dylan ground the heel of his hand into his forehead and groaned. "Fuck, Taryn. I'm so sorry."

Indignation forced me upright, and I tapped out a reply to Metro with numb fingers. "Don't say another word. For all of Beckett's bull-shit, he's never put me in this kind of trick bag."

A moment of silence stretched into several, and just when I got my bearings, the door to my office flew open and Tori stormed in.

"Have you seen the email from Metro?"

For a second, I breathed a sigh of relief because I thought she was talking to Dylan. But that fierce amber gaze was settled on me.

"I just got it. Why?"

Tori gaped at me, incredulous. "Because you hired Trent. You gave him artistic control. Have you heard the tracks? This guy obviously doesn't know what he's doing. And if you weren't so busy avoiding Beckett, you would've been in LA overseeing the album."

"Belle," Dylan interjected, taking hold of her arm. "It's not—"

"It's not *what?*" she roared, shaking off his grip. "Did you forget how to sing? No. This guy is a hack. He doesn't know how to blend." Vibrating with anger, she dug her fist into her hip and said, "You need to fix this, Taryn"

A reply so venomous crawled up my throat, I felt it burn all the way to my lips. But at the last moment, I caught sight of the one inch scar on Tori's neck where they'd inserted her trach tube all those years ago. My focus shifted to Dylan, hanging his head and waiting for the fallout that would never come.

"I will," I said calmly.

In the wake of the easy victory, I thought Tori might soften, but instead she turned on her heel and left.

Dylan shoved to his feet and, lingering by my desk, he said quietly, "I'll talk to her, T-Rex. I'll make it right."

But he wouldn't. And we both knew it. Still, I gave him a nod to assuage his guilt.

And with that, he was gone, chasing after Tori. Like always.

Swiping away an angry tear, I sent an email to Trent, begging for more time.

When my phone buzzed, I picked it up without thinking and my heart slammed against my ribs when I read the message from Harper.

You've got a deal.

Chapter 18

TARYN

The next morning, I stepped outside the air-conditioned lobby of the Omni Hotel clutching the thumb drive full of evidence. Harper stumbled out a moment later, glaring at me when the valet coasted to a stop in my Mercedes.

"No limo?"

I waited until we were in the car to ask, "Have you looked at your contract, Harper?"

She rolled her eyes. "My attorney went over it with a fine-toothed comb. What do you think took me so long?"

I knew every worthwhile attorney in Austin, and her guy? Yeah, no. He was an ambulance chaser who would take anyone's case. But then, in my plans for Armageddon, I'd contacted, and retained, every attorney that could damage me or Twin Souls.

"Well then," I said as I pulled away from the hotel, heading south towards the airport. "You do understand what constitutes a 'hit' album, legally speaking?"

Harper was looking out the side window, but in the reflection, I saw her brow crease in response to my question. "I know what a hit album is," she huffed.

"Do you know how many hit albums it takes to afford twenty-four-hour limos at your disposal and first-class tickets, and let's say—a little house in LA?"

Harper's face fell by increments. By the time we hit the freeway, her bottom lip was in her lap.

"If you wanted money, Harper, asking for a hit album wasn't the way to go."

Panicked, she whipped her head around. "You mean I won't make *any* money?"

Sad truth? Promoting Harper would be easy. I wouldn't have sent her to Metro if I didn't think she had it—that special thing. I might not have it, but I recognized it in others.

With my help, Harper's album would be a success, and she would make money. Unfortunately, the girl was stupid and greedy, and she'd blow it all on Chanel purses and shoes from Louboutin's latest collection. And without another album to back it up, she'd burn out. All I had to do was sit back and wait for the inevitable fizzle.

After waiting the appropriate amount of time to watch Harper squirm, which in this case was the ten minutes it took us to get to Austin Bergstrom Airport, I said, "You'll make money." And something about the recollection of her trailer park roots and hand-me-down clothes softened the rough edges for two seconds. Long enough for me to add, "Get a financial advisor."

And then the bitch rolled her eyes again, and I was done.

Because we were short on time, I dropped Harper off with her suitcase and went to find a parking space. Honestly, I couldn't stomach being around her any more than I had to. I'd even booked our tickets on opposite sides of the first-class cabin.

After my car was secured, I pulled out my phone and, rolling my head from side to side, I tapped out a text to Tori. *Not feeling well. I'll be in tomorrow.*

I winced as I hit send. I'd be *back* tomorrow, so a follow up text would be needed. And I never lied to Tori. My last lie was such a whopper, it haunted me to this day.

Wake up, Belle. We're waiting for you. Rhenn's waiting for you.

I had whispered that deception every day she was in her coma. *Selfish.* I didn't want to lose her. Couldn't bear it.

Shaking off the memory, I pulled up Chase's contact information, smiling at his last text.

Miss your face, friend. Call me.

Blowing out a breath, I swiped my finger over his name.

"Where are you?" he rumbled in that sexy morning voice of his. "And why did you leave so early?"

"Good morning to you too," I said as I unfolded myself from the seat. "I had an unexpected business trip."

Hauling my rollaway out of the backseat, I headed for the bank of elevators.

"How long will you be gone?"

"I'll be back tomorrow night." I winced at the background noise, his and mine. "Where are you."

"I'm on a job site. What time tomorrow? Nine?"

"Oh ..." I glanced at my ticket as I walked into the terminal. "About that. Eight fifty-five, actually."

I smiled at the attendant in the first-class line who promptly took my ticket and ID, proffering a boarding pass a moment later.

"Will you call me when you get back?" Chase asked.

I walked to the front of the security line and then turned over my ticket. "Of course."

"Have a safe trip, Sweet Taryn."

Grinning like an idiot, I threw my rollaway onto the conveyor belt and then tossed my phone into the bin with my laptop.

When I retrieved the device, I was surprised to find a text from Tori.

Do you need me to come over? I can bring soup.

Guilt swamped me as I tapped out my response.

No, I don't want you to catch anything. My fingers hovered over the keys, and with my anger gone, I added: *I love you.*

On the plane in my plush leather seat, I sipped my orange juice, staring out the window at the Austin skyline.

The flight attendant paused and said to me in a whisper, "You'll need to set your phone to airplane mode. We're about to push back from the gate."

"Oh ... yeah. Sorry."

When I picked up my phone, the four words on the screen from Tori made the trip almost bearable. Almost.

I love you too.

Chapter 19

CHASE

I dropped a case of Shiner Bock onto the bar, then reached into my pocket for the box cutter.

"Top me off?"

My hand froze as I looked into Laurel's piercing blue eyes. Shifting my gaze to Calista, sitting at a table a few feet away with her arms crossed over her chest, my apprehension waned a bit.

"Depends on what you're drinking," I said.

She rolled her eyes. "Just club soda, warden."

I sprayed a shot of seltzer into her glass. "I ain't your warden, darlin'."

Casting off my sarcasm, Laurel brightened at the playful term of endearment. "But Logan says you're everyone's keeper." Sliding her gaze to the side, she muttered, "Even if you are farming it out in my case."

The fuck?

Placing my palms flat on the bar, I waited patiently for her to look back at me. "What's that supposed to mean?"

"Calista?" Lauren tinkled the ice in her glass, barely containing the sneer curling her lip. "Your hired gun."

Smirking, I pulled a bottle of beer from the vat. "Sober companion is the proper term."

Considering the sour look twisting Laurel's mouth, "companion" was a stretch.

"I was thinking more like pit bull," she spat. "She's certainly got the face for it."

My anger roared to life as I leaned across the bar. "Listen, princess. I don't care whether you like Calista or not, she's trying to help your ass. Show some respect."

Eyes round, Laurel's mouth fell open and then her gaze dropped to my fingers, balled into a fist around the bar towel.

"Geez, I didn't mean anything." Lifting her glass, she took a drink. "Get a grip."

Regret settled over me despite the lingering irritation. Laurel was damaged. To what extent I wasn't sure. The private investigator Logan had hired to find Laurel uncovered numerous hospital visits for everything from broken ribs to a dislocated shoulder. Whether it was a boyfriend, a pimp, or the strip club owner she worked for, someone had abused her.

Dropping my forearms onto the bar, I lowered my head to catch Laurel's eyes. "Has Calista shared any of her story?"

She shook her head.

I grabbed a ticket from one of the cocktail waitresses and then pulled out a couple of shot glasses. "Ask her, she'll fill in the details. But I'll give you the highlights. Addicted before she was old enough to drive. Two kids by the time she was eighteen. And one hell of a nasty drug habit."

Filling a shaker with vodka and lemon juice, I smiled. "Don't let the business clothes fool you. And I wouldn't let her hear you call her a pit bull. Calista's actually pretty graceful. Made a lot of money as a dancer."

Letting that nugget sink in, I poured the Lemon Drops into the shot glasses and finished loading the tray with bottled beer.

"You mean a stripper, right?" Laurel asked after the waitress picked up the order.

"Yep."

"But, I thought ..." Suspicion threaded her tone. "She works for you."

I barked out a laugh. "I own two bars and three restaurants. A few buildings. But no strip clubs. Calista is VP of Human Resources for the Phoenix Group."

Laurel's cheeks flamed as she stared into her drink. "Must be nice."

I bit my tongue. Laurel still didn't get it. Nothing about Calista's life was nice. Or easy. Calista fought tooth and nail to get clean, stay clean, and piece her life back together. And now she was trying to pay it forward. Because I asked her to.

Shaking my head, I strode to the cash register to run the night's receipts, keeping one eye on Laurel in the mirror. She looked around, her gaze flitting over all the women and lingering on the groups of unattached guys interspersed throughout the crowd. Clearly, Laurel was on the prowl, which I guess was better than the alternative. Setting her sights on a guy who took a seat a couple of stools down, Laurel adjusted her top, allowing the swell of her breast to spill from the V-neck T-shirt.

I twisted to take a closer look at Prince Charming. Clean-cut. Longhorn T-shirt and faded denim. No tats.

Laurel scooted down one seat, smiling at the kid, and I chuckled to myself. Sex on the brain twenty-four seven, just like her brother.

Not that I had any room to talk. Flashes of Taryn and the look on her face when I was buried between her thighs kept me semi-aroused all fucking day yesterday. Hell, I had to forcibly contain myself from jerking off like some hormone-riddled teenager.

I finally gave in when I was in the shower this morning, visions of Taryn on her knees, working me over with that pretty mouth spurring me on. But my spank session was more about ego than anything else. I had to let off a little steam or I'd blow the second Taryn was under me. And she would be under me. Tonight, some-time after eight fifty-five.

I motioned for Calista to come over. "I thought we agreed that the kid would steer clear of the bar?"

"She's not a prisoner, Chase. I took her to a meeting, and she mentioned that she wanted to hear a little music. She *told* me that." When I couldn't muster more than a blank expression, Calista sighed. "If she wanted to get wasted, she wouldn't have told me. And that's why I'm sitting here. No, it's not ideal." She scratched her arm absently. "For her or for me. But she was going to go tonight, regardless. Believe that."

I covered Calista's hand with mine. "You know I appreciate this, Cal."

She smiled. "You can appreciate the hell out of me on my birthday. I'll make you a list.

After Calista returned to her post with a fresh club soda, Seth tapped me on the shoulder.

"Everything's in the back of your car, just like you asked." He handed over my keys. "I threw in some dessert. It wasn't on the list." His brow arched. "Unless you've got something else in mind for dessert."

I did, but there was no way I was going to let my asshat bouncer in on the plan.

"Thanks."

Sifting through a bowl full of peanuts on the bar, Seth grabbed a handful from the bottom. "So, who's the chick? Is she smoking hot?" He tossed the nuts into his mouth. "Sharing is caring, my brother. Tell me all about it."

I caught Seth's arm when he went rooting through the bowl for a second time. "Other people have to eat those. Stop digging around. I have no idea where those fingers have been."

Clueless as ever, Seth leaned a hip against the cooler. "Whoever this chick is, does she have a sister? Because anyone who's got you this worked up—"

"I'm not worked up," I growled. "And I'm not running a dating service. There's a bar full of women here."

But none of them were Taryn. And the fact that I was crawling out of my skin because I hadn't seen her? Yeah, that wasn't sitting well with me.

Grabbing a bar towel, I went to work scrubbing some imaginary stain. "Sorry, it's not you," I grumbled, lifting my chin to Laurel, making goo-goo eyes at Joe College. "Can you keep an eye on that for me."

One corner of Seth's mouth quirked up as his attention shifted to Laurel. "I didn't know you had a thing for Logan's sister. You want me to go break that up so you can take her upstairs?" Tilting his head, his smile grew. "She is really hot. I wouldn't mind—"

Before I knew it, I had Seth backed into a corner, my finger an inch from his nose. "Laurel is family. And she's a fucking baby. So, if you have any thoughts about tapping *that*, think again. After I got through with you, Logan would work you over so good you'd be taking your meals through a straw."

Bridgette slid between us, her fingers coiling around my arm. "You boys fighting over me again?"

Strain infused her bubbly tone as her gaze volleyed between Seth and me. The bouncer outweighed me by a good thirty pounds, all muscle, but you'd never know it by the way his hands flew up in surrender. "Jesus, Chase. I was only messing around."

Tearing my murderous gaze from his face, I looked down at Bridgette. "I have plans. I'll see you tomorrow."

Muttering a hasty goodbye to Laurel, I sized up her new friend, who seemed harmless enough.

On my way out, I pulled Seth aside. "I'm going to let that shit back there slide this one time. But I swear to you, man, Logan ever sees you look crossways at li'l sis, he'll kill you."

Seth's hearty laugh faded when he saw the serious set of my jaw. Anyone but Logan and the threat would be idle, and Seth knew it.

Bits of random conversation from the crowds meandering down the sidewalk filtered through my open car window as I waited at the light a block from Taryn's building. But I couldn't hear anything beyond the whir in my head.

Taryn's last text promised a call when she got home. That was an hour ago.

She's blowing you off.

The thought lingered as I eased to a stop at the hidden gate in back of her building. My fingers hovered over the keypad. Only five people had the code so the blip would definitely show up on the security print out.

Punching in the code, I threw up a smile for the camera in the corner, trained on my car window. And then I drove through the gate.

Chapter 20

TARYN

*E*xhausted, I battled with my rolling suitcase as I stepped off the elevator. "Work with me, here," I muttered.

Head bowed, I trudged along, feeling around inside my purse for my keys. For such a tiny bag, everything got lost.

"About time you got here."

My heart stalled when I spotted Chase sitting in front of my door. Climbing to his feet, he strolled toward me. And then his hands sunk into my hair and his mouth covered mine, tongue diving between my lips with wild abandon.

Sliding his hand to my nape, he touched his forehead to mine. "Missed this mouth." He nipped my lip to prove the point.

Still dazed from his kiss, I ran my hands over his broad chest to his shoulders. Cursing the hormones, or the pheromones, or whatever it was that made me want to hold onto Chase so tight that he'd never leave, I smiled. "I missed you too."

"You okay?"

The gentle tone and concern clouding his gaze made me squirm. "I'm fine. Just tired. What are you doing here?"

The pads of his calloused fingertips dug into the tension knots on my neck. "Waiting for you." He pressed another kiss to my lips, gentle this time. "You said you'd call when you got in. Your plane landed over an hour ago."

"Yeah, I had to stop by the office."

A heavenly scent wafted up, and I blinked at Chase as I tried to place the aroma. Wrestling from his hold, I pushed him aside, searching. He chuckled low in his throat as I rushed blindly toward the three large bags with the familiar turquoise script propped against the wall next to my door.

"Franklin's?" I gushed, nearly falling to my knees in worship. "You brought me barbecue ... *from Franklin's?*"

Somehow Chase managed to grab the handles on the bags before I ripped them open. "I take it you're a fan?"

A fan? Franklin's was hands-down the best barbecue joint in the city. Lines formed around the little shack at sunrise on most days. And when the food was gone, the owner placed a homemade sign in the window that simply read "Out." That usually happened before noon.

"How did you manage to get Franklin's Barbecue at this time of night?"

I scrambled to get the key into the lock, missing the target when Chase's lips brushed my neck. "I told you." His free hand slid to the juncture of my thighs. "I'm a resourceful guy."

The heel of his palm slid against the layer of satin lining my skirt. The maneuver was bold, possessive ... and totally hot. I thought about protesting. A brief notion that floated away as he applied more pressure.

"Open the door," he growled into my ear. "I'm starving."

Chase's voice, raw with need, sent a quiver down my spine. If he was acting, it was an Academy Award winning performance. In the early years with Beckett, I felt wanted, cherished. But later I was more like his anchor. A familiar port in the storm that was his life. As much as I hated to admit it, I'd read the accounts in the tabloids from the other women who described a wild man that I'd never known. With me, Beckett was gentle, and I thought it was my fault, that I didn't evoke that response.

But this—the way my stomach flooded with desire—it was all new.

Arm wrapped possessively around my waist, Chase followed me inside. The bags hit the floor with a thud and containers rolled in every direction. And then I was off the ground, pinned to the wall, his hips holding me in place.

His mouth claimed mine, and his hands were everywhere. "So fucking sweet."

The slit on my skirt gave way with a loud rip as he wedged himself between my legs. Fingering the lace on the top of my thigh-high stocking, he hissed. "Fuck. Didn't expect these."

"Wait ... the food!" I protested when Chase scooped me into his arms. "I thought you were starving."

He brushed a kiss to my lips as he carried me up the stairs. "I am."

After setting me on my feet, he turned on the faucet and went about finding my favorite bubble bath.

"What are you doing?"

He wiped his hands on his jeans. "Making sure you're good and relaxed."

His lips ghosted mine as he fumbled with the seed pearl buttons on my blouse. Next came my skirt, and then I was standing in front of him in only my stockings, matching bra and panty set, and fuck me heels high enough to make a stripper blush.

Dropping to his knees, he kissed the swath of skin on my thigh, directly above the lace on the stocking. "Is there someone in LA I need to worry about, or are these for me?"

"N-no ... they're for me," I stammered. "I mean, they match the outfit, and I like them."

"Baby, I'm not complaining. In fact, I think you should wear them every day." Eyeing the lace once again, he bit his lip. "Yeah ... *every day.*"

He removed one shoe and then the other before making quick work of my bra. Lacing our fingers, he pulled me toward the tub and, pressing his lips to mine, he eased me onto the side. When he removed the two chopsticks holding my loose bun in place, my hair tumbled down my back.

"Interesting use of utensils," he said.

I grabbed the sticks from his hand. "They're not to eat with. They're for decoration. I got them in China when—"

Silencing my rambling with a soft kiss, he knelt in front of me and then dragged my stockings down my legs.

Fuck me.

I had no idea removing my clothes could be this hot.

He popped to his feet, taking me along with him. "Up you go."

Hooking his fingers into the side of my panties, he shoved them down in one swift move He fisted the back of my hair as he scored his teeth along my jaw, to my neck, and finally my breast.

"Oh ... God ..."

Fireworks danced behind my lids as he nudged my legs open and sank two fingers into my slick heat.

"Baby, you better get into the tub or it's you and me against the sink."

"Come in with me."

His lips curved into a smile. "Bathtub sex isn't all it's cracked up to be." I blinked up at him, because I had no idea. "Get into the tub, Taryn."

When I still didn't move, he swatted my ass. Hard. "Ouch!"

Rubbing the tender spot, he pressed another kiss to my lips. "Get in the tub."

I placed one foot in the sudsy water. "Fine ... but only because I want to."

Easing into the fragrant bubbles, I groaned as the water slid between my legs, meeting the bundle of nerves dying for attention.

Chase was gone for less than two minutes, and when he returned he pressed a goblet of wine into my hand. "Found this in your fridge."

"Oh, God ... Thank you."

After downing half the glass, I sank low enough that only the peaks of my breasts were visible. My nipples tightened as Chase dragged a soft sponge from my shoulders to the tips of my toes.

Kneading the ball of my foot with nimble fingers, he asked, "How's that feel?"

I mumbled something unintelligible as he worked his way up to my calves, and farther up to my inner thighs.

"I want to make you come, baby."

My lids fluttered open, and my mouth curved into a drowsy smile. "I thought bathtub sex wasn't any good."

He tipped forward, stealing the gasp that escaped when he eased a finger inside my channel. "This isn't sex."

His tongue slipped into my mouth as he added another digit, circling my clit with his thumb.

"Ahhh ..." My head fell back, my toes curling as the pleasure rolled through me. "Oh ... God ... I'm coming ..."

When I floated back to earth from the unexpected orgasm, he was smiling down at me. "I love the way you do that."

"What?"

"Let me know exactly what's going on inside your head."

My cheeks flamed. "I do?"

A quick kiss, and he pushed to his feet. "You do. Now, stay put. I'll be back for you in a few minutes."

Boneless, I managed a nod, and my lids fluttered closed.

"Ugh ... It was just getting good," I complained moments later when Chase's hand coiled around my arm to help me to my feet.

He laughed as he wrapped me in a fluffy towel. "I thought you were hungry?"

Franklin's!

His arm banded around my waist. "Easy. The floors are slippery."

Despite a mild protest, he swept me off my feet and carried me to my bed. The smell of jasmine from my favorite Yankee candles warred with the faint scent of mesquite that had my full attention. That is, until Chase stripped off his jeans.

He eased on top of me, his rock-hard erection digging into my thigh.

"Franklin's or me?" When I hesitated for a millisecond, a laugh erupted from his chest. "Don't worry, I'll be quick."

After sliding the condom in place, he took my hands and pinned them to the headboard. My back bowed, and he smiled, sucking one nipple into his mouth.

Wrapping both my wrists in one of his large hands, he kept me immobilized as he moved to the other breast. "Stop squirming." He bit down on the pebbled peak. "Or no barbecue for you."

He slid inside me with one thrust. My fingers throbbed as he tightened his grip. "I missed you," he growled. "Fuck ... I did."

Our eyes met, and for a moment I felt a connection so deep it took my breath away. Before I could question it, his mouth was on mine and our tongues collided. His hand snaked between us, and with only the lightest touch to my needy bud, I shattered, taking him along with me.

"Fuck ... *fuck* ... Taryn ..." He released my wrists as the spasms wracked his body. "What are you doing to me?" Rolling onto his back, he threw his arm over his face. "I think you're trying to kill me."

"That was ..."

Chase propped on his elbow and his smile evaporated. "Jesus, did I hurt you?"

I stopped rubbing my wrist, which I wasn't aware I was doing. "No, I didn't even notice."

Entwining our fingers, he brought my wrists to his lips for a kiss. "Just ... you know ... tell me next time."

Tugging his hair, I forced his troubled gaze to mine. "You didn't hurt me. I would've said something. I don't like pain."

The admission rang in my ears. Pain had been my constant companion for five years. An unwelcome guest. And I didn't feel it as acutely when I was with Chase. But I couldn't tell him that. That probably crossed some kind of friendship boundary.

I was still mulling it over when he returned from the bathroom. He scooped up the bag on his way to the bed. "Let's see what we have in here."

Pulling a piece of brisket out of the Styrofoam container, he took a bite and then groaned. "Damn, this is good."

He pulled box after box from the bottomless bag.

"You know ..." he said, feeding me a piece of brisket, "indulging in comfort food can be a sign of sexual frustration."

The sheet slipped to my waist when I sat up, staring at my rapidly disappearing dinner. Chase had managed to inhale three ribs to my one.

"I wouldn't know since you're eating all the food."

He laughed as he prepared another heaping serving. Propping some pillows behind him, he reclined against the headboard. "There's plenty, baby. Come here."

Since there was no way I could match his pace, I grabbed the plate, growling when he reached for a home fry.

"Greedy girl."

We inhaled the entire contents of the bag in minutes, and then Chase ripped open a towelette, wiping the grease off my fingers. Rolling onto my back, I absently rubbed my belly. "That was so good."

Chase dug around in the bag and produced one final treat. "Mmm ... pie."

Swiping a pillow while he was busy looking for the discarded packet of plastic ware, I shoved it behind my head.

Placing the container with the pecan pie on my stomach, Chase scooped a bite onto the spoon. The morsel wobbled as he lifted it to my mouth, but it slid off before it reached its target, landing with a plop on my chest.

Sweeping his tongue over the gooey sweetness, Chase winked. "Now that's some good fucking pie."

I brushed a lock of hair out of his eyes, and when he smiled, I knew—he *was* going to kill me. Break my heart and leave it in a million pieces when this all faded away.

Chapter 21

CHASE

I stared at the shadows on the ceiling in Taryn's loft, the cherry on my cigarette glowing brightly as I took a big puff. I'd given in and bought a pack on my way here. But only after Taryn fell asleep did I feel the need to smoke one.

She quieted my mind, even as her presence spoke to everything wrong about what I was doing. What I was risking.

She stirred, snuggling into my side. "This is new," she mused, taking the butt from my hand. Smiling, she lifted the Marlboro to her lips and took a drag. "Fall off the wagon, did you?"

And though I knew she was talking about the cigarette, my stomach dropped.

I threw back the covers. "Nope. But I have to take off. I've got an early meeting."

Taryn propped on her elbow, and I saw it on her face. The disappointment. "Okay ... call me tomorrow."

It came out like a question, so I nodded. She dropped back to the pillow and watched me step into my boxers. I stalked to the bathroom, avoiding her gaze and that damn magnetic pull. Loitering as I gathered the rest of my clothes, I took stock of myself in the mirror.

I needed to spend the night in my own bed. Get my head clear. Wash Taryn's scent off my skin.

But I did none of those things. Instead, I grabbed the bottle of Chardonnay from the ledge of the tub and inspected the contents. Half full.

The crisp, fruity liquid slid down my throat easily, but didn't provide the courage I desired.

Go.

My brain barked the order, but it only took seconds for the alcohol to argue the logic. Shuffling back to Taryn's bed, I slipped under the covers, keeping my back to her. A small compromise.

She pressed a kiss to my shoulder. "I thought you were leaving?"

I am. I *was.*

I rolled over, and the tendrils of hair in her face begged for my touch. "You want me to leave?" I tucked a wayward strand behind her ear. "Say the word, baby."

She smiled a dreamy smile. "No. I want you to stay."

Pulling her forward, my hand slid to her ass. "Why's that?"

"Because I want you to make me breakfast in the morning."

I traced a finger along the ridge of her spine, cursing my inability to keep my hands to myself for one fucking second. "Is that all you want?"

Despite the wine fogging my brain, my cock sprang to life when her fingers coiled around my shaft. "No."

She gave me a saucy grin, so I pinned her on her back. "You *are* a greedy girl. Twice in one night."

Grabbing a condom from the nightstand, she pressed the foil packet into my hand. "You're one to talk."

She kissed my neck, and any bit of resolve fell by the wayside. I rolled the latex into place and, positioning myself at her entrance, I sank in an inch. "Is this what you want?"

All you want?

I pushed all the way in, swallowing the small cry when she moaned. As I moved inside her, it was easy to forget all the things that made this—whatever it was—such a bad idea.

In the dark, there was nothing but her. The feel of her skin and the sound of her voice. But things that happened in the dark had a funny way of forcing themselves into the light. I knew that better than most, and still, I couldn't stop myself.

But then, I never could.

Chapter 22

TARYN

*B*right sunshine poured through the window, warming my skin and coaxing me from sleep. My smile fell away as I patted the empty space next to me. I sat up and looked around with bleary eyes.

A tray sat on the bench at the foot of my bed, a piece of paper tucked between the cup of coffee and plate of waffles.

Frowning, I recalled the notes Beckett used to leave strewn around the loft before he'd go on tour. As if his abandoned trail of breadcrumbs and sweet nothings would cushion my fall after they led me off the cliff. And there was always a cliff.

He's not Beckett.

I picked up the lukewarm cup of coffee and stared at the frothy contents. Sweet with extra cream, just the way I liked it.

Gazing at the note, I took a sip, but before I got the nerve to sneak a peek, my phone shrilled.

Scrambling to retrieve the device from the pocket of my jeans, I debated answering Tori's call.

"Hey, Belle."

"Do you know what I'm looking at?" she asked without preamble.

I picked at the crispy edges of the waffle. "No clue."

"A bill from the Omni Hotel, charged to Twin Souls for a four-night stay."

Groaning inwardly, I kicked myself for using my corporate American Express card to pay for Harper's room. "And?"

When I heard teeth gnashing, I could almost picture the vein bulging in Tori's neck. "What was she doing here, Taryn? I told you—"

My guise of serenity crumbled into a cloud of anger. "I didn't meet her in the office." Shoving to my feet, I stormed to my desk. "She's my client, for fuck's sake."

"*Our* client, apparently, since she's signed at Twin Souls."

Not really, but oh well. I wasn't going to bother explaining the finer nuances of Harper's contract to Tori at the moment.

Yanking open the desk drawer, I searched for my super-secret hidden pack of cigarettes. After sneaking a couple of puffs of Chase's smoke last night, I was craving a hit. Big time.

I stopped digging when I pulled out a long-forgotten photo shoved in the back of the drawer. Damaged, Leveraged, Revenged Theory and Drafthouse, all standing below a banner for the Sixth Street Takeover Tour.

And me, wrapped in Beckett's arms, with Paige on one side and Tori on the other.

"Nothing happened between Harper and Dylan."

The lie slipped out in a whisper as I closed the drawer.

Tori sighed. "What's done is done. I just ... I don't want ..."

To lose anything else.

Knowing her as well as I did, I could finish the sentence that she never would. But Dylan wasn't Tori's to lose, not when she'd never claimed him.

Sinking onto the bed, I stared out at the wisps of white fluff dotting the blue sky. "There won't be any publicity. I've already told the label the story's bullshit."

After a long moment, Tori cleared her throat. "I saw the article in the *Statesman*. The one about you and Beckett."

My stomach twisted. "Really, it's out?"

She hummed. "Yep ... this morning."

In the end, Beckett's misguided loyalty wouldn't do any good. The next time he was spotted with a supermodel or a fangirl, the speculation would start again. The whispers.

I wonder what happened? I bet it's Taryn. Poor Beckett.

I released a staggered breath. "Beckett doesn't want to be linked to Maddy. So he just ..."

Used me.

"I don't think so. He said—"

I picked up my fork and stabbed at the waffles. "I know what he said. It doesn't matter. I've moved on."

"Yeah, he told me about that guy," Tori said quietly. "Are you still seeing him?"

Since I'd yet to provide any details, the hurt edging her tone was justified.

My focus shifted to the note on the tray. "We're just friends."

Friends, at least ...

"Well, you can tell me all about your *friend* tonight."

"What's happening tonight?"

"Caged is playing the Parish. They're down a manager."

"I know. I've gotten a few emails from Logan Cage. But there's something ... Hold on..." I plucked my iPad from the nightstand and then did a quick search. "Here it is. Their last manager said they were trouble." Scanning to the end of the article, I rolled my eyes. "Never mind. I know that bitch. She's the problem. Dylan mentioned them a few months back, but I've been too busy to set up a meet."

"Yeah, I know." Sarcasm infused Tori's tone. "Anyway, I think we should sign them."

"Sign them?" I laughed. "That's not how it works, Belle. You know that. I need to take a look and then—"

"That's why I'm asking you to come along. I want to be involved in the vetting from now on."

Tori was serious about extracting a little payback for Harper. And I had to wonder if she'd resort to such immature tactics if we hadn't been friends since kindergarten. But the stakes were higher now. Higher than she realized.

"So, do you want to go, or what?" Tori pressed.

A headache threatened, and I rubbed my temple. "Of course, I want to go. What time?"

"We'll pick you up at eight."

Fuck.

Dropping my head into my hand, I rubbed my temples. "Who's 'we'?"

"Dylan and Beckett and me."

"Why would you invite them, Belle?"

"Because I want their opinion," she snapped.

Since my opinion was the only one that mattered, I needed to remind Tori of that by going along on her little adventure. "Fine. I'll see you at eight."

Ending the call, I tossed the phone on the bed, and since my day couldn't get worse, I plucked Chase's note from the tray.

Taryn,

Enjoy your breakfast. We'll talk soon.

A brushoff ...

I guess a week and a half was the shelf life for a fling. Especially one involving a superstar ex and newspaper articles full of angsty confessions.

At least he made me breakfast.

Disappointment swam in my gut as I dropped the note on top of the waffles. I watched the ink run as the butter spread across the paper. And when the scrawl was too opaque to read, I pushed to my feet and shuffled to my closet to choose my suit of armor for the day.

Chapter 23

CHASE

*T*he bouncer covering the back door at the Parish leaned against the wall, his heavy boot scuffing the paint. Chuckling as he looked down at his phone, he didn't notice me until I was on him. Eyes wide, he fumbled to pocket the device.

"Keep that damn thing out of sight while you're working," I barked as I marched past him. "I'm not paying you to watch videos."

Ignoring his stammered apology, I kept on walking, the copy of the *Statesman* burning a hole in my back pocket.

Once inside my office, I tossed the rag onto my desk and dropped into the chair, glaring at the headline.

Beckett's Side: Leveraged Guitarist Sets the Record Straight on Fame, Music, and Taryn.

Yanking open my bottom drawer, I found the bottle of Jack and poured a liberal amount into my coffee cup before spreading the paper out. I nearly choked on my first sip when I read Beckett's opening quote.

"There's been a lot of rumors going around about my personal life," Brennin said. *"False reports from people who know nothing about me. For the record, Taryn is the only woman in my life."*

Ignoring the rest of Beckett's delusional ramblings, I scanned the rest of the print for anything resembling a response from Taryn.

Ayers has been tightlipped about the status of her relationship with Brennin. It has long been speculated that the two are secretly wed. Though a license was issued in Nevada in 2014, no marriage was ever recorded.

I chuckled dryly into my next gulp of bourbon.

Nothing about Taryn's life was private. Her darkest secrets and deepest pain were out there for anyone with an Internet connection or the price of a newspaper. Something as monumental as a wedding couldn't be covered up.

Like a stint in rehab? Having a rock star for a brother? An unfulfilled six-figure record contract?

The anxiety over my undisclosed past drifted away when I found the only quote ascribed to Taryn at the very end of the piece.

"When asked for a comment, Ayers simply stated: I love Beckett. Always."

I should have been happy. Or at least relieved.

Every minute I spent with Taryn made it just a little easier to believe that we were something more than casual. But now I had proof that the feeling wasn't mutual. So there was no reason to risk continuing our little fling.

Resolved, I downed the rest of my drink and then tossed the newspaper in the trash on my way out of the office.

Maria, my back of the house manager, rushed toward me as I made my way to the dressing room.

"You'll never believe who's coming tonight."

Distracted, I checked my phone. "No clue."

A flush colored her cheeks as she exclaimed, "Dylan Booth, Beckett Brennin, and Tori Grayson! Can you believe it? "

The world slowed to half speed along with my steps. "Party of three?" I asked, hopeful, because surely, I couldn't be that unlucky.

Glancing at her clipboard, she shook her head. "Four."

I exhaled a slow breath, mostly to see if there was oxygen in my lungs.

"Make sure we have security in place."

She jotted down a note, her grin still intact. "No worries. Logan asked me to have Zeke keep an eye out. His sister's here tonight."

Shit.

Against my better judgment, I blew past the dressing room and hit the main floor. The bartender shot me a smile when I slid a hip onto the stool.

"Shiner?" he asked, dropping a cocktail napkin in front of me.

"Jack, three fingers. Straight up."

As I waited for my drink, my gaze traveled over the crowd to the VIP area, and I glimpsed Laurel and Calista at a small table.

"Anything else?" The bartender asked, pocketing the ten spot I left for a tip.

"Nope."

Skirting the crowd, I emerged by the stage where Logan was sucking face with a girl in a pink wig. I nudged him as I passed. "Don't you be making any plans for after the show. Calista's not taking care of Laurel all night."

Logan made eye contact long enough to acknowledge my comment while Pinkie continued to nibble his neck.

Rolling my eyes, I joined Cameron a few feet away.

"I thought you were cutting out early tonight?" he said as he tuned his guitar.

"Changed my mind."

When the house lights dimmed, the guys formed their usual huddle to go over the set list. And that's when I saw the four figures climbing the stairs in the VIP area. Dylan Booth was in the lead, Tori Grayson a step behind. But all my attention was on Beckett's hand, resting at the small of Taryn's back as he ushered her to the table. I'd never wanted to break someone's hand so badly in my life.

"Good crowd, huh?" the DJ mused when he ambled up.

Catching his arm as he pushed the curtain aside to make the announcement, I said, "I've got this one."

In all the years I'd owned the Parish, I'd never taken the stage. Not to make an announcement. Or to play. It was a line I'd never crossed. Until I did.

Ignoring my brother's look of surprise, I strolled across the weathered hardwood, chants from the crowd thundering in my ears as I stepped into the spotlight.

What the actual fuck are you doing?

The rage simmering under my skin answered the question as I shifted my focus to the VIP section. I couldn't see anything beyond the colored lights, but they sure as shit could see me.

"How y'all doing tonight?" I roared into the mic. "I'm Chase Noble, the owner of the Parish. It gives me great pleasure to welcome to the stage, Sixth Street's own ... *Caged!*"

Beams of light swept over the audience in slow circles, and I caught sight of Taryn's face. Surprise coated her features. I felt no measure of satisfaction, but I smiled nonetheless. That is, until I felt Cameron's arm snake around my shoulder.

"No, you don't." Laughing, he tightened his grip as I tried to give him a playful shove.

"Hey guys!" he shouted, whipping the audience into a greater frenzy. "Give it up for the coolest bar owner in Texas and one helluva musician, my brother, Chase!"

Frozen in my spot as the light show began a second revolution, my stomach clattered to the floor when I saw Taryn stumbling down the steps of the VIP seating.

The magnitude of the clusterfuck snapped me out of my stupor, and my feet moved of their own accord. Fighting the crush of people in the pit, I spotted Taryn's head bobbing in the sea of strangers.

She ducked into the small alcove with the pay phones that nobody used. When I followed her inside, the weight of a large body shoved me out of the way.

"Leave her alone," Beckett spat. "She ain't interested."

"Mind your business, dude. She's interested."

I stopped short of telling the fucker how very interested Taryn was last night when she was under me.

Beckett wagged a finger in my face. "She is my business. Now back off."

Before I could wrap my hand around his throat, Taryn slipped between us. "Go back to the table," she said to Beckett. "Before someone figures out who you are."

Dropping a possessive hand on her hip, he sneered at me. "I ain't leaving."

Taryn slanted a gaze his way. "This isn't a date, Beckett. Tori wanted you here. Not me. Now go watch the show."

"You heard her," I rumbled.

But more importantly, *I* heard her. Taryn wasn't here with Beckett.

He hesitated for only a second before brushing a kiss to the top of Taryn's head and stalking away. She didn't notice, though. All her attention was on me, those stormy eyes filled with questions.

"You're Cameron Knight's brother?" she finally asked, her brows pinched tight in disbelief.

"Let's talk someplace more private."

I took her arm, but she shook off my grip. "Answer me!"

After a long moment, I let out a shuddering breath. "Yes."

The same word that held such promise when we were standing on that street corner put an end to us.

"I thought we were friends," she said as the tears gathered.

Drawn to the first raindrop that fell onto her cheek, I took a step toward her. "We are. Of course we are."

Friends at least ...

Excuses danced on the tip of my tongue, but before I could offer even one, Taryn shook her head. "Friends don't lie to each other."

Residual anger coalesced with the alcohol that had yet to burn its way out of my system. "Guess Beckett didn't get the memo."

This time when I crossed the line, I didn't feel the rush. Only regret when Taryn brushed past me and walked out of my life.

Chapter 24

TARYN

I stormed to the table, fighting to keep my anger from boiling over and burning everyone in the vicinity.

"I'm leaving," I yelled over the music as I snatched my purse from the back of the chair. "I'll take a cab."

Tori leaned forward, cupping her ear. "What?"

"Leaving!"

Beckett grabbed my wrist. "Give me a minute," he shouted over the drum solo, eyeing the crowd with apprehension. "There's too many people ... I can't ..."

I shook off his hold. "I didn't ask you to."

Before he could respond, I dashed from the VIP area. The humid air hit my face like a blow dryer when I finally made it outside. Bypassing the line of cabs, I headed north. In a city the size of Austin, my entire life was limited to a three-mile radius. And maybe that's why I couldn't breathe. The air was tainted with every memory of any consequence. And Chase Noble just added to the swirling tornado of emotions.

Chase is Cameron Knight's brother.

And why wouldn't he just tell me?

A horn blasted, and I looked around.

"Taryn!" Beckett hissed through the open window of Dylan's Hummer. "Get in the fucking car."

I waved my hand. "I'm fine. Just go."

Please go.

"Get in the car, T-Rex." Dylan's tone held less bite, but urgency underscored his plea.

It was then that I noticed a few people at the sidewalk cafe, eagerly taking in the show.

Is that Beckett Brennin?

Oh my God, Dylan's driving!

It's Taryn!

Chairs scraped the pavement as the casual observers abandoned their seats, inserting themselves into my private hell. Self-preservation kicked in, and I moved toward the Hummer.

Beckett jumped from the truck, his body shielding me as he nudged me inside. "Really smart," he growled. "You want to get us mobbed?"

I scooted to the end of the seat, Beckett's proximity irking me. "You're going to get yourself mobbed. I didn't ask for your help."

Dylan gunned the engine, and two minutes later he bypassed the front of my building and drove straight to the gate on the visitor's side of the parking garage. If I thought I was going to get out of this without a major discussion, I forgot who I was dealing with.

Dylan pulled the Hummer into one of my designated spaces and, without a word, he slid out of the truck and strode toward the elevator. Tori followed suit.

"You just gonna sulk out here all night?" Beckett asked as he hopped out of the truck. "Because we all have keys to your place. You're the only one that's going to be sitting in the dark."

And this was my life.

Gathering my resolve, I joined the trio in front of the infernally slow elevator.

"That was some stunt you pulled," Tori muttered as she stepped onto the lift. "I'm getting really tired of your personal shit interfering with my business."

My voice echoed off the metal walls as I followed her in. "And what about your personal issues, Belle? And don't try to act like you don't have any."

She muttered something under her breath, and I did the same. When the doors slid open, Beckett slipped an arm around my waist, digging his fingers into my side. "Out," he coaxed. "We'll discuss this in the loft."

The man with the attention span of a fruit fly was now giving me lessons on etiquette and decorum. Yeah, no.

"Get off me, Beckett." I shook off his grip. "You've got no dog in this hunt."

Dylan had Tori out of my reach, ushering her down the hallway. He shoved his key into the lock and then pushed open the door, yanking her over the threshold a second later.

The boys had witnessed their share of fights between Tori and me in the past. The distant past. For five years I'd given in. But tonight, I was ready to hash it out. Because, come hell or high water, things were going to change.

My rage abated as I paced the floor in my loft.

"I've already signed Harper," I said. "If you want to keep punishing me for that, feel free. It was a business decision."

Tori tapped her finger against her knee impatiently. "I'm sure she'll be a welcome addition to the team. Just like Caged."

On the imaginary scoreboard hanging over our heads, Tori and I each had one point. A dead heat.

"They're a good band," I conceded. "No loss there."

Shifting in her seat, Tori settled against the cushions. "And ... I want Chase Noble to join the team as well."

I didn't blink, even when the ground shook as Beckett jumped to his feet. "No way," he growled as he attempted to sidestep Dylan. "What the fuck, Belle?"

"Calm down, dude," Dylan said as he grabbed Beckett's shoulder. "I told you, Logan said Chase is the best producer out there."

"I don't give a fuck," Beckett seethed. "Taryn isn't going to manage the dude that used her to get his brother a shot. Is that what you want, Belle?"

Tori said nothing as Beckett continued his objections.

Tuning out the white noise, I crossed my arms over my chest in defense. From Tori.

"We don't need producers," I said. "I've got that handled."

Tori sat back, assessing me with a frosty glare. "Obviously you don't since you let Trent roll over you on the Leveraged project. We need a musician to oversee the tracks."

Dylan's eyes found mine, beseeching. And since defending myself would only lead to questions I couldn't answer, I dropped into my seat. "Fine, Belle," I said. "If that's what you want."

Ignoring the yawning silence, I glanced at my laptop on the dining room table. Inside, there were twenty or more offers from headhunters across the country. I never read them, just tucked them in my little electronic file. Because I never considered leaving. Until now.

Dylan cleared his throat. "Do you have anything set up for this weekend?" he asked me as he took a seat next to Tori.

"This weekend?" I croaked.

I followed his gaze to the calendar on my fridge, where a big red circle marked the date for our annual pilgrimage down the Guadeloupe River. The Spring Float.

"Maybe we should cancel this year," Tori said quietly, and when our eyes met, I saw the girl behind the cloud of anger and discord. My best friend.

"Of course we're not going to cancel," I said, grabbing a pen and paper from my backpack. "Has everyone confirmed?" Dylan nodded. "Then I guess I should start with tent assignments. Preferences?"

Beckett sat up, suddenly enthralled with the conversation.

"I'm with you, babe," he said casually.

I scribbled notes without looking up. "Nice try. You can sleep in Dylan's tent, or bring your own. You're a big boy."

He pulled me to his side, tickling my ribcage until I squirmed.

"I am a big boy. That's why you need to be sleeping in my tent."

Just talking about the trip cleared the air, and we were teenagers again. We'd done the float every year since we were freshmen in high school. Before the accident, it was a tradition. Now it was a tribute.

The year after Rhenn died, Tori made her first trip down the river alone. The doctors had advised against it since her bones were barely healed. But I tied her tube to mine, and we made the journey together, with all our friends cheering us on.

Overcome by the memory, I chanced a peek at Tori and found her staring at me with soft eyes. "I don't care what we eat," she said. "Or what campsite we stay in, as long as you and I are in the same tent. And on the same path."

Our lives were like that damn river. Always flowing in one direction, leading to the same spot. And if I had to change that, I didn't know who I'd be. So I pushed aside any foolish notion about the file in my computer and went back to planning our trip.

Chapter 25

CHASE

*T*he guys busted through the door of the dressing room, high-fiving and patting each other on the back.

"Do you know who was in the audience tonight?" Cameron asked me as he pressed a bottle of beer into my hand. "Of course you did. That's why you made the announcement." He narrowed his eyes in mock irritation while wagging a finger in my face. "You should have said something. We could have really fucked up. Lucky for you we're ready for anything."

I winced inwardly, certain they weren't ready for what I had to tell them.

"Listen, Cameron—" I began, but his attention was diverted to the door when Laurel walked in.

She was off the ground, scooped into Logan's arms a second later. After swinging her around in a celebratory hug, he looked down at her in anticipation. "Did you hear anything?"

"About what?" she asked, glancing at me out of the corner of her eye.

Logan laughed. "Tori Grayson was sitting right next to you. Didn't you see her?" When Laurel didn't say anything, he added, "Dylan Boothe and Beckett Brennin were there too."

His smile melted when she looked down at her toes. "Oh, um ... they left."

Logan's arms dropped limply to his sides. "Left? When did they leave?"

"About ten minutes after the show started." She offered a hopeful smile. "Maybe there was an emergency or something."

The guys let out a collective groan as they digested the information.

Sean sank into the folding chair against the wall. "Obviously, they didn't like what they saw," he said with a sigh. The brooding drummer usually kept his feelings to himself. But even he couldn't hide the disappointment as he stared into his bottle of water. "Maybe we didn't sound as good as we thought we did."

"Fuck that," Logan bit out as he stomped over to the table to grab a beer. "We were tight. I don't know what's going on, but—"

Wrangling his phone from his pocket when an old Leveraged tune echoed in the room, he said, "It's Dylan," as he headed for the door. "I'm going to find out what the hell happened."

Since I didn't want to go through my confession twice, I decided to wait until he returned. I drained my beer, then poured a shot of Jack for good measure. When the stay of execution dragged on for several minutes, I fortified myself with a second shot.

Infusing steel into my spine when Logan reentered the room, I braced for his anger.

"Well?" Cameron asked. "What happened?"

"It's all good," Logan said as he sifted through the cooler for a beer. "Tori liked what she saw so they didn't need to stick around."

"What about Taryn?" Sean chimed in. "She handles the talent, right? What did she think?"

"No clue," Logan said as he eased onto the sofa. "I'm sure she's fine. They're going to draw up a ninety-day agreement, and then we'll see how it goes."

When the chatter started up again, I poured another shot—my fourth? It was all blurring together.

Cameron's hand came down on my shoulder, and I almost

jumped out of my skin. "We're going to take this party over to Nite Owl," he said frowning at what I could only believe was my sour expression. "Is that all right?"

I shrugged. "Sure. Whatever."

Once we got to my loft, I grabbed a couple of beers and sank onto a chair on the periphery of the party with my phone in my hand.

To text or not to text?

Chuckling at my own joke, I dropped my head back. Even with the amount of liquor dulling my senses, I could still see Taryn's face behind my lids, her sun shower eyes clouded with pain. Pain that I put there.

Hours later, I cracked open a bleary eye when Cameron shook my arm. "We're heading home," he said, glancing over all the bottles on the table that I didn't remember drinking. "Are you okay?"

Fuck.

A few beers and the kid was looking at me like ...

Sobered by the thought I couldn't finish, I shoved to my feet and tried not to sway. "I'm good. Just a little too much cheer, I guess."

Logan strode into the room, zeroing in on his sister. "You," he said, pointing at Laurel. "Upstairs."

Rolling her eyes, she pecked her brother's cheek on the way to the stairs. I stayed upright long enough to wave at everyone as they left. Then I dropped back into the chair.

My lids snapped open when Logan's boots met the coffee table with a loud thud.

"What?" I mumbled groggily, glancing around the empty room.

He crossed his arms over his chest, glowering. "When were you going to tell us you're fucking Taryn Ayers?"

Taryn's name on Logan's lips swept away some of the haze. My mind raced for an excuse and, finding none, I let my head fall back.

"Aren't you going to answer me?" Logan asked, after a long moment.

And say what? That even with everything that happened I'd do it again if I had the chance?

With the last thought swirling in my head, I hauled myself upright. "Who I fuck is none of your business, Logan."

Disgust curled his lip, and he looked away. "Do you know how long I've been trying to get this shit squared away with Twin Souls."

I rose on unsteady legs and walked to the kitchen to get something for my pounding head. "I know exactly how long since I've been carrying the band while you work out your management issues. Let's not forget how you got into this mess."

Thundering to his feet, he closed the gap between us in seconds. "Don't lay this shit on me. You're the one who jeopardized the bands future over a lay."

My fingers balled into fists, and I rounded on him. "It wasn't like that."

Logan searched my face. "What was it like, then?"

When I couldn't find the words to explain, he shook his head. "Yeah, that's what I figured."

I fished four aspirin from the bottle I found in the drawer. "I won't be seeing Taryn anymore, so you got nothing to worry about."

Logan took a seat on the barstool. "It's not that easy. Dylan invited us to go to the spring float next weekend. Apparently, their whole crew does it every year. Tori Grayson insisted that you come along and make things right with Taryn or she's going to pull the offer."

Chapter 26

TARYN

*G*ravel crunched under the tires of Dylan's Hummer as we coasted to a stop. He knocked my foot from its perch on the back of his seat to get my attention. "Want anything?"

I sat up and glanced around the parking lot of the bait and tackle shop, smiling when I spotted Pedro, the guy who had run the place since we were kids, greeting customers from his spot on the redwood deck.

"Skittles, Red Vines, and Starburst," I said. "Make it two."

Dylan reached over and pulled an earbud from Tori's ear. "You want anything?"

She sat up with a start and wiped her mouth with the back of her hand. "Huh? Oh ... cookies."

Dylan jumped out of the truck and sauntered toward the shack, oblivious to the girls who stopped mid stride to gawk at his rock-hard abs and broad shoulders.

Amused, Tori shook her head at the spectacle. "Hope he doesn't pick up a girl in there."

"He won't."

With you around.

Tori tugged off her oversized *I'm With The Band* T-shirt and then adjusted her bikini top. "When's Beckett coming up? Tonight or tomorrow?"

Averting my gaze from the scars on her back, I sighed. "I don't know. I'm not his keeper."

She snorted. "Since when? You might not be riding the boy anymore, but you two are still up in each other's business."

Annoyed, I plucked one of the three remaining Starburst from the package. "Beckett does what he pleases."

"That doesn't mean he's not telling you where he's at and what he's doing." She turned in her seat. "Especially after what happened with ..."

My glare stopped her from finishing the thought. In the six days since I'd walked out of the Parish, I'd spent my time planning the float and tending to business. Twin Souls business. At the moment that didn't include Chase Noble.

Tori swiped her sunglasses from the dashboard. "Have you talked to him?"

"I'll talk to him when there's a reason to talk to him."

A business reason.

"Fair enough," she said.

We sat in companionable silence until Dylan climbed into the truck.

"Don't go into a sugar coma, T-Rex," he warned as he pitched a small bag at me.

Dumping the contents on the seat, I gleefully examined the assortment of Fireballs, Laffy Taffy, Lemon Drops and other non-chocolate items. I'd learned the chocolate lesson the hard way when I was fourteen and my Hershey bar melted in the pocket of my cut-offs. I'd walked around all day looking like I had a serious case of Irritable Bowel Syndrome. Rhenn was forced to defend my honor, holding some kid's head under the murky water until he apologized for insulting me.

My lips tugged into a smile at the memory.

Tearing open a Butterfinger, Dylan popped a piece into his mouth and then fired up the engine. When he looked over his shoulder to maneuver the big truck from the parking space, he caught sight of the longing in my eyes.

"Don't get this all over." He tossed the remainder of the candy into my waiting hands. "I'm not kicking someone's ass if they dredge up your old pet name, *Shitty Kitty.*"

Tori fused her lips around the straw of her Big Gulp, her eyes widening as she tried to choke down the mouthful of soda. Giving up, she let loose, spewing Dr. Pepper all over Dylan's pristine dashboard.

"Damn it!" she screeched, pulling long strands of raven hair off her chest.

"That's what you get." I smirked, popping in my ear buds to block out Tori's grumbling and Dylan's laughter.

We got back on the highway, and moments later, my stomach fluttered at the first sight of the Guadeloupe, peeking through the trees lining the road.

On days like this, none of us wore the personas we donned for the outside world. We were just us. The same group of kids that had climbed these rocks and floated this river since we were old enough to convince our parents to let us navigate it alone.

"What the hell is he doing here?" I shrieked as Dylan pulled to a stop in front of the campground.

Chase glanced our way as he lifted an ice chest from the bed of the Dodge Ram truck.

"Fuck, Taryn, don't kill me," Dylan pleaded.

I slapped the back of his head. "Why would you invite him?" I growled.

Dylan's eyes darted to Tori. "It was her idea. I mentioned the float trip to Logan the night of the show, and she said to invite them."

He jerked when I kicked the back of his seat. "And you didn't think to tell me? What the hell were you talking to Logan for anyway?"

Dylan squeezed the back of his neck. "I called them," he admitted. "I didn't want them to think we didn't want them."

"We?" I challenged. "Did you suddenly decide to leave the stage and start managing talent?"

"You know what I mean," Dylan said.

Dropping my head into my hands, I sighed. "Yes, Dylan, I know what you mean. Now drive me home. This isn't my idea of a good time."

A light tap pinged off the glass, and I lifted my gaze, a handful of my hair still clutched in my fists. A smiling blonde stood at the side of the truck.

"Who's that?" Tori asked, teeth clenched into a smile.

"How the hell do I know?" I replied as I hit the button to lower the window.

"Hey y'all. I'm Lily. Cameron's girlfriend," she said. "Which of you is Taryn?"

Lifting a hand as if she'd just called roll, I mumbled, "Here."

Her smile grew, if that were possible. The girl was downright perky. "Chase sent me over to ask if you have a mallet."

"Why?" My stone-cold gaze shifted to Chase, leaning against his truck and sipping a beer. "Does he want me to bury it in his head? That could be arranged."

Lily frowned.

"That was a joke." I showed some teeth to prove the point.

"No," Tori deadpanned. "It really wasn't. But I know we've got a mallet in the back somewhere."

Lily gathered her long, blond hair in a pile at the top of her head. "Glad to hear it. We need to set up the tent so I can change. It's hot as balls out here."

Hot as balls? I snorted a laugh despite myself.

Dylan jumped out of the truck. "Nice to meet you, Lily. I'm Dylan, and that's Tori." He stuck a thumb over his shoulder. "And you've already met Taryn. She's our own little ray of sunshine." He cocked a brow at me as he turned Lily toward the back of the Hummer. "Let me get you that mallet before Taryn finds it and gives it to Chase herself."

As soon as the liftgate closed, I crawled over the seat. "Get your shit out of the back, I'm going home," I declared. "You guys can catch a ride with one of the other guys."

Tori shook her head vehemently. "No way. I'm not getting stuck out here with these idiots. Do you know what can happen in three days on the river?"

Nothing was going to happen, and Tori knew it. It was one of the few places the boys could go without being accosted. Everyone was too interested in making sure their inner tubes didn't spring a leak to worry about our group of rock stars.

"Look at Chase!" Tori exclaimed. "He doesn't know what to do with himself. He keeps looking over here like you're going to climb out of the window any second."

She craned her neck to get a better view, so I slapped her arm.

"Quit looking over there." I dropped my forehead to the steering wheel. "This isn't high school, Belle. And Chase isn't Beckett. I don't have to have him in my life."

When I turned to peer at Tori, she looked very much her age. "You're right. Chase isn't Beckett. So maybe you shouldn't treat him like he is." When I blinked first, she swung the door open. "Come on. You know you're staying."

"Debatable."

"Suit yourself." She hopped to her feet. "But if you take the truck I'll have Dylan report it stolen."

As soon as Tori joined the group, Chase broke away and walked right over. Reluctantly, I hit the button, and the glass slid down.

Lifting the bottle of beer to his upturned lips, he said, "Why are you hiding over here?"

"I'm not hiding. I'm probably not going to stay."

His tongue swept his bottom lip. "Don't let me run you off."

Glaring, I pushed open the door, knocking him backward. "You couldn't run me anywhere," I called over my shoulder as I headed down the path.

He fell into step beside me, suddenly serious. "Why won't you talk to me. I've called and—"

"There's nothing to say. You lied to me and I—"

"I didn't fucking lie." Gathering his composure, Chase blew out a breath. "I just didn't tell you everything. There's a difference."

Tori was right. Chase wasn't Beckett. But the excuses were the same. "No, there isn't," I said, unshed tears burning my throat. "And if you were me, you'd know that."

Rather than embarrass myself, I turned away and trotted down the path. And when Chase called my name, I broke into a run and didn't stop until my side ached and I couldn't breathe.

Chapter 27

CHASE

*T*he morning sun crept through the mesh window in my tent, and I threw my arm over my eyes to block the blinding dawn.

Sweat trickled down my skin, sour from the beer and whiskey I drank last night.

Last night ...

After Taryn arrived and we had our little falling out, I took solace in Shiner Bock. And now my head felt like someone had buried a hatchet in my skull while I was sleeping.

Feeling around for the bottle of aspirin, I found a handful of stray tablets on top of the sleeping bag.

I popped a few into my mouth, blanching at the taste as I chewed. When the pain was tolerable, I hauled myself up and ventured to the row of faucets on the edge of the campsite to brush my teeth. Skipping the shave, I stashed my supplies in a plastic bag, securing the gear in the pocket of my loose-fitting board shorts.

Alcohol wafted from my pores, so I headed to the river to hose off. When I cleared the tree line, I spotted Taryn waist deep in the still water, chestnut hair glistening in the early morning sun. And her skin ... fuck ...

She jerked when I snuck up behind her. "What the hell, Chase?" she screeched, loud enough to shake the birds from the trees. "You scared me."

I dropped my hands on her hips. "That's one way to get us some privacy."

"Not private enough," she muttered as she wiggled out of my arms. "Just leave me alone."

"I would if I could," I said truthfully.

Since I had no power over my body when Taryn was around, I sank to my knees and let the murky water hide the evidence of her effect on me.

She crossed her arms over her chest and pouted. "So you're just going to sit here."

I squinted up at her. "Yep."

When she made no attempt to leave, I took her hand and pressed a kiss to her palm. "Afraid you can't control yourself?"

"I can control myself just fine," she said softly, without a hint of conviction.

"So, this doesn't do anything for you?" I kissed her knuckles, then the back of her hand. A gentle tug, and she fell forward, her knees digging into my thighs. "What about this?" I brushed my lips over her neck and up to her ear.

She said nothing, just stayed still as the water lapped against us.

"Damn, I missed this smell," I said as I breathed in her sun-soaked hair.

Taryn pushed away, and my arms fell to my sides. Then, to my surprise, she turned and reclined against my chest.

After a long moment, she whispered, "I love it here."

"Me too."

I doubt we were talking about the same thing. She was taking in the scenery, her gaze fixed on the sycamore and elms cupping the opposite shoreline, while I was content just holding her.

"I've always wanted to live by the water," she mused. "I have a lot at Lake Travis."

Since I didn't know how long the magic would last, I took full advantage of the conversation. "I know a good builder if you're interested."

She released a tremulous breath. "Already have one. The house has been framed for six years." Dropping her head back, she looked up at me with a sad smile. "Paige designed it. It was her house."

I swept a curl behind her ear. "I could help you finish it."

Turning her attention back to the trees, she shrugged. "Why? It would just be an empty house. I couldn't sell it. And I can't live there. It's better to leave it unfinished. Like Paige."

Her voice cracked, so I tightened my hold, coaxing her back from wherever she was.

"Maybe it's better to have a short life filled with great things than a long life full of unfulfilled promises."

"Why can't you have both?"

I chuckled. "I wonder that every time I pick up a guitar."

She settled into the crook of my arm so she could see my face. "What do you mean?"

Pondering for only a moment, I finally said, "I've been playing the guitar since before I could remember. My dad was in a band." She nodded, and I could tell it was no surprise. "He used to make me go onstage before his shows. And it was so lonely up there. Just my guitar echoing off every wall, with only the techs and roadies to serenade."

Her brow furrowed. "You don't like to play? But you're so good."

I pressed a kiss to the little crease on her forehead. "I like a small stage where the audience can breathe with me. If I try to go bigger—"

Whatever thought was about to escape receded into the dark space in my head when a group of ten or so kids bounded into the water.

Taryn let out a little sigh as she climbed to her feet.

"We should get back," she said, squinting down at me.

We. I liked the sound of that.

I hauled myself up, nodding. "Yeah."

We'd just reached the shore when Laurel appeared at the tree line.

"Where's that green canvas bag?" she called. "I packed my extra bathing suit in it before we left the loft."

I was still trying to figure out what bag she was talking about and where it could be when I caught sight of Taryn looking down at her toes.

She couldn't think ...

But when she brought her gaze to mine, I knew that she did.

"No, no," I said, chuckling. "That's Logan's sister. She's just a friend."

My explanation didn't seem to matter because Taryn nodded and turned on her heel. She passed Laurel as the kid trudged to the beach.

Tamping down my anger, which had nothing to do with Laurel, I dug my keys out of my waterproof bag and handed them over. "Look in the truck."

She tossed me a smile and then took off at a run.

Shaking my head, I took a step, grazing my foot on a jagged rock protruding from the silt. I dug the stone from its hiding place to keep some unsuspecting kid from cutting themselves.

The plain little rock had obviously broken away from one of the larger boulders. Jagged on one side, bright veins of color burst from the smooth surface on the other.

The stone was too beautiful to throw back, even with its jagged, imperfect edges, so I stowed it in my pocket.

Trudging back up the worn path, the rock bit into the skin on my thigh as I followed Taryn's muddy footprints until they were no longer legible.

We were already an hour late pushing off when I tossed my tube into the river. Sinking onto the float, I looked around.

Spotting Laurel at the water's edge talking to someone outside our group, I nudged Cameron's shoulder. "What's that about?"

He followed my gaze, then shrugged. "No clue." Securing his float to Lily's with thick twine, he tested the knot. "Let's hope Logan doesn't get all twitchy," he said. "We don't need him throwing any punches."

A dry chuckle bubbled from my chest when my brother tied the knot again. And again. "Dude, I'd worry more about Lily's narrow ass sliding through the tube than losing her on the river."

His brow creased. "I didn't think about that." He glanced at Lily, packing snacks in a waterproof bag a few feet away. "Maybe I should have her ride with me."

"She's not a toddler," I said.

Cameron ripped a hand through his hair. "I know, but she's never done this before."

"And you've been doing it since you were eight. She'll be fine."

His concern was admirable, but at the moment, I just wanted to get this show on the road. The sooner we got to the campsite, the sooner I could disappear into my tent. It was easier to avoid Taryn when she wasn't standing four yards away in a bikini.

Hidden behind my sunglasses, my gaze roamed the length of her body, settling on her erect nipples. The pebbled peaks were barely visible, but of course, I noticed.

Glaring at me, she folded her arms over her chest.

Yeah, baby, I'm looking ... sue me.

I groaned as the tide pulled me closer to their group.

Dylan pushed off the shore, sliding his float between Tori's and Taryn's. "Beckett's tied up," he said. "He'll be here when he can.

Taryn stared off into the distance as Tori and Dylan floated toward the open river.

Sucking down the last of my beer, I tuned out the revelry surrounding me and then let my head fall back.

A couple hours later, Taryn cut in front of me, kicking purposefully.

"What's your hurry?" I asked.

She broke to the far right and continued to paddle. "No hurry."

From her position, a few yards ahead on the left, Tori called out to Taryn, "Hey! You said you weren't going to do the drop! Get over here!"

Repositioning herself atop the tube, Taryn waved at Tori. "I want to grab a shower before it gets too crowded so I'm taking the shortcut."

Tori cursed as she floated to the left at the bend along with the rest of the group. It was the easier route by far, with calm water that spilled out onto the clearing where we would make camp.

I drifted to the right at the last moment, and followed Taryn.

She looked over her shoulder and rolled her eyes. "Have you ever been this way?"

"Many times." I dropped a hand into the water, paddling toward her, but the tide picked up, widening the gap. "I've probably been doing this float longer than you have."

Minutes later, the trees became denser, blocking out a little of the sun. I sat up straight and examined the shoreline. The water was up at least a foot—maybe two—from the norm. This route was by no means treacherous. Tricky? Sometimes. But the sound of the falls ahead was louder than I remembered. Louder than it should be.

A sinking feeling hit my stomach and kept right on going,

"Taryn!" I yelled. "Wait for me, baby."

"I ... I can't stop," she said through gritted teeth. "The water's a little choppy."

A little choppy? I was being thrown around pretty good, and I was six three and two hundred pounds. Taryn was almost a foot shorter and couldn't weigh more than a buck twenty.

"Just hold on, baby." I tried to mask the urgency in my tone as I wiggled to free my legs so I wasn't a slave to the tide. Head first in the tube was never recommended. In calm water it was fine. But in chop, you could slide under. I didn't even want to think about what could happen in this position going over the drop.

I kicked furiously, but Taryn slipped over the falls before I could reach her. My leg scraped the jagged rocks as I followed her over, landing with a splash at the bottom.

I looked around in a panic. "Taryn!"

Spying her empty yellow float, I dipped under the water line. All matter of debris swirled in front of me as I tried to make out any shapes in the murky depth. Spotting her red bikini, I surged forward.

Please ... please ... please ...

Grabbing her around the waist, I held on tight until I felt the muddy ground beneath my feet. A cough wracked Taryn's body as I laid her on a patch of tall grass under a canopy of trees.

"Baby ..." I slapped her cheek lightly. "Taryn, talk to me."

"Chase ..." She coughed out my name along with a mouthful of water.

"I'm right here. Open your eyes for me."

Her hand shot to the back of her skull, and she winced. "Ouch."

"Taryn, talk to me." I slid my fingers into her hair, feeling around for a bump. "What day is it?"

"Saturday ..." she mumbled.

"Where are we?" My stomach sank when she looked at me in confusion. "Do you know where we are?"

She nodded, her brow pinched tight. "On the river."

I grazed the large goose egg hidden beneath her tangled locks, and she hissed a breath. "I think I hit my head," she mumbled.

I pulled my hand away to check for blood. Nothing. Thank fuck.

Holding up two fingers, I asked. "How many?"

Taryn rose to her elbow and winced. "Two."

"I think you're okay. But I want to get downriver so I can take you to urgent care."

"It's just a bump on the head," she grumbled. "I'm fine."

Ignoring her protests, I tried to remember all the signs of a concussion.

Tipping forward, I examined her eyes. "Look to the right." My heart sank when she looked to the left. "The other right."

A bubble of laughter tripped from her lips. "It's a thing. Right and left are hard for me. Even if I hadn't bumped my head, I probably would've missed that."

My shoulders sagged with relief when I realized she was okay.

"God, you scared me." I rested my forehead lightly against hers. "Don't ever go alone like that."

She curled her fingers into my hair, and her free hand slid to my chest. "Your heart is beating so fast."

"Yeah ... well ..."

Smiling, she pressed a soft kiss to my lips. "Thank you."

Since she was the one who kissed me, I laughed. "For what?"

"For following me."

I'd been following Taryn from the first day we met, and there was no reason to believe I wouldn't continue the trend.

"I'll always follow you."

Her brows turned inward, and she cupped my cheek. "What was Logan's sister doing at your loft?"

Apparently, I was right about her assumption. Blowing out a breath, I took her hand and then fell onto the grass on my back. "Laurel's had some problems. She's staying in the space above mine for a little while until she gets on her feet. And don't ask me why she put anything in my duffel because I have no clue."

For a long moment, there was only the sound of the rushing water and the rustling leaves. And then Taryn said, "I don't think I can be just your friend, Chase."

When I rolled onto my side, her eyes were closed, like she was bracing for a storm.

Grasping her chin, I turned her face to mine and smiled.

"Then let's renegotiate."

Chapter 28

TARYN

I cracked open one eye and groaned as a sharp pain traveled to my temple. Running my fingers through my tangled hair, I winced when I grazed the bump on the back of my skull.

"How's your head, baby?" Chase's voice drifted across the tent. "Do you need some aspirin."

"No. That pill the doctor gave me upset my stomach. I told you I didn't need to go to urgent care."

Not that I had a choice. When we got to the campsite, Chase threatened to forcibly put me in the car and take me to the nearest hospital, and nobody raised a finger to stop him.

I sat up. "What are you doing over there?"

"Watching the sunrise."

The Fender rested on his knee like a favored pet. He slid his fingers across the frets absently as he gazed out the mesh window.

I stood up and stretched before joining him. "How long have you been up?"

He set the guitar aside, then pulled me into his lap. "A while. You sure you're okay?"

"Just tired."

After the third time Chase woke me up to ask me what day it was and if I knew my birthday, I'd stayed awake, and we drifted in and out of conversation until a couple of hours ago.

When he brushed a kiss to my mouth, my senses ignited at the taste of coffee lingering on his lips. "Oh my God, where is it?" I looked around, zeroing in on the mug next to him. "You made coffee?" Before he could answer, I lifted the lukewarm brew to my lips and took a huge gulp. My eyes bugged as the liquid burned a path to my stomach.

"What is that?" I coughed.

Chase took the cup from my hand. "It's Irish, baby."

"Irish," I spluttered. "Irish *what?*"

"Irish coffee. I couldn't sleep, so I thought ..."

I smoothed the tension lines bracketing his mouth with my thumb. "You didn't sleep at all? Why?"

He forced a smile. "Who knows? I've got regular coffee. Let me get you some. Tori is probably going to bust the door down when she wakes up."

"I know, right?" I chuckled. "Rhenn should have nicknamed her 'Tenacious T' instead of 'Belle.'"

"Where did that come from ... the 'Belle'?"

"Um ... it's from Beauty and the Beast. Rhenn found out that Tori was obsessed with the movie. I mean, she still watched it, like, all the time until we were thirteen. So he started calling her Belle." I shrugged. "Then we all did. He used to say she was the beauty to his beast."

Chase rested his chin on my shoulder. "What's with the T-Rex?"

"Ugh. You had to bring that up? Tori's boyfriend names her after a Disney character and mine ..."

When I snapped my mouth shut, he pressed a kiss to my temple. "And yours?"

"Apparently I roar like a Tyrannosaurus-Rex when I'm mad."

"And what do you call Beckett?"

Becks. "Asshole."

His chest rumbled with laughter. "I like that. Let me get you that coffee."

I slid off him and grabbed a blanket.

"This area is clothing optional. At the discretion of the owner." Chase's hands slid south, and he cupped my ass. "No covering up."

"Then why are you wearing pants?" I tucked my thumbs into his belt loops. "Hardly seems fair."

"If you want to get me naked, baby, all you got to do is ask."

I did ask. I practically begged. I did everything but jump his bones, but he wouldn't give in. My little bump on the head scared Chase more than it did me.

He poured us each a cup of coffee, adding a teaspoon of powdered creamer to mine. "I didn't think the cream would keep. So, you're going to have to settle for Coffee-Mate."

He handed me the mug and then took a seat on top of the sleeping bag.

"Thanks." I stared into my drink as I sank down beside him. "You don't even like cream. Why do you have Coffee-Mate?"

"Because you make a face when you're forced to drink black coffee. I learned that after our sleepover."

It was such a small thing. And maybe I should've be offended that Chase had planned to lure me into his tent for a romp and serve me coffee with instant creamer the next morning. But really, I wasn't.

"So you assumed that sometime during this trip I'd be drinking coffee with you?"

He smiled into his next sip. "You can't blame me for hoping."

The cicadas serenaded us as we sat in companionable silence.

When he finished his coffee, Chase swirled the grinds in his cup. "Why is Twin Souls so interested in getting me to work with them? Is it you or Tori that's pushing this?"

It was Chase's decision. And I didn't want him to think the offer had anything to do with a stupid fight between Tori and me.

"You know your brother's work," I said. "And you're also really talented, so it makes sense."

"You still didn't answer me. Are you trying to make me over in someone's image? Is that what this is about?"

"No. But Twin Souls offers representation to a select few. It's a great opportunity to have your music showcased in front of a larger audience."

"And you'd be in that audience?" he pressed. "You like that kind of stuff? That life?"

A tremor, like a tiny earthquake, rumbled beneath my skin. "Not really."

Chase tipped my chin to look into my eyes. "I wouldn't mind doing some arranging. But I'm not sure." He took a big breath. "The music business ... for me ... it doesn't really ..."

It took a second to register the thundering voice outside the tent.

"Where is she?" Beckett roared. "Which tent?"

"Dude, leave her alone," Dylan implored. "She hit her head. Chase is just making sure she's okay."

"I'll bet," Beckett replied sarcastically. "Why didn't you call me?"

"Because I don't think that's what she wanted. Even if they are, you know, seeing each other again, it's her choice. And I wouldn't get all possessive and push up on the dude. The whole bunch of them can brawl. Haven't you heard the stories about Logan?"

"He ain't Logan," Beckett snarled. "He's a fucking wannabe. And he's a suit. He runs a fucking business. Chase Noble doesn't have the juice to go three rounds with me."

"Stay here," Chase growled as he jumped to his feet.

He yanked the zipper on the entrance with such force the whole tent swayed in protest.

"You want to find out how much juice I have? I'm right here!"

"Whoa, let's calm down." Cameron's voice entered the fold as I tugged the Night Owl shirt into place and stumbled out of the tent.

Dylan stood between Beckett and Chase, while Cameron had his arm wrapped tightly around his brother's chest.

"Get off me, Cameron," Chase warned.

"Let him go," Beckett taunted. "You think I'm concerned that the CEO is going to land a solid punch?"

Thick veins bulged on Chase's neck as he strained against his brother's grip. "I'm not the one that just made the cover of People Magazine for their looks, asshole. Or maybe that's because of your girlfriend." He laughed wryly. "Your new girlfriend, that is. She's the supermodel, right?"

The verbal blow ricocheted off Beckett and hit me square in the chest.

"Enough!" I croaked, staggering toward them. "Both of you."

Beckett glanced me over. "How's your head? Did your friend kiss it and make it better?"

Anger tightened my throat. "Beckett ... Jesus. What's wrong with you?"

"Why don't you tell him the truth?" Beckett said. "Tell your boy here that you're not going to get all hot and bothered if he makes the cover of The Wall Street Journal. That's not what does it for you."

Out of the corner of my eye, I saw Tori jogging toward us. Everyone was out of their tents, the campsite silent as they watched the spectacle.

"Beckett," I said. "Shut up. Now."

Ignoring me, he continued. "You don't want someone 'close' to the music. That's why you dropped that record producer in LA after a couple of dates. You want a musician." He shifted his narrowed gaze to Chase. "And this guy ain't it."

Shrugging off his brother's grip, Chase took one giant step into Beckett's space. "Don't pretend that you know what Taryn wants just to make yourself feel better."

Beckett laughed. "I've known Taryn most of her life. You're the one who doesn't have a clue."

The silence stretched as the two assessed each other, and then Chase turned and brushed past me. I flinched when a loud crash sounded in the tent.

Beckett took a step toward me. "Babe—"

"You may be right," I choked. "I might not know what I want. But I know what I don't want." I closed the small gap between us and spoke in a voice that was only for him. "And that's you."

Beckett's lips parted, but I didn't give him a chance to retort. I stormed to the tent I shared with Tori, rage and embarrassment quickening my steps.

Grabbing my toiletries from the open duffel, I emerged a moment later and made a beeline for Dylan. "I need the keys to the Hummer."

He pulled the fob from his pocket. "You're not going home, are you?"

I shook the bag of shampoo and face wash. "Clearly, I'm not. I just need a shower."

"Are you going to finish the float?"

"I don't know," I said quietly. "Let me find out what Chase wants to do."

"Go grab a shower," Tori said as she slipped her arm around my shoulder. "Do you want us to wait?"

I looked around the campsite at all my friends. And then at Beckett.

"Nope." I slipped out of her embrace. It was time to step away. Break away. Make a choice.

Head down, I walked slowly to Chase's tent while Beckett's gaze followed me. It was like I was crossing enemy lines.

Cameron and Logan fell silent as I approached.

"He's not in there," Cameron said quietly when I reached for the flap.

"Where is he?"

"Good question," Logan replied, fury tensing his jaw. "He took off with my sister a few minutes ago. Neither of them are answering their phones."

My stomach clattered to the soft ground. "Um ... just tell him ..." There was nothing to say, so I shook my head. "Never mind."

Nausea accompanied me as I made my way to the Hummer, and on autopilot, I drove to the RV park a few miles down the road.

I stripped out of my clothes behind the thin curtain in the communal shower. My hope washed away with the trickle of water from the ancient showerhead, then pooled at my feet and swirled down the drain.

Numb, I dressed and headed back to the campsite where Cameron was loading his gear in Logan's Mustang.

Holding the keys so tight I could feel the metal edges bite my palm, I wandered over to him. "Did Chase come back?"

"He's on his way to Austin with Laurel," Cameron said as he met my gaze.

A tight smile on my lips, I declined the apology he was sure to offer. "Okay, have a safe ride home."

Acid burned in the pit of my empty stomach as I stared down at the trampled grass on my way to the campsite. A pair of well-worn boots came into view, and I looked up into Beckett's cobalt eyes.

"Are you headed back to Austin?" I asked.

"Yeah, I'm—"

I held up my hand. I didn't want to hear his voice. But at least he was here. Beckett would always be here.

"Can you give me a ride?"

Chapter 29

CHASE

*P*acing around the loft, I waited for Logan and Cameron to arrive. I pulled out my phone to text Taryn. But what would I say?

Sorry I left without a word, dinner tonight?

I stared down at the blank screen as the apprehension bubbled inside.

Laurel groaned, so I abandoned the text and edged toward the couch.

She'd followed me into the tent after my dust-up with Beckett. High on who knows what, she'd babbled incoherently and tried to crawl all over me. Before she could do any more damage to herself or her brother's reputation, I put her in the car and headed home. She'd slept most of the way, throwing up twice in the truck.

I crouched in front of her.

"You lied to me," she mumbled, looking around with unfocused eyes. "You said we were going to go party."

I also told her I wouldn't call Logan, which I did, the minute she passed out. My hard ass approach wasn't working.

"It's a private party, darlin'." I swept a lock of hair from her face. "Tell me what you took."

Her heavy-lidded gaze turned sultry. "Why, you want some, baby?"

I gave her the most genuine smile I could muster. "Depends. Show me the goods."

She reached into her bra and fumbled around, producing a small, clear baggie.

I glanced at the little yellow pills. OxyContin. One of those bad boys could knock a grown man on his ass. Unless the grown man had a habit. Back in the day, I could take plenty.

"Oxy?" I chuckled, keeping up the charade. "Good choice. How many of these did you take, baby?"

If she said more than one after being clean for a couple of months, we were in trouble.

"Just one," she mumbled. "So good ..."

I shoved the pills into my pocket before tilting her chin with my knuckle. "You got any uppers?"

As bad as it was, it could get worse. She could be speedballing, mixing the Oxy with amphetamines.

"Nah," she slurred. "Dude didn't have any s-speed."

"You score this at the river?" Her eyes fluttered to half mast, surveying me with caution. Cupping the back of her neck, I leaned close to her ear. "I thought you wanted to party? There are only three pills here. We can't party with three pills."

"I know a guy," she said as she pulled me closer. "He delivers."

Footsteps thundered in the narrow stairwell as Logan topped the stairs, his frantic gaze shifting from Laurel to me.

"What the fuck are you doing?" he roared. "Get your hands off her."

Before he could lunge, Cameron was on the landing, his arm snaked around his best friend's neck.

"You called him?" Laurel croaked, confusion furrowing her brow.

I gave her a nod as I disentangled myself.

Logan's furious blue eyes tracked my movement as I walked toward him.

"She took an Oxy," I said. "She scored them at the river."

Logan fought to even his breath but remained still in Cameron's hold. "You said she was fine," he bit out through gritted teeth.

It wasn't important that I didn't say it, only that Logan believed that I had.

I rubbed the back of my neck. "Yeah, she wasn't ready—"

Logan shrugged off Cameron's grip. "Maybe if you weren't so busy fucking around with Taryn you would have noticed."

"Dude, he's allowed to have a life," Cameron said. "Yeah, maybe he should have told us to watch Laurel, but you know how it is. He was attracted to the chick."

Bitter laughter rumbled from Logan's chest. "He was fucking Taryn before we went to the river. You just didn't know it. That's why she stormed out of the show the other night. Tori told Dylan if he didn't make things right with Taryn we wouldn't get our deal. That's the only reason Chase was invited—to get his shit straight with Taryn."

Cameron blinked at me, too stunned to speak.

"Yeah," Logan continued. "Your brother's got his own agenda. Seems Tori wants to offer him his own little piece of the pie. Executive Producer or some bullshit. That's why my sister didn't get the attention she needed."

The sleeping giant yawning inside me roared to life. "You little fucker. It's not like that. I told you—"

Logan shoved me to the floor, then dropped a knee to my chest.

"I left as soon as I saw what was going on with Laurel," I snarled. "Now get the fuck off me. We need to deal with this situation. Your sister needs more help."

More help than I can give.

Logan hauled to his feet. "I shouldn't have trusted you to begin with. I'm taking Laurel home with me."

He yanked a blanket off the back of the couch, swaddling his sister like an errant child.

"I wouldn't do that, dude," I warned. "She needs to go back to rehab. You can't help her."

"I can do a better job than you," he shot back, pulling Laurel to her feet.

When footsteps echoed in the stairwell, I prayed it was Vaughn, but it was Calista who appeared on the landing.

"I did a sweep of Laurel's apartment like you asked," she said. "I found these in the refrigerator."

Calista handed over a prescription bottle and a small bag of weed and then wiped her palm on her jeans for good measure. She never broke a sweat, not even when faced with a room full of junkies shaking off their last high. But holding the weapons of your own destruction would make anyone twitchy.

Calista had demons under her skin—sleeping—waiting. Like mine.

The Oxy in my pocket called to that empty place where my demon crackled to life. I'd felt him there for days. Even tried to drown him in alcohol. But the booze only fortified the bastard.

I shoved the small weapons in my pocket, adding them to my growing arsenal. "Thanks, Calista. Logan's taking over Laurel's care. You might want to give him some information—"

"I don't need anything from y'all," Logan said as he marched past us with his sister in tow. "I'll send someone over to collect Laurel's stuff. I'll see you Thursday if we still have our gig at the Parish." Doubt flickered in his eyes when he realized what his disrespect might cost him.

I blew out a resigned breath, my failure tainting the air. "You're solid. That's got nothing to do with this."

Laurel's eyes found mine. For all of her excitement about leaving with her brother, she knew what it meant. There was a reason she came to me, drunk or high. She wanted to be saved. And Logan couldn't save her.

I smiled, noting the defeat in her eyes. Or was it mine? My own defeat reflected there?

Calista's brow furrowed in concern as she looked at me. Really looked at me. "Chase, do you need anything before I go?"

The little pills in my pocket promised the absolution she couldn't offer. "I'm good."

She nodded, then followed Logan down the stairs.

Cameron dropped on the floor next to me. He looked very much like the little boy that lived in my memory, always seeking me out for guidance. "Why didn't you tell me?"

"About?"

There were so many things I hadn't told him. Starting with Taryn and ending with the craving that boiled beneath my skin. The craving was winning. My tone was already shorter than I intended. I wanted to be alone. With my demon.

"Your thing with Taryn," he said quietly. "And Tori's invite. You can't really be thinking about doing that."

The sane part of me tried to conjure an answer. But it was the dark bastard taking over, inch by inch, that turned to my brother. "Why?" I smirked. "Afraid of a little competition?"

Cameron's face fell as he collided with the side of me that disappeared all those years ago. "No, man. That's not ..." He shook his head. "You just can't."

Pushing to my feet, I towered over him, fingering the plastic baggie in my pocket.

"I can do anything I want." I walked casually to the fridge and grabbed a beer. "I don't need your permission. And I didn't ask for your advice."

Cameron nodded slowly. He knew who he was dealing with. Or he suspected. We'd done this dance before, and he'd never won.

"I guess you didn't." He cleared his throat. "Why don't you hand over that little stash, and I'll be on my way."

Determination sharpened his features. Cameron couldn't win, but he'd fight. He fought for me when he was a kid, and now he was a grown man. Six two if he were an inch, he'd use that bulky frame to impose his will. Not that it would work. I pulled the prescription bottle and small baggie of weed from my pocket, careful to leave the Oxy where it sat. Tossing the stash to my brother, I smirked when he caught it with one hand. "Good save."

But not good enough.

He visibly relaxed as he tucked the goodies in his pocket. "Why don't we go grab something to eat?" he offered. "We can talk."

I lifted the beer to my lips. "Dude, I'm tired. I've been babysitting Laurel all fucking afternoon. Just ..." Grinding my teeth, I fought like hell to keep from slashing too deep. "Go home. I'll call you tomorrow."

Cameron lingered behind me for a long moment. "I'll see you tomorrow, then?"

I nodded.

As soon as the door clicked shut, I picked up my phone. Scrolling through my contacts, I cursed when I couldn't find the number I was looking for. Sinking onto the couch, I directed my browser to a website for the dive bar where one of my old band mates was playing a gig.

A woman's gravelly voice barked over the loud music. "Yeah?"

"Is Havok playing tonight?"

"They go on at nine."

"Thanks, darlin'." I reclined into the cushions. "Hey, is Pierce around?"

"Who's this?" she asked suspiciously.

"Noble."

She dropped the receiver and bellowed for Pierce.

A breathless voice boomed over the line a moment later. "Noble, dude, how the fuck are you?"

"Good, man." I pulled the Oxy from my pocket, turning the baggie over in my palm. "I was thinking about catching your show tonight. Maybe we could jam afterward. Party a little."

The demon currently wearing my face smiled. I didn't know how to party "a little."

Pierce laughed. "Come on down Noble; it's pretty freewheeling over here. You can hit the stage with us."

I took out a pill. Closing one eye, I held it up to the light. A forty. Forty milligrams. Eight times the strength of one Vicodin. I broke the pill in half, then washed it down with a swig of beer.

"I'll see you at nine, Pierce."

The sun beat through the window, warming my skin. I squinted, then looked down at the stain on my shirt. Vomit. I barely made it to my feet before the bitter taste of bile filled my mouth.

Hunched over the toilet, I spewed last night's beer into the bowl. The shower washed off the stench but not the guilt. Not even close. I wiped the steam from the mirror and gazed at a reflection I almost didn't recognize. It had been a long time since I'd seen him. Or me. The *real* me. The guy that lost chunks of time in a drug-fueled haze. The only thing I remembered about last night was floating on a cloud. And the call to Pierce. Then nothing.

Fuck.

I never made it to the bar. Which was probably a good thing. Half of a forty milligram Oxy knocked me on my ass. If I'd managed to make it out of the loft, I'd probably be in the hospital.

I dressed quickly, the walls in the small bathroom closing in on me. I'd spent too much time on dirty tile, hugging a toilet or propped against a metal door in my old life.

I found my phone wedged in the cushions of the couch. Twelve o'clock. I'd slept through the night and half the day.

Checking the texts, my heart sank. Nothing from Taryn. My fingers hovered over the keyboard, but I lost my nerve, so I headed to the fridge for some liquid courage.

The bottle was halfway to my lips when I saw him. My father.

Tyler assessed me from the landing, looking me over with a narrowed gaze. We had the same eyes, Tyler, Cameron, and me. But my father's hazel orbs held no life.

"Is that the only old habit you've given in to, boy?" he asked with a laugh.

One look at my father and the demon in me ran for cover, so I strode to the sink and dumped the beer.

Methodically, I placed the empty bottle in the trash, then took a deep breath, meeting my old man's gaze. "What do you want, Tyler?"

Chapter 30

TARYN

I pulled into the parking lot behind Chase's building, but instead of getting out of the car, I waited to gather my resolve. Exhaustion blanketed me like a thick coat, stifling and oppressive.

After returning from the river yesterday afternoon and fighting off Beckett's attempt to comfort me, I fell into a fitful sleep on my couch.

Most people came back from the float with a glowing tan. My parting gifts? Dark circles and frown lines.

I squeezed a couple of drops of Visine in my tired eyes, blinking as the saline tears slid down my nose.

Resigned, I headed for the back door, my steps faltering when I met Bridgette's gaze across the lot. The bar manager blew out a plume of smoke, tapping her ash into the large standing ashtray.

"Hey, Taryn." Curiosity piqued her tone. And wariness if I was reading her correctly. "What's up?"

"Not much. Is Chase around?" I smiled tightly. "I need to pick up something I left in the loft."

My heart. Or a piece of it anyway. But, I'd settle for my silk blouse and La Perla bra and panty set I threw in his hamper. The price of my "no regret" policy wouldn't be my favorite lingerie.

Bridgette cocked her head, casually leaning against the door-frame to block my entry. "Does he know you're coming?"

"Nope. But, feel free to warn him if you'd like." I reached for the door, looking her in the eyes when her fingers coiled lightly around my forearm. "Look, I don't care who he has up there. I'm getting my stuff, that's it."

Her eyebrows shot to her hairline. "Oh, shit ... you think he's got a girl up there?"

"Laurel lives upstairs, so technically she's always up there, right?"

"Not anymore. She moved in with Logan."

"Oh ..." I resisted the urge to ask when. It was none of my business.

Bridgette tipped her chin to the older model Mercedes parked askew in the handicapped zone. I noted the personalized license plate on the beat-to-shit bucket of bolts.

Noble 1s.

The Noble Ones. Tyler Noble's band. He had one hit a million years ago, but he milked it for all it was worth. During one of my surreptitious Google searches, I'd found a bevy of articles on Chase's dad. The descriptions of the elder Noble were far from flattering.

Arrogant, maniacal, fame whore—and that was from the main-stream press.

Bridgette's lip curled in disdain. "That's Chase's daddy's ride. The guy is a piece of work. He only comes around to pump Chase for information on Cameron, or pick up a few dollars in spending money." She took another drag of her smoke, then muttered, "Fucking loser."

"You know Chase's family?"

Nodding, she dropped the butt in the ashtray. "Sure." Smoke swirled from her coral-tinted lips as she pulled her long tresses into a ponytail. "I've known Chase since I was in high school. Actually, I'm a friend of Cameron's. We used to date." A nervous smile curved her mouth. "Can we keep that part between us? Cameron is engaged to this girl, Lily. I don't want to end up on the wrong side of that situation. Nothing is going on with Cam and me. But I love my job. The way he feels about Lily? I'd be out of here on my ass if she said the word. *Believe.*"

"I won't say anything, but Lily doesn't seem like the type." I smiled reassuringly. "I've only met her once, though, so I don't know."

"She's sweet, but with Cameron's past, I don't want to push my luck. The boy put the 'whore' in 'man-whore.'" Her brow arched. "Know what I mean?"

Bridgette fell for the good-looking bad boy in high school and look where it got her. She worked in a bar. Granted, she was the manager, and by all accounts seemed very happy, but I couldn't help but draw similarities to my situation.

I patted her on the arm as I slipped past. "Your secret's safe with me."

The door to Chase's loft was ajar, but I knocked anyway. Hearing no response, I trudged up the staircase, pausing when angry voices spilled into the small space.

"I don't know what you're asking me for, Tyler," Chase said, anger infusing every word. "If Cameron wanted you to know what was going on in his life, he'd tell you."

A second voice, gravelly with a strong twang replied, "That's the problem, son. Y'all two are ungrateful sum-bitches, you know that?"

"You do realize that's my mama you're insulting?" Chase snarled. "Why don't you get out of here before I throw you out. Go sleep it off somewhere."

Tentatively, I climbed the last few steps. From my vantage point below the landing, I could just see into the large space. I caught a glimpse of Chase's profile as he sat at the grand piano in the alcove, his father hovering behind him.

"I said it's time to go," Chase said, tension furrowing his brow. "I'll have Bridgette call you a cab."

"A cab?" Tyler snorted. "My big shot son is going to call me a cab. That's rich. If you would've stuck to the plan, you'd have a limo and a driver. Like your brother." He leaned down and tinkled the keys on the piano. "I guess I bet on the wrong horse. You've got twice the talent as that little pisser, but he's the one on the radio. He really made it. And here you are, living over a bar."

"My bar," Chase bit out, rising to his feet. "You know damn well I've got more money than Cameron. But it's not about that, is it? I'm not famous." Chase's hands clenched into fists at his sides. "Do you know how many properties I own around this city, old man? And in Dallas? Hell, I've even got a beach house in California. The only thing that Cameron owns is half of this bar and the house I gifted him."

"Why you reading me your résumé, boy?" Tyler barked out a laugh as he looked up at his son. "You applying for a job or something? Your brother doesn't need to own anything. He's living the life. Staying in them five-star hotels, with room service and hot and cold running pussy. I bet—"

I startled when Chase shoved his father out of the way.

"Stay away from him, Tyler." He paced in a small circle, rubbing the back of his neck. "How much is it going to cost me this time to buy us a little peace?"

"You wound me, son."

Tyler's smile widened when Chase sank back onto the piano bench.

"How much, Tyler?" he asked quietly.

"A couple thousand."

Without a word, Chase walked across the room. Pulling back an oriental rug, he crouched in front of a floor safe.

He looked over his shoulder when Tyler advanced. "Stay the fuck over there," he snapped. "I don't trust you."

Returning to the piano bench, Tyler's leg bobbed in anticipation. Greed painted his features when Chase pulled out a stack of bills.

A pained expression crept onto Chase's face as he held the bounty just out of his father's reach. The old man didn't notice. He was too enthralled with the money.

"Stay away from Cameron, or I swear to God, I won't give you another cent." Chase held tight to the cash even as Tyler tried to pull the stack from his son's hand. "Are we clear?"

"Always, son."

With a satisfied smile, Tyler staggered to his feet. He weaved as he made his way to the stairs, holding tightly to the loot.

Chase's mouth went slack when he saw me. I climbed the last couple of steps, then stood awkwardly on the landing. My gaze shifted to Tyler when he stopped to look me over.

"Hey," he slurred, the smell of whiskey faintly seeping from his pores when he leaned toward me. "I know you." He pointed a finger at my face. "I do—I do know you. You're that record manager I seen in the papers with my boy." He shot Chase a look. "My other boy. You're from that company. The one that girl started when her old man got run down."

Now that Tyler was up close, I noticed the familiar jawline and the similar nose. And those eyes. Tyler's hazel eyes swam in a sea of red, and they were glassy, but they were Chase's eyes nonetheless.

My hand went to my stomach as I tried to form a sentence. "I ... I'm ..."

Chase vaulted across the room, positioning himself in front of the horrible man. "Get out of here right now. Or I'll throw you out on your ass."

Tyler whistled and shook his head, ignoring Chase's warning. "I knew you had some of my blood pumping through those veins." He lifted a brow. "Looks like they didn't beat all the sense out of you at that fancy school. Did you finally decide to use some of that God-given talent of yours or is she just warming your sheets?"

Chase grabbed the front of Tyler's shirt. "You can walk out of here on your own, or I'll throw you down the fucking stairs." He lifted his father until they were nose-to-nose. "Your choice."

"What are you getting so riled up about?" Tyler wheezed. "I'm trying to pay you a compliment, you little shit. That's good business. Get your girlfriend to line up a couple of gigs. Smart. If I would have hooked up with someone in the business instead of wasting my time with Callie—"

Chase shoved Tyler to the ground. "Ten seconds, fucker. I'm counting. If you're not gone in ten, I'll bust your ass."

Pushing to his feet, Tyler scurried down the stairs, cursing all the way. Chase stomped to the window, his footsteps thundering through the loft.

I closed the distance between us, stopping a foot from where he stood gazing down at the busy street. "Chase ..."

Resisting the urge to comfort him for as long as I could, I finally gave in and slipped my arms around his waist. The muscles in his back, knotted and tense beneath his T-shirt, relaxed as my hand skimmed his chest.

Bracing his palm against the glass, he dropped his gaze to the floor. "Sorry about that."

"Do you want to talk about it?" I asked.

There were so many "its," I didn't know where to start.

Chase spun around. And then his hands were in my hair, and his tongue slid between my parted lips. Hitching my leg around his waist, he reversed our positions. I fought for balance, gripping his shoulders.

When he finally pulled away, he said, "Talk is overrated, baby."

Peeling me off the glass, he walked us to the bed and eased me onto the mattress. Stunned by the sincerity in his hazel eyes, I folded him in my arms. "It's okay," I whispered. "It's okay ..."

It wasn't. But there was nothing else to say.

After a moment, his fingers found the button on my jeans. Searching my face, he waited for my ascent.

I nodded, my voice too choked with emotion to find any words. He finished undressing me and then stood, shucking off his clothes with a singular focus. Reaching into the nightstand, he took out a condom and then slid it into place.

"Sweet Taryn," he whispered, easing on top of me. I gasped when he buried himself with one thrust. "So fucking sweet."

He set a frenzied pace, gripping my thighs as he pulled my legs to his waist.

"Come, baby," he grunted through ragged breaths. "Please."

His mouth found mine as I tipped over the edge, spiraling to a place where there was no pain and no regret. For either of us.

I flipped on the light in Chase's bathroom. Reaching into the hamper, I picked through the mangled heap of discarded towels and cotton T-shirts until I ran across my silk blouse and lace panties. Stuffing the garments into my tote, I tiptoed back into the loft.

A halo of smoke hung above Chase's head as he sat on the edge of the bed, puffing on a cigarette.

He lifted his gaze, studying me impassively. "I thought you left." He flicked his ash into a half-empty bottle of beer on the nightstand.

I walked toward the bed, cursing my flawed memory. I had a speech prepared when I got here. But our romp negated most of what I'd intended to say anyway.

"I'm just getting my stuff." I took a seat on the mattress and, unable to stand the awkward silence, I blurted, "Why did you leave without telling me anything?"

He stared straight ahead. "When?"

I studied his profile. *When?*

"Yesterday, at the river."

Blowing out a breath, he shoved to his feet and then stepped into his jeans. "I had something to take care of." He ambled toward the kitchen without a backward glance. "You want a beer?"

"With Laurel?"

He flopped on the couch. "Yep."

"You said she came with Logan."

"And she left with me."

My stomach fell to the floor. "Bridgette said she moved out. I thought ... I thought y'all were just friends."

Friends ... at least.

Pain lanced through me when a smile curved his lips. "I have all kinds of friends, Taryn."

"I don't understand."

He dropped his head against the back of the couch. "I don't

suppose you do. It's pretty simple, though. Laurel's a fun girl. No complications. I don't want to hurt you, Taryn. So it's better if ..."

You don't let the door hit you on the ass on the way out.

Stepping into my shoes, I forced a smile. It nearly broke me, that smile. "I get it. There's nothing else to say. See you around, Chase."

As I said it, I realized it was true. I would see him. Chase would be on the fringe of my life. And if I did my job well, promoting his brother, he'd taint any triumphs with his presence. Excruciating pain spread through me at the thought.

Awkwardly, I gathered my things while he waited, elbows propped on his knees, staring at the ground. He never looked up.

In a daze, I drove the short distance to BlueBonnet Towers, stifling the sobs until I was safe inside my loft. But even there, I felt his presence. I could see the top of his building from every window.

Too much.

With shaking hands, I opened up my laptop. Tears fell on the keyboard as I tapped out an email to Trent, the record producer at Metro.

Change of plans. I want to speak to you in person. I'm flying out tomorrow.

Chapter 31

CHASE

*T*he shit hole of a dressing room stank to high heaven. Sweat and alcohol and desperation clung to the worn-out furniture and filthy carpeting.

I looked up when the haggard waitress peeked her head in the door, her gaze fixed on Pierce.

"Havoc—you got ten minutes!" she boomed, her lip curled into a sneer. "And nobody better pass out tonight. You're wearing out your welcome."

"Got it, Cruella," Pierce snickered as he reached for the blunt. "We'll be there."

She flipped him the bird. "And don't call me Cruella."

He looked her up and down with glassy eyes. "You're right, sweetheart. Cruella Deville was kinda hot."

She slammed the flimsy door, nearly knocking the cheap plywood off its one good hinge.

The bar had seen better days. It was a dive when I played here at sixteen, and if possible, it was worse now. Not that I cared much about my surroundings at the moment. I was too high to notice. But apparently not high enough. I could still see Taryn's stricken face as she stood in my living room. No amount of drugs could wipe the image from my mind.

Which was ironic, since drugs were the reason I sent her away in the first place.

When she showed up last night and witnessed the scene with my old man, I saw it as a sign. I buried myself in her sweet body, hoping that she'd save me from myself and the cravings. It worked for a minute. But sure as shit, as soon as she slipped out of my arms, I started bargaining.

Just a little something to take the edge off.

After formulating an elaborate scheme to sneak away and feed the beast, the truth hit me. Taryn couldn't save me. Nobody could. So in a moment of clarity, I lobbed a few verbal grenades, hit all the soft spots. And she left.

Then I took an Oxy and waited for the void to swallow me. But it didn't. She was there, like a sliver embedded in my mind.

"Noble." Pierce jabbed me in the ribs and shoved a small mirror into my hand. "Take a bump. You look like you're ready to pass out."

Closing one eye, I looked down at the powder. "Coke?"

"Not unless you're buying, dude." He laughed. "That's Crystal."

Shrugging, I took the straw. Meth. Coke. It didn't really matter. The Oxy was kicking my ass. And besides, I was only going to do a line.

The white granules hit the back of my throat, and I winced, tears springing to my eyes.

"Hurts so good, don't it?" Pierce chortled.

As soon as the euphoria crept over me, all my good intentions fell by the wayside. One line was never going to be enough.

I clutched the mirror when Pierce made a grab for it. "I'm not done,"

I gave him a smile to hide the edge in my voice. My heightened awareness brought with it the notion that four of us were sharing this paltry stash.

I snorted the next line before Pierce got any ideas. "Does your guy deliver? This shit ain't gonna last."

He clapped me on the shoulder. "No worries, dude. My guy will get someone to make a run, as long as you got cash."

Cash I had. It was my common sense that had left the building. My gaze shifted to the door when a familiar voice scratched the inside of my brain.

"Get out of my way, or I'll put your ass on the ground," Cameron bellowed, knocking someone aside as he barreled through the door with Logan on his heels. They wore equal looks of disgust as they scanned the room.

"Cameron, dude!" Pierce exclaimed as he jumped to his feet. "Long time no see."

My brother tore his heavy gaze from mine for a second to take in my friend. "Pierce," he muttered.

Frenetic energy crackled between Cameron and me. Even in my fucked-up state, I felt it.

"We got a show," Pierce said, stepping out of the line of fire. "Y'all stick around. We'll party when we're done."

I thought about responding, but the effort was beyond me. Rooted to the shitty couch, I watched listlessly while Pierce and his crew scurried to gather their stuff.

"You want me to make that call, Chase?" Pierce raised a brow. "The dude does business at that titty bar off Airport Row. I could always go for a lap dance."

I nodded. "Sounds good."

"You can come too, little brother," Pierce said as he headed for the exit. "Good drugs and easy women. We'll make a night of it."

As soon as the door slammed shut, Cameron grabbed the mirror I didn't realize I was holding. "What the fuck are you doing?" he seethed. "Are you fucking crazy?"

I grabbed a beer from the table. "You need to run along. This is a private party. By invitation only."

Cameron laced his hands behind his head and muttered to himself while Logan leaned against the wall, his features schooled into a mask.

I reached for the blunt, and Cameron grabbed my hand. "Don't make me drag you out of here," he growled.

It took all of three seconds before I was on my feet, nose-to-nose with my baby brother and his ticking jaw.

"You'd need a forklift to drag me anywhere." I felt the scowl coat my face, the combination of the speed and adrenaline pushing me over the edge. "Get out of here. I don't need a chaperone."

Logan pounced like a cat, his fingers coiling around my bicep. "You're going to need a fucking doctor if you don't come with us."

The madman currently in control of my body caught Logan's wrist and twisted hard. "We can get a room for two." I smiled, tightening my grip. "Because you know I ain't going down alone."

"Fine by me," Logan spat. "I got a few minutes to kill, and I'd love to put you on your ass. You've been asking for it for days."

The door burst open, and the owner of the bar stepped in, a Louisville Slugger at his side. The old man hadn't changed a bit since I was sixteen.

"You having a problem with these guys, Noble?" His brow furrowed as he gave Logan a once over. "Cage," he grumbled. "You're not any more welcome in my bar than your old man. I told you that years ago."

"I'm just here for my friend." Logan looked down at the bat in the old man's beefy paw. "And that little toothpick you're carrying don't scare me one bit."

When the rational side of my brain made one final attempt to assert its will, I lifted my hands in surrender.

"We were just leaving." I patted the old man on the arm as I strode by.

My attempt at a carefree swagger was hard to maintain as I bounced off the walls, the red exit sign at the back of the building growing closer with every stride. I pushed through the door, sweat pouring off my brow as I staggered to my car.

Cameron grabbed the door handle when I slid behind the wheel. "Where do you think you're going?"

"Back to the loft," I said, my most reassuring smile in place. "You didn't give me much choice now, did you?"

"Get out," he ordered. "You can't drive."

I shrugged, and Cameron loosened his grip. It was almost too easy, fooling my brother with that lame ploy. I slammed the door and then turned the key.

"Chase!" He beat on the window, his hazel eyes blazing with fury. "Open the fucking door."

Cameron took futile steps to block my path. But he wasn't fast enough. Dirt and gravel spit from my tires as I careened toward the entrance, leaving my brother under the street lamp.

I popped the last Oxy into my mouth as Cameron's silhouette grew smaller in the rearview mirror. The farther I drove, the fainter the shadow became until it disappeared altogether and there was nothing left but my own eyes, staring back at me in the reflection.

My smile melted as I took stock of what I'd become. I no longer feared the monster inside of me. I embraced him.

Chapter 32

TARYN

I got off the plane at LAX, dragging my worn suitcase behind me. My stomach churned, the strong smell of airline fuel wafting into the cramped hallway.

Dread washed over me as I thought of the photographers congregating at the bottom of the escalator, hoping to get a shot of the flavor of the week so they could auction it off to the highest bidder.

Standing in the corner of the crowded bathroom, I tucked my long hair under an LA Dodgers baseball cap.

I slipped through the throngs of people unnoticed, breathing a sigh of relief when the automatic doors whooshed open, and I spotted my regular driver hovering next to the unassuming black sedan in passenger pick up.

Out of nowhere, a paparazzo stepped in front of me, walking backward with a video camera trained on my face.

"Taryn! Where's Becks?" He pulled the lens away to judge my reaction. "Are you here to confront Maddy?"

Another cameraman joined the fray. And another.

Sidestepping the boldest reporter, blocking my path with his thick body, I passed the driver my bag. "You guys must be really desperate."

"Come on, Taryn," he pressed, nearly falling off the curb in hot pursuit as I ducked into the backseat. "Are you here with Beckett?"

I slammed the door on the interloper.

"Sorry about that, Ms. Ayers." The driver met my gaze in the rearview mirror, a sympathetic smile lifting his lips. "You know how they are."

I nodded wearily and looked out the tinted windows. The LA skyline, with its blanket of haze, deepened the gloom settling on me. Tori's ringtone pierced the air.

Not now, Belle.

I hit ignore, sending the call to voicemail. Likely, her tone would mimic the flavor of the dozen texts she'd sent since this morning when I apprised her of my plans. Resting my eyes for what I thought was a second, I jolted awake when the sedan pulled to a stop and the driver lowered the partition.

"Sorry to wake you. We're here."

I punched in the code for the wrought iron security gate, glowering at the girls loitering on the perimeter of the property. Drained and bone tired, I stepped into the perpetual California sunshine.

"There you go, Ms. Ayers." The driver said, exchanging my suitcase for a generous tip. "See you next time."

I surveyed the façade of the two-story, six room Mediterranean mansion. A shit ton of bad memories overshadowed the opulence of the charming estate. But since I was only going to be here a couple of days I didn't see the use in going to a hotel.

I dragged my suitcase over the threshold, the wheels sliding on the polished marble as I made my way to the staircase.

A cloud of stale perfume assailed me as I stepped inside the guest room. Assuming Harper Rush was the previous occupant, I threw my suitcase on the bed, ignoring the cloying floral scent. I froze when I pulled open the dresser drawer and came face to face with a stack full of publicity shots of Maddy Silva.

Gathering my things, I did the only thing I could do. I walked straight to the double doors at the end of the hallway. As I glanced around the room I never wanted to see again, I spotted several pictures of me on the dresser.

An eight by ten glossy of me at seventeen sat on the nightstand, facing the bed. Beckett's tribute fell flat when I thought of all the women that must've seen the photo and felt sorry for me. But I was too exhausted to care.

I caught a whiff of Beckett's soap, lingering on the feather pillows. It was strangely comforting in an odd way. Whatever else Beckett was, he was home to me.

Taking a deep breath, I blocked out the sound of Tori's ringtone. I'd deal with the fallout when I was rested.

My eyes drifted shut, and Chase's smile awaited me in a dream. The fifteen hundred miles that separated us wasn't far enough to drive him from my mind. But it was a start.

I took the last bite of my Hershey bar and then began the search for my laptop. It was somewhere in the bed. As much as I dreaded sleeping here when I'd arrived, I hadn't left the safety of the room in thirty-six hours.

Throwing back the heavy comforter, I spotted my MacBook. A glimmer of hope resounded in my chest when I saw the little yellow "away" symbol next to Tori's Skype handle. Maybe she wouldn't answer. Gingerly, I hit the button and held my breath.

"Taryn!"

I could hear her voice, but there was no live feed. Thank God.

"I'm here," I replied dully.

"I can't see you."

"Hit the button with the camera in the middle of the ..."

"Where have you been?" she demanded. "And why haven't you picked up the damn the phone?"

"I did," I protested. "I sent you a text. I'm in LA."

"No shit." She lifted the energy drink to her lips, the aluminum can crunching under the pressure of her grip.

"I've got to handle that business with Trent."

I conveniently omitted the fact that I'd skipped the meeting and had yet to reschedule.

"And you had to fly out there personally—without telling anyone where you were going?"

"We just talked about this." My diplomatic tone edged with irritation. "You told me to handle Trent, and I am."

"We've got a meeting with the vendors about the memorial show. That's the priority."

At the moment, I was the priority. But Tori didn't see that. She didn't even ask.

"You don't need me for that," I bit out. "I'll be back in a few days."

Tori contemplated for a moment, then lifted her chin. "No."

I arched a brow. "What do you mean 'no'?"

"'No' means 'no.' I need you here. Come back now."

In the span of a day and a half, my best friend had morphed into a querulous child. Well, the metamorphosis took longer, but the edicts were fairly new.

Relaxing against the pillows, I crossed my arms over my chest. "That's not your decision, Belle."

"It's my company. And I didn't authorize this trip."

"I'm not a child. I don't need your permission to take a meeting."

"As long as you work for Twin Souls you do."

The knife sank into my skin, burying itself between the sword that Beckett slipped in years ago and the blade that Chase planted two days ago. A tiny garden of sharp metal.

"If you feel that strongly about it—" The screen shook violently under my bobbing leg. "Then maybe I shouldn't be working for Twin Souls."

Tori's jaw dropped, but she quickly recovered. "What are you saying, Taryn?"

She bit out my name like it left a bitter taste in her mouth. And maybe it did.

Ignoring her question, I took in a lungful of air so I could continue. Finish this without dissolving into a puddle of tears.

"I don't have much protection when it comes to the company. But I do have first right of refusal on any Leveraged project." I swallowed hard. "But I'll relinquish all rights to anything else, if you'd like." I lifted my chin added as an afterthought, "Except Harper Rush."

She pulled off her reading glasses, revealing her rich, amber hued irises. "Harper Rush?"

"She's not a client of Twin Souls. She's my client. I have a contract with her personally." Tori's lips parted, and I shook my head. "You never wanted her, Belle. So I made sure you'd never be saddled with her if I ever left."

"You mean quit," she bit out.

I meant died. But I wouldn't tell Tori that. Because when I signed that paper, I believed a freak accident would be more likely than me leaving Twin Souls.

My fingers dug into my ribs as I hugged myself tighter. "Resign. There's a difference."

She assessed my resolve with a narrowed gaze. "And if I decide to replace you on the Leveraged project?"

I smiled sadly. She'd painted me into a corner, and I had no leg to stand on. Except for the fact that Beckett would likely refuse to finish the project without me. Maybe.

"Legally, you can't. And if you tried, you know what would happen. Beckett would side with me, and Dylan would side with you."

She raised a brow. "You sure about that?"

I wasn't sure about anything.

"I've been with Leveraged since the beginning. Since Damaged." My voice broke when I thought of Rhenn and Paige, and everything we'd created in their memory. "I won't make them choose. I'm asking you as my friend. My best friend. Let me finish this project, and I'll be out of your hair."

"Out of my ..." She blinked, then fused her lips shut for a long moment.

I said a silent prayer that she'd give in because I couldn't.

When the stone set in Tori's eyes, I knew it wasn't meant to be.

"Fine, Taryn," she said through clenched teeth. "Finish out the project."

The screen flickered, and all that was left was her photo. It was an old picture. And she was smiling that carefree smile she used to wear.

As I closed the laptop, a piece of me fell away. Tori didn't know she had it—that piece of my heart. But I could feel the hollow spot in my chest where it used to reside.

Climbing back under the covers, I dragged a pillow over my head. And then the sobs came. Thick and hot, tears rolled down my cheeks in waves.

I'd lost everything. Or threw it away. Hell, maybe whatever I had was never mine to begin with. It was a borrowed life. Like everyone said.

Who was I, if I wasn't Beckett's girl, or Tori's best friend? Maybe I'd wither and fade without them.

No, that wouldn't happen.

As the tears continued to fall, threatening to drown me where I laid, I had my doubts.

Chapter 33

CHASE

*T*he bottle slipped out of my hand and fell on the floor. Cracking one eye open, I looked around the dark room. Voices drifted in from a wall away. It was business as usual at The Phoenix Group, despite the fact that the CEO was holed up in his office on the tail end of a three-day bender.

Snatching the bottle from the floor, I took wobbly steps toward my large mahogany desk and then slid into the oversized chair. I glared at the monitor as I brought the whiskey to my lips.

Wiping my mouth with the back of my hand, I read the latest blurb on the Leveraged fan site from yesterday afternoon. I clicked on the link, and a picture of Beckett outside the terminal at LAX bloomed.

"Beckett and Taryn together again! Sources close to the band confirm that Beckett hopped a plane and joined his longtime love in Los Angeles. Hit the link after the jump for a sample of Leveraged's latest single on their yet untitled album."

My finger hovered over the mouse button while I tried to decide how much of a masochist I really was. Smiling wryly because the answer to that particular question was obvious, I pressed the back of my head to the soft leather chair and stared at the ceiling when the music began to play.

"I breathe your name; you move with me. My future, my past, you'll always be. Stay with me, baby. I want you near. Inside you is the only peace. My only love, my sweet release. Stay with me, let me drown in you. Stay, won't you stay, no one else will do. I need you to stay. Stay ..."

Though it may have been Dylan's voice bleeding from the speakers, they were Beckett's words. When the credits flashed at the end of the sample, it confirmed what I already knew.

"Stay"

Copyright 2018—Leveraged

Words and music: Beckett Brennin

The fucker might as well have written it in the sky. Or painted it on a billboard. The song was for Taryn.

Sweet Taryn.

My attention shifted to the door. "Chase ... are you in there?" my assistant inquired warily.

Her shadow retreated, and I finished the whiskey, throwing the bottle into the trash on my way to the armoire in the corner where I grabbed a clean shirt. Inside the sanctity of the small bathroom, I stood in the utilitarian shower, the water washing away three days' worth of debauchery.

I dressed quickly and then fumbled with the keys to my truck.

My truck? Shit.

I was worse off than I thought. I must've gone to the loft and dropped off my Mercedes. Or I left it somewhere. Contemplating last night's whereabouts, I strode past my assistant's desk.

"Chase," she said as she grabbed a handful of messages. "Cameron's been calling all day."

"I'll call him."

"There are some checks for you to sign for the Arboretum project," she called after me. "What should I—"

Since the only thing on my mind was getting something in my system to keep from jumping out of my skin, I couldn't be bothered to answer her. Sliding behind the wheel of my truck, I found my phone in the center console, vibrating. Unknown number.

It's going to take more than that, baby brother.

When I reached into the cupholder to turn it off, my fingers grazed the rock I'd picked up at the Guadeloupe during the float trip. I ran my thumb over the jagged edges as the words to Beckett's song tumbled around in my head.

I need you to stay ...

A bitter smile tugged at my lips. Maybe Beckett was getting his wish. Slamming the car into gear, I sped out of the lot and then raced down the freeway toward the opposite end of town. Liquor stores and pawn shops flew by as I searched for the street. When I turned down Crack House Row, I slowed to a crawl.

Spotting an old man seated on a folding chair in front of a dilapidated house, I screeched to a stop.

"You holding?" I barked, walking straight up to the guy with a wad of cash in my hand.

"Get your ass out of here, boy." He snickered, his eyes darting around to take in his surroundings. "I don't need no trouble from some rich prick looking to have a little party with his country club friends."

I peeled a couple of hundred dollar bills off the stack. "I asked you a question. That requires a yes or a no. Are. You. Holding?"

"You got some attitude, huh?" He whistled. "Or a really bad jones. You got a monkey on your back, boy?"

Two men emerged from the ramshackle house, walking toward me with matching smiles on their faces.

"What's the problem, Pops?" Thing One said as Thing Two stepped to my side. "You need some help out here?"

"Nah. The rich boy was just leaving. Ain't that right?"

Rubbing his stomach, Pops revealed the butt of his gun in the waistband of his pants.

"You might want to check his pockets, though." Pops yawned. "He said he wanted to donate a little cash to one of our local charities."

When Thing Two made a move, I stepped forward, and whatever was hiding behind my eyes gave him pause.

"I wouldn't do that," I growled.

He blinked without backing down, but he didn't advance. Which was encouraging.

"I'm going to ask you one more time," I said, my attention back on Pops. "You got something I need? That's the only way you're going to get this from me." I held up the bills, fingering the corners as I stared at him.

When he failed to respond, I headed for the truck. Thing Two grabbed my arm just as Thing One decided to advance. My fist made contact with Thing Two's face, and he fell to the ground.

"Stay the fuck down before I really hurt you," I growled, my arm cocked in preparation for the next assault.

"Get off me," he mumbled.

I looked up when Pops hooted with laughter. Stunned, Thing Two looked over his shoulder as blood gushed onto his shirt and dripped on the cement.

"Come back over here, boy," Pops said to me. "You're all right, you know that?"

Smiling, I stepped over Thing Two to make my way to his daddy. Or his surrogate daddy. Hell, the guy might have only been his employer—but one thing was for sure—he didn't give two shits about the kid bleeding on the sidewalk. And neither did I.

"Whatcha need?" Pops smiled through rotting teeth when I crouched at his side.

I looked up at Thing One, returning his slow smile as Thing Two hobbled toward the house.

Shoving six one-hundred-dollar bills at Pops, I asked, "What do you got?"

Chapter 34

TARYN

*H*earing my name, I sat up and looked around the dark room. "Who's there? Chase?"

The mattress dipped, and Beckett's scent settled over me.

"No," he said as he crawled under the covers. "Not Chase. Just me."

"What are you doing here?"

His cobalt eyes came into focus as he laid his head on the pillow. "You haven't answered your phone in three days. Did you think I wouldn't come looking for you?"

Memories of my last conversation with Tori itched at my brain. I clutched Beckett's T-shirt as the enormity of my decision closed in on me. "What did I do?" I choked. "Becks ... what did I do?"

Beckett cupped my cheek. "You did what you had to do, I guess. If it makes you feel any better Tori's freaked. She didn't expect you to quit."

I didn't expect it either.

"I couldn't ..."

He folded me in his arms when a sob escaped. "Quiet, babe. It's all right."

Sliding my arms around his neck, I buried my face in his chest. His long fingers twined into my hair as I burrowed closer.

"Make it stop," I whispered.

"What?"

"Everything."

As my breathing evened, I thought of all the times Beckett had comforted me. Everything he meant to me. And when our eyes met, and he lowered his mouth to mine, I didn't stop him. The callouses on his fingertips, rough and familiar, blazed a path down my back.

"I love you," he murmured. "Only you."

Reality hit me with brutal force.

"No," I choked.

He rose to his elbow. "What is it, babe?"

Only the concern in Beckett's eyes kept me from spilling a truth so harsh that we would never recover from it.

I don't want you.

He pressed a kiss to my forehead. "I get it. You're not ready."

I nodded, my stomach lurching when he rolled away from me.

He's leaving.

I sat up in a panic.

"Come here, babe," he urged, settling against the pillows. "Control yourself. I'm trying to be a gentleman."

I laughed, tears spilling onto his T-shirt when I laid my head on his chest.

"I love you, Becks."

It wasn't a lie. I did love him. Just not the way he wanted.

Not yet, anyway.

Not ever.

My heart sank a little deeper in despair when I realized that even as I lay here, comforted by Beckett's familiar scent and touch, the notion of us was already a distant memory.

Chapter 35

CHASE

*S*itting in my car in the parking lot at Nite Owl, my eyes
darted around.

Fuck it.

It was my building, and I needed sleep. I'd been holed up at The
Phoenix Group off and on for the past week. I guess my brother
finally got around to remembering that my office had an oversized
couch and a private bath, because he'd shown up, threatening to bust
down the door.

I had to laugh because my assistant actually believed my wild
rocker sibling was the one with the issue. She followed my orders and
had Cameron escorted from the property. I had no doubt he'd
be back.

My hand shook as I slid my key into the lock on the back door.
Safely inside, I walked up to a full case of liquor and pulled out a
bottle. Jim Beam. It didn't matter—the alcohol was interchangeable
at this point.

Something to wash down the pills.

I sank onto the bed in my loft and, digging the plastic baggie
containing the mini pharmacy from my pocket, I turned it over in my

palm. Twenty or so Oxys, a dozen Xanax, some speed, and a couple grams of coke.

It was almost easier to moderate things before, even though I was addicted for years. Because I didn't have money. I depended on the kindness of strangers and the good graces of others.

I'd be dead in a few months the way I went about things now.

The unsettling thought tumbled around inside of my brain, and just before I drifted off, a hazy figure appeared at the foot of the bed.

"Who's there?" I mumbled.

Logan's pale blue eyes flashed in front of my face a second before he jerked me to my feet. Despite the chemicals that slowed my reflexes, my survival instincts kicked in, and I wrapped my fingers around his throat. A pain shot to my shoulder when he grabbed my wrist and wrenched my arm behind my back.

He threw me face down on the maple hardwood, pressing his knee into my kidney. "Checkmate, son," he said, the smile in his voice unmistakable.

"Get off me, Logan," I wheezed. "Don't make me hurt you."

"That's funny. I was about to tell you the same thing." He leaned close to my ear. "But I really don't care at this point. You can walk, or I can carry you. Your choice."

By the time Logan wrestled me down the stairs, I was fully alert. His smile was gone, replaced by fury.

"Get off me, fucker!" I bellowed, thrashing as he pushed me into the back seat of a car.

Expecting to find my brother behind the wheel, my stomach sank when Calista turned to look at me. "Stop fighting, Chase," she said quietly. "You know the drill."

"Fine, take me to rehab," I spat. "If y'all are dead set on fucking with my life."

In a last-ditch effort to break free, I clawed my way across the seat. Prying my fingers from the silver door handle, Logan twisted my arm behind my back.

"Can we get a move on?" he muttered, using all his strength to hold me in place. "I'm going to knock his ass out soon if we don't get to the fucking hospital."

Hospital ...

"I'm not going to the fucking hospital!" I fought harder as the words sank in, cracking the woodgrain door panel with my boot. "Take me to rehab!"

Calista was too smart for that trick, and I knew the minute I saw her that I was truly fucked. If it were Cameron driving the car, I'd likely be on my way to one of the many cushy rehab facilities in the area. And by tomorrow morning I'd be breathing free air.

"Their not going to keep me, Calista," I snarled, craning my neck to get a glimpse of her. "You're fucking fired, by the way."

"I can always get another job." She laughed softly without humor. "And with all that shit you're holding, you better hope they keep you. A seventy-two-hour mandatory hold is a lot nicer than the floor of the Travis County jail."

And there it was.

As I suspected, Calista was taking me for an evaluation, and given my current state, it was a good bet I'd be remanded for a seventy-two-hour hold. Seventy-two fucking hours. An eternity.

Adrenaline kicked in, and soon I was fighting harder than I had in years. But Logan was a brick wall. When I managed to land a solid blow, his head snapped back, and I smiled.

Until I saw his fist. And then everything went black.

I propped up on my elbows and spied Cameron through the small window in the door to my hospital room. His face was drawn and full of worry as he spoke to the doctor.

Groaning, my head slammed into the pillow when the next wave of nausea hit.

The door creaked open, and I turned to the wall as heavy footsteps approached.

"You know most of this is in your head, right?" Cameron said as he pulled out the chair next to my bed.

"How do you figure?"

"You haven't been using that long. It's only been a hot minute. I saw you go through withdrawal the first time. You chipped a front tooth you were shaking so bad."

I pulled the blanket up to fight the chill. Phantom or not, my legs were trembling. "Thanks for the trip down memory lane. Now get the fuck out."

"So you're just going to lie here and wallow?"

"Until ten o'clock." I groaned inwardly when sweat popped out on my brow. "Then I'm walking out of here. Seventy-two hours is up."

"Whatever."

The chair scraped across the linoleum, and the door slid shut a couple of seconds later.

I closed my eyes, banishing my brother from my thoughts. Guilt was wasted on someone like me. Eleven years, and it wasn't enough to keep me on the straight and narrow. My teeth chattered in earnest, so I conjured up a thought to warm me. A hint of rain soaked skin wafted to my nose, and a flash of stormy blue eyes drifted through my head. And that was worse.

Ten o'clock couldn't come fast enough.

Chapter 36

TARYN

*B*enny Conner surveyed me with his slick, used car salesman smile. He wore the moniker of salesman with pride, so it wasn't like he'd be offended by my description.

Benny C, the most sought-after concert promoter in the business.

I'd booked my first major tour with his company on behalf of Damaged when I was nineteen years old. The Damaged debut album had just reached the platinum mark, and I wanted to strike while the iron was hot. In all my naïveté, I'd contacted the publicity department at Conner Productions and offered the group up on a silver platter.

It was my first coup. My first major score. In truth, the only thing I'd asked for, besides a huge chunk of change for the band, was to have Leveraged on the bill as the opening act. In exchange for an eighteen-month tour where we visited every corner of the globe, Damaged became superstars and Leveraged was launched.

I'd stayed close with Conner Productions throughout the years. Their tours were grueling, and Benny himself was the biggest shark in the tank, but they served their purpose in the business. And if I wanted to re-invent myself and break away from Twin Souls, I couldn't take a step down.

The people at Conner were quick to respond when I'd sent my

résumé, setting up the interview within a day of my initial query. But I might have overreached just a tad. Even in my nine-hundred-dollar business suit and Louboutin pumps, I felt underdressed. Hell, the secretaries dressed as well as I did.

Mandy, the head of Benny's public relations team, surveyed me from her spot across the conference table, a frown tugging the corners of her collagen-enhanced lips.

I tried to hide my disappointment. If the head of PR wasn't a fan, it would be challenging to get a job here.

"Taryn, we're so happy you agreed to meet with us before you went elsewhere," Benny said smoothly.

"I've only been here a few days," I joked. "I haven't even unpacked yet. Y'all work fast."

"That we do." Benny chuckled. "I asked Mandy here to sit in on this meeting. If you decide to take the position I'm prepared to offer, she'll be one of your most valuable resources." He gave her a smile that she didn't return. "Having someone work for you with Mandy's credentials could lead to some great opportunities."

Work for me?

My knees shook beneath the conference table, rattling the chair, so I took a large swallow from the green bottle of Perrier to calm my nerves.

"I'm sure once you take a look at what we have to offer," Benny continued. "You'll realize that Conner Productions is the best place for you to showcase your talents." Benny slid a thick, elegantly bound book across the desk.

I didn't know whether to open it, or just admire it. My fingers slid along the cover, which was not paper, but soft leather.

"I've outlined the responsibilities for the position, along with the compensation and bonus structure." Benny's smile widened. "Of course, we can always negotiate the compensation. Money is not an issue. We want you on the Conner team, Taryn."

I opened the cover, fusing my lips together when I saw the salary. And the job title.

Senior Vice President.

Apparently, of everything, from the amount of responsibility diagramed. But the actual job title was: Senior Vice President/Talent Acquisition

"This is …" I cleared my throat, "a very generous offer, Benny."

"I've had my eye on you since the first contract you negotiated with us." He leaned back in his chair. "I never thought we'd be able to steal you away from Tori Grayson."

Prickling, I took another drink of water and then smiled tightly.

"It wouldn't really be theft. Tori and I are partners."

Sort of. Kind of.

Benny's gaze shifted to the folder in front of me. "In that packet, you'll find a very generous profit sharing package. I'm a believer in rewarding my team with profits, not titles." Releasing a chuckle, he shrugged. "Of course, there was no VP of Talent Acquisition before I got your résumé, so I guess I'm a believer in titles as well. Because they are important."

Mandy glared at me. Apparently, she wasn't happy with her title. Or with me. Whatever it is that she did, Mandy was well paid if the diamonds dripping from her ears and her wrist were any indication.

"I'm going to need to look this over." Keenly aware of its weight, I picked up the folder. It could double as a telephone book in a small city. "There's a lot of information here."

Benny laughed, nodding to an assistant who tapped on the open door.

"We wanted to give you the full meal deal." He waved her in. "Some of the perks that aren't mentioned include the use of our private jet. That's at your discretion. Say, if you'd like to fly home and visit your old team." He laughed. "As long as you bring back a signed contract for a tour, that is."

I jumped when the cork popped on the champagne bottle. Benny's wide-eyed assistant handed me a flute before passing one to Mandy and Benny.

"Here's to future alliances," Benny toasted.

When my glass was empty, Mandy steered the conversation from pleasant chatter about my trip, and Austin, to business.

"We're in the process of looking into a band that's just signed with Twin Souls," she said casually, her finger wicking the side of the crystal flute. "Would you have any insight as to what it would take to get Caged to sign on for the European leg of our next tour?"

Benny feigned indifference, though he seemed just as interested in my answer.

"Any information I have concerning past clients at Twin Souls is proprietary." My gaze shifted to Benny. "I'm sure you understand."

While Benny nodded, Mandy kept the pressure on.

"Do you have a confidentiality agreement?" she prodded. "A non-compete? Given your friendship with Tori Grayson, I would think those stipulations wouldn't be in place."

I cemented on a smile. "They aren't. That's my stance on the matter. Nothing is in writing."

Agitation etched Mandy's brow. At least I think it was agitation. I suspected Botox was to blame for her inscrutable features.

"What I'm getting at," Mandy said as she leaned forward and clasped her hands, "is that your close personal relationship with the members of the Big Three, as well as Caged, would go a long way in easing the bands' minds when it comes time to negotiate. Tori seems intent on picking and choosing the schedules, and she hasn't been inclined to hear any proposals from Conner Productions. I'm sure you can see how that might be a detriment to all the bands' future growth."

Defensiveness stiffened my spine. "Twin Souls manages all their clients with an eye toward their future," I bit out. "As far as the bands' schedule, that was my area. It wasn't Tori blocking your efforts. Conner tours are not for the faint of heart, and the Big Three all have a lot on their plates."

"Well, I'm sure that once you join the team, you'll be able to handle all the pesky details, so the bands' will feel comfortable signing up," she said as she held out her glass for a refill. "Our tours are rigorous, but the rewards can't be denied."

"It depends on the kind of reward," I said quietly. "And what you have to give up to achieve it."

For a minute, I almost forgot who I was dealing with. Why I stayed in Austin—and why I put my heart and soul into the company I started with Tori.

"Of course. I just ..." Mandy looked to Benny for guidance.

She needn't have bothered, since I suspected he was in on it. And if they brought me in, this is how it would be. They'd be paying me half of that fat salary so I'd convince the boys that Conner was the place to be. And it wasn't. I'd kept the Big Three on top of the music industry for years without selling their souls.

My heart sank a little as I gathered my things.

"Leaving so soon, Taryn?" Benny sat up, confusion furrowing his brow. "I thought we could have lunch. Kind of a pre-celebration."

At the Ivy, I'm sure. With a contingent of press snapping photos for the news story that would "accidentally" leak about my new job.

"Thanks, Benny." I rose from the cushy leather chair. "But you know I'm here on business. I wanted to meet with you, and I'll definitely take a look at your offer. I've got to get back to the studio."

I rolled my eyes, as if it was a bother. The real bother was sitting in the room with these two clowns.

In all fairness, Conner Productions was typical of the industry in general. But I didn't want typical. I wanted awesome. Hell, I'd started awesome from the ground up.

An idea popped into my head, the notion so brilliant I nearly squinted.

"I'll let y'all know." I was suddenly relaxed enough that my southern twang, the one I tried to hide at all costs when I was anywhere near the west coast, came shining through. "Thanks."

I rushed out, the receptionist and the grand foyer a blur as I made my way to the elevator. Powering up my phone, I scrolled through the contacts, smiling triumphantly when I found the number I was looking for. I waited until I was in the parking garage to get a clear signal before I placed the call.

"Elise Donnelly."

Smiling at the familiar voice, I slid behind the wheel of the rental car. "Elise, it's Taryn, you can drop that fake ass generic accent," I joked. "If I don't hear someone say 'y'all' in the next two minutes, I'm going to scream."

"Howdy, Taryn," Elise drawled, using her best down-home Texas twang.

I laughed, straight from the belly. And it felt so good. "Even better. How would you like to meet me so we can discuss a little business venture? As long as it's not tofu or sushi, I'm buying." I pulled onto the busy street, leaving the Connor Productions building behind. "Is there any place to get a decent slab of ribs around these parts?"

Chapter 37

CHASE

I threw my knapsack on the small twin bed and stepped back. The orderly dumped the contents while I looked out the window.

"Standard procedure," he said apologetically. "But, I gotta ask, any needles?"

I shook my head and lifted the water bottle to my lips with a shaking hand. The setting sun shimmered through the dirty screen turning the whole world shades of gold, red, and orange. My gaze fixed on the sliver of water in the distance where the trees parted.

"Group therapy tonight at eight." The orderly stuffed the items back inside the green canvas bag. "Breakfast is at six. Miss it, you don't eat."

Without waiting for me to acknowledge him, he left the room, his tennis shoes squeaking on the polished floor behind him. I sank into the uncomfortable chair, the plaid tweed itching me through the thin fabric of my board shorts as I continued to stare at the scrap of shore. My jaw ticked when the door swung open again.

"Great view, huh?" Dr. Briar's voice sounded behind me. "You can earn a two-hour pass after your first twenty hours of group."

"Gee, thanks."

The guy must've forgotten that I'd checked myself in voluntarily. I could walk out the door and call a cab from the nearest pay phone.

They still had pay phones, didn't they? The random thought trailed off.

"Our counselors are pretty familiar with the Guadeloupe," he continued. "If you bank a few hours, you can take an afternoon and float the river. It's very relaxing."

"You don't say." My chest ached as the sun sank behind the rocks, and I squinted to catch the last ray that danced off the water.

In my periphery, I saw him lay the beat up black guitar case on the small bunk. "We made an exception for this. But we can just as easily rescind the privilege if you break the rules."

My fingers curled around the armrests. I ached for the feel of the wood in my hands. The guitar was the only thing my old man ever gave me, and I'd kept the Fender when I'd sold or traded everything else I owned. The guitar was a beacon of light. My assurance that when it was said and done, the music would be waiting for me.

I shot him a bitter smile. "So, I guess that means I should cancel the party in the mess hall?"

Dr. Briar chuckled as he pushed his glasses up his nose.

"I know you're here of your own accord, Chase." His tone turned serious. "But there aren't any shortcuts. You can't buy sobriety. You've got to put in the work."

My Fender called to me. More than anything I just wanted the fucking dweeb to take a powder so that I could play. Briar crossed his arms over his chest and held his ground, waiting for a reply. These kind of doctors were big on acknowledgment—"owning" your disease.

Swallowing against the metallic taste that lingered in my mouth from the non-narcotic medication that was supposed to help with my transition, I pulled out my guitar. "I get it."

The tips of my fingers tingled when I laid them against the strings.

Since I had no say so in the matter, it was futile to tell Briar to take a hike, so I went about my business.

The first strum sounded tinny to my ears, so I adjusted the tuning pegs until I got the right sound. Then I began to play. "Blue Eyed Summer," the song I wrote for Taryn. Unable to help myself, the words poured out in a soft whisper.

I forgot the doctor was there, only coming back to myself when the last chord died on my strings.

Briar sank down onto the edge of the bed. "That was really beautiful. Did you write it for someone in particular?"

I could lie. It's not like he'd ever know.

"A friend."

Friends ... at least.

"Does your friend have a name?"

Sweet Taryn.

"Taryn." The ache in my chest spread, and my temples began to throb.

Briar eased his back against the metal headboard. "Do you want to talk about that?"

Pondering the question, I strummed absently without looking at him. Did I want to talk about Taryn? No ... it hurt too much.

"Not really."

Another song took form in my head as I stretched the musical muscles that had been dormant for the past few weeks.

"Is your friend an addict?" he ventured.

I barked out a laugh. "She's addicted to beautiful." The lyric popped out in answer to his question, turning around in my brain.

"That's not what I meant."

"No," I grumbled. "She's not and addict, or an alcoholic, or a co-dependent. She's normal."

"So are you."

"Can we leave her out of this?" I shot Briar a fierce look, but he remained neutral. "She's not in my life anymore."

He nodded, surveying me with a placid smile that I wanted to wipe off his face with my fist. "So she didn't mean anything to you?"

I bristled, my fingers frozen on the frets of the guitar. "I didn't—" Biting my tongue, I averted my gaze. "I said she's not around."

"Your choice or hers?"

"Mine."

Some of the tension left my shoulders as Briar stood.

"One more question?" he asked.

Like I had a fucking choice.

"Yeah?" I laid the guitar in the case and picked up the notebook with the curled pages and tattered edges.

"Do you love her?"

I stared out at the Guadeloupe, the sliver of water now lit by the full moon that hung low in the sky. The answer was clawing at the back of my throat, but still, I pondered.

"Yeah," I finally said.

My shoulders sagged, the weight of my confession like a ton of bricks I'd just strapped to my back. Taryn was part of it now. My "process." The road to recovery would include lengthy sessions about the girl that never knew how I felt.

When the lock clicked shut behind Briar, I flopped onto the bunk and closed my eyes.

Taryn was there. Inside my head. She'd inhabited the same spot ever since I woke up at the hospital. Before, even. I fingered the smooth side of the small stone that I'd picked up during the float trip.

You're the smooth surface to all my jagged edges.

My vision clouded as I wrote down the lyric. I'd used music before to soothe the savage beast. But right now, I needed to learn to deal with the ache.

Drugs hadn't taken Taryn far from my memory, but I'd use them nonetheless. But instead of seeking a high, I'd be chasing oblivion. And if I wasn't careful, I'd find it.

Chapter 38

CHASE

SIX MONTHS LATER

$\mathcal{T}$he blood rushed to my head as I made my way to the lectern, and the steady drone of the air conditioner accompanied me on my path. Though, from the temperature, you'd never know the small church basement had the amenity. Since the weather in central Texas fluctuated between hot and boiling hot with humidity, the heat was nothing new. But today, I had serious doubts that I'd be able to get through my speech without soaking through my T-shirt.

I wiped my palm on the front of my jeans before shaking John's outstretched hand.

"You ready?" he asked.

I nodded, then clasped my hands in front of me while he addressed the group.

"We've got an anniversary today," John said through a wide smile. "I'd like y'all to welcome Chase Noble. He's celebrating six months of sobriety today."

He paused when the room erupted in cheers. Some of the tension left my body as I scanned the faces of my addicted brethren. The pride I felt came from a different place than being applauded for my music, but it was gratifying nonetheless. More so since recovery was a hard-fought battle and singing and playing the guitar was as easy as falling off a log.

It wasn't necessary to make some big confession, but at some point, we all did it. When we were ready. I went over the monologue in my head while John spoke a little about support and the challenges we all faced.

I'd made the speech before, in group the day I left rehab. But that was kind of a cop-out. I would never see those people again. They would never ask me about my regrets, the ghosts of all the people I'd hurt. I made my confessions with the assurance that they would stay locked in that little room with the pale green walls and the tattered couches that overlooked the Guadeloupe. The place I felt closest to Taryn.

The door creaked open, drawing my attention. Fresh sweat popped out on my brow when Logan stepped in. Pulling the baseball cap low on his head, his eyes darted around, then locked onto mine. Acknowledging me with a smile, he took a seat at the back.

"Chase?" John smiled, holding out his hand.

I shifted my attention to the dark blue chip. Six months of sobriety and all I had to show for it was a piece of plastic. And my life. Yeah, there was that.

He dropped the disk into my open palm, patting me on the back when I stepped in front of the microphone.

"Hi y'all." I took a deep breath and smiled, my focus on Logan. "I'm Chase and I'm a dope fiend."

A few chuckles broke out at my turn of phrase. We all had our own little words we used to describe what we were under the skin. Since I was a fiend when I used, dope fiend seemed as appropriate a brand as any. When everyone settled, I took a sip of water and then continued, "I'm six months clean today." More cheers and a few whistles. Logan nodded, silently offering his support.

"I've been using drugs off and on since I was twelve. I'm a musician, and I started playing in bars and clubs when I was a teenager.

By the time I was fifteen, I'd developed a taste for prescription drugs. But y'all know how that goes." More chuckles. "Since I couldn't convince a doctor to prescribe me any without breaking a couple of bones, I moved on to heroin at sixteen. My brother found me one night after I'd taken a little too much. I nearly died."

Cameron had obviously never shared this sordid little piece of our family history, if Logan's slack jaw was any indication. My brother, fiercely loyal until the end.

I blew out a breath. "That didn't stop me, though. I'd just signed a record deal, and the first leg was in Germany. So I ... uh ... I scored this stuff." I scratched my head. "And I didn't really know how strong it was and I ended up overdosing backstage before a show. I was in full withdrawal when I got back to the States, and I ended up at the hospital. That's when I went to rehab for the first time. I was eighteen. And I stayed clean for over ten years."

I bowed my head when the applause rang out again, accepting the praise as much as it chaffed.

"Thanks," I shifted my feet, turning the six-month chip over in my hand. "I can't really pinpoint the exact moment I fell off the wagon. But I do know when I started using, though." More laughs and I chuckled myself. "Anyway, if I had to guess, I fell off about two years ago when I ... um ... forgot." Looking over each of the faces, I saw reactions ranging from confusion from the younger members to deep understanding from some of the veterans. "I forgot that this isn't something I'll ever beat. That I'll never be cured. The most I can hope for is a better understanding of myself and my disease."

My disease.

I cringed inwardly at the weakness I felt admitting it out loud. But I was getting used to that too.

"My family and close friends never gave up on me," I continued. "When I hit rock bottom, I had someone there to help me back up."

Rubbing my chin, I grinned while Logan just shook his head, suppressing his own smile. Logan did help me up that day, but not before he knocked me on my ass. The ache in my jaw and the bruise that refused to fade for a month were testaments to his strength.

"I'm doing my best to make it up to the people I hurt." My fingers curled around the podium when I thought of the one person I'd hurt most. Sweet Taryn. The biggest casualty of my little war. "I'm trying—"

A loud chorus broke out from the crowd. "Trying is lying!"

Trying is lying.

I nodded. "*Yeah ...* So, *I am* taking it one day at a time." I held up my chip. "Thank y'all for listening."

A weight lifted off my shoulders as I stepped off the stage. John clapped me on the back, the pride on his face evident. Of all the people in our little group, he'd helped me the most. And he had the most to lose. John recognized me the minute I'd stepped foot in the church. And I'd recognized him. I'd met him years ago when I needed a variance to develop some land around Lake Travis. John was a state senator that sat on one of the most prestigious committees in Texas. And he was a cokehead. His word—not mine.

"You've got my number if you need anything." He leaned in. "And I mean anything."

"Thanks." I nodded. "I'll see you next week."

A trickle of sweat ran down my back as I made my way to the exit where Logan propped up the wall.

"Fancy meeting you here," I said with a smile when he looked up. "If I would have known you were coming, I'd have baked a cake."

Logan released a chuckle and followed me out the door. I gave him a sidelong glance as we walked.

"What?" he asked, burying his hands in his pockets.

"Just didn't expect to see you here." I veered onto the garden path, taking the long way to the parking lot when I spotted a couple of chicks with wide eyes trained on Logan. "How did you find out?"

"Cameron told me." Staring down at the crumbling red bricks, he frowned. "I hope you don't mind me coming. I just ... you know ... wanted to support your sobriety. And since Cameron went to your other graduation, I figured ... um ... I'd come to this one." I strolled along, unhurried, so that Logan could find his words. This kind of stuff was hard for him. Hell, it was hard for me, and I'd been in intense therapy for months.

"I know it wasn't your fault," he finally managed to get out. "Laurel. I know it wasn't your fault."

A smile tugged at my lips, equal parts pride and gratitude. Logan had grown a lot in the last few months. Laurel was back in rehab after showing up at his door, strung out and broke. Foregoing the country club facility he'd sent her to the first time, he drove her ass straight to a sobriety boot camp. The same one I opted to go to when my seventy-two-hour hold was up, and my head was clear.

I pulled out my car keys. "How is she?"

"Hating life at the moment." He shrugged. "She's complaining about the accommodations at rehab."

"I suspect she was couch surfing for the past couple of months." I chuckled. "The fresh air will do her good. And when she gets out and goes through sober living, I'll set her up in one of my buildings. She can pay reduced rent, but she's got to work."

Logan nodded, biting a hole in his bottom lip. "I can't help her if she doesn't want to help herself," he begrudgingly admitted.

For a man who prided himself on bending people to his will, this was a huge step.

"I'm glad you realize that, dude."

He lingered at the bumper of the car, his eyes roaming around the parking lot.

"What aren't you telling me?" Leaning against the trunk, I lifted a brow. "I know you, Logan. What's up?"

"You're building that new recording studio with Tori, right?"

His lip curled inadvertently at the mention of my new business partner.

"You know I am."

"Is that what's got her so worked up—or is she just naturally bitchy?"

I laughed, and his scowl intensified. Tori Grayson was fiery, no doubt. And demanding. From what Cameron had relayed to me in passing, she was putting the group through their paces.

"She's intense," I conceded. "But y'all knew that when you signed on."

"I didn't know she was crazy." Logan ripped a hand through his hair. "Dylan said Tori was easier to deal with when Taryn was in charge. I guess we came on board at the wrong time."

I flinched inwardly. Rarely did anyone speak Taryn's name aloud. Since I'd gone into partnership with Tori on the studio, I'd spent two or three days a week at Twin Souls working on designs. Between Rhenn, Paige, and Taryn, it was like the offices were inhabited by ghosts that no one talked about. Seeing Taryn smiling down at me from one of the many photos that lined the walls was the sweetest kind of torture.

When Logan met my gaze, I surmised I wasn't as successful as I thought at hiding the grimace.

"I'm sorry, dude." He shook his head. "I wasn't thinking."

"It's fine."

"Maybe Tori will chill when she gets out to LA," he groused. "If I don't kill her on the fucking plane."

The question popped out before I could reel it in. "What's in LA?"

Besides Taryn. She was there. It took all my willpower not to fly out and throw myself at her feet. I'd gone as far as booking a ticket. Twice.

"The Leveraged album is finally done." Logan rolled his eyes. "You know Tori wouldn't miss that. If Dylan was releasing a fart she'd be there, let alone a new album."

I almost choked on my tongue. Cocking my head, I noted Logan's petulant tone. And then it hit me.

"Tori's kind of hot, though, don't you think?" I asked casually.

His blue eyes turned frosty, homing in on me with laser like precision. "That's not cool, Chase."

"What?"

"Taryn's her best friend. Isn't there some kind of chick-code?"

"I'm not a chick." Unable to keep up the ruse, I clapped Logan's shoulder and laughed out loud. "Don't worry, bro, my interest in Tori is all business."

He feigned indifference, though his features visibly relaxed. "If you're interested in keeping me from choking out your new partner, you'll fly out to the coast with us and keep her out of my hair."

Logan Cage was nothing if not crafty. And I suspected keeping Tori out of Dylan's hair was more what he had in mind.

"I suppose I can take a few days off." I suppressed my smile and the pang of apprehension that followed. "We can stay at the beach house. There's plenty of room."

Logan slumped against the car, contemplating. "I guess that would be all right. I was thinking we could stay in town. Tori's going to be staying at Dylan's house, from what I hear." His scowl returned with a vengeance.

"Really?" I tried to hide my surprise. "How's that going to work? Isn't Taryn staying with the band?"

With Beckett ...

For someone who was as clear as a pane of glass when it came to his fascination with Tori, Logan had no right to chide me when it came to Taryn. But from the smirk on his face, he was about to do just that.

"Taryn isn't staying at the Hollywood Hills house," he said with an I've-got-a-secret tilt to his lips. "Dylan said she rented a place on the beach."

The shock wiped away any guile I possessed. "Which beach?"

"I don't know," he replied with a shrug. "All those beaches sound the same to me."

"Logan," I growled. "Cut the bullshit."

When I pushed off the car, ready to wrestle the information out of him, his blue eyes flickered with amusement.

"I'm just fucking with you, man." The smile dimmed as he toed the pavement. "But I don't think Taryn would have rented the place if she knew."

"Knew what?"

"That the guy who broke her heart owns a house two miles away."

Chapter 39

TARYN

The door to my cottage blew open, the chuff of air spreading a fresh dusting of sand on my wood floors.

Groaning, I made a grab at the stack of papers on the table in front of me.

Beckett strode in, checking the label on the box. "This says 'bathroom.'" He glanced at me. "Which bathroom?"

"There are only two bathrooms," I grumbled. "Take your pick."

Shrugging, he headed down the hall.

"If you're so concerned about space," he called, "maybe we should have rented a bigger place."

We. My stomach knotted at Beckett's choice of words. We weren't together. In the six months I'd been at the Hollywood Hills house, I'd displaced him from his room, taken over his private bathroom, and made the kitchen my own. But we weren't a couple.

He ambled into the kitchen, humming to himself as he grabbed a box from the floor. As he unpacked the glassware and plates, he stumbled upon a couple of wine goblets. "Red or white, babe?" His long fingers turned the bottles in the built-in wine rack to examine the labels.

He wanted merlot, which I hated.

"On the left." I settled into the chair, bringing my knees to my chest as I drank him in. He was beautiful, as always.

"You didn't answer." He replaced the cork, then swirled the burgundy liquid around the glass while he assessed me. "Do you want cabernet or something white?"

I dropped my gaze to the bottle in his hand. "How do you know I don't want merlot?"

"Because you hate merlot."

And yet, bottles sat in the half-empty rack. I'd stocked up at Trader Joe's on my first shopping trip. Along with pistachio nuts and his favorite cherry ice cream. Neither of which I particularly cared for. A Beckett-friendly house. If there was such a thing, I had it.

Abandoning the glass, he crossed the room and knelt in front of my chair.

"Babe, what is it?" His fingers twined my hair as he examined my face with a look of concern so genuine, I winced. "Is it your stomach? You shouldn't have eaten the—"

"The what?" My feet hit the floor with a thud. "The dried tomatoes on my pizza ... is that what you were going to say?"

His palm trailed down my arm, and he took my hand. "Yes."

"Why?

"What do you mean?"

"Why shouldn't I eat the dried tomatoes?"

Confusion lined his brow. "T-Rex ... what's the matter?"

"Just answer me." A tear spilled onto my cheek. "Why?"

"Because there's too much acid," he said cautiously. "And it upsets your stomach. Is that what this is. A stomach ache?"

I'm not fifteen, I wanted to yell. The stomach aches that brought me to my knees as a teenager were no more. But Beckett knew everything about me. Everything. There was no getting away from our history.

"Is it something else?" he asked, reaching to check my temperature.

I batted his arm away. "We're not together, Becks."

I said it more to convince myself than him, since I'd apparently turned one of the most sex-crazed rockers on the planet into my sexless husband.

I'd expected Beckett to fall back into his old ways, staying out all night or sneaking a girl into the house when I was at work. But he never did.

"I know that," he snapped. "You don't have to remind me."

He stared out the window, not meeting my gaze, but deeply aware of my every look. Like always. I softened as I took in the hard edges of his profile. He jolted as my fingers traced the stubble on his jaw. I'd picked up razors too. They were tucked in the box he'd just stowed in the bathroom, ready for him to use.

"Beckett. This isn't—"

Fair. Right …

"I'll wait." He closed his eyes, leaning into my touch. "I'm waiting. For you."

My fingers trailed into his hair, testing the consistency. The rich, brown locks were silky and as familiar to my touch as my own.

"I'm sorry," I whispered.

"Don't be. You're worth it."

My attention turned to the grains of sand on the floor.

"Ugh," I groaned. "It's everywhere."

He rose, more sand joining the pile when he stomped his feet. "You wanted to live at the beach."

"You never see this part on TV." I grabbed the broom. "I'm not going to last out here."

Beckett scrutinized me while I swept up the mess. "Don't you think you should start getting ready?" Glancing at my rumpled T-shirt and messy hair, he lifted a brow. "I know you're going for a casual vibe with the new agency, but there are limits. We're still your clients."

As I dumped the sand into the trashcan, some of the grains blew back and landed on the floor, and I scowled. "I don't think I'm going to go tonight."

His boots thundered against the hardwood as he marched to my side. "What are you talking about?" Prying the dustpan from my hand, he threw it on the floor and then dragged me to the couch. "You have to go. You're the publicist. We need to discuss the arrivals for the party tomorrow night. It's your project."

My last project. The end of an era. Now that the Leveraged album was complete, my business with Twin Souls was concluded as well.

I shrugged and smiled at him. "It's just dinner, right? I don't need to be there."

He ripped a frustrated hand through his hair, his blue eyes flashing with anger. "How long are you going to keep this up, T-Rex?" Exasperation laced his tone. "You can't avoid her forever."

Like everyone else, Beckett had grown accustomed to speaking about Tori in the generic. "She" or "her." For the most part, I managed to avoid the subject altogether. During my months of self-imposed exile, I went about my business setting up Ayers Public Relations, and Tori did ... whatever it was she was doing.

"I'm not avoiding her," I lied. "I'm going to see her tomorrow night at the launch party, babe."

I swallowed hard at the endearment I didn't mean to bestow. Old habits die hard, and in the natural progression of our path from lovers to friends, sometimes I lost track of where we were. Or *when* we were.

Beckett didn't notice, his focus on the picture window overlooking the shore. "I just want things to get back to normal." He slipped his arm around my shoulder. "You two need to get over ... whatever it is that *this* is."

I glanced around at all the boxes littering the floor of the small beach house. *This* was not something we could sweep under the rug like the grains of sand that blew in from the shore. Tori and I would eventually speak. It was inevitable. She was my best friend. But truth be told, we would never be what we were. I no longer lived in Austin, and I didn't work for Twin Souls. That part of my life was over.

I shifted, creating some distance. "I'm going to talk to Tori privately next week when I go home. If I can get past Stacia."

My lip curled inadvertently around the name of Tori's assistant. Since Stacia came on board at Twin Souls, she'd taken it upon herself to run interference between Tori and me. For all I knew, that was in her job description—keep Taryn out of Tori's hair—in big bold letters on the top of her offer letter.

"Just give me the word. I'll take care of Stacia for you." Beckett paled when I shot him a speculative glare. "I didn't mean it like that. I meant—"

"I know what you meant."

Beckett shut off the ringer on his phone when a Damaged song broke the silence. I glanced at Tori's picture, still lighting his screen.

He scrubbed a hand over his face, then looked around glumly. "How did everything get so fucked up?"

"It's not fucked up ... it's life." I smiled sadly. "People change. They grow apart. They—"

"*Die*," Beckett said softly, turning his attention to the framed pictures on the sofa table.

Most were photos from the first tour. Rhenn and Paige were in every one.

I swallowed past the hard lump in my throat. "Life goes on. Even if you don't want it to."

Like an unwelcome visitor, Chase Noble flashed in my mind. He was the bookend on the painful chapter of my life that closed the day I left Austin. I couldn't think of him without smiling. Or crying. The fact that I thought of him at all was the greatest irritant.

Beckett stood, adding in a dash of guilt to try and change my mind about dinner. "Every song on that album is for you." He took my hands and pulled me to my feet. "Take a shower and come with me. It won't be the same without you."

Biting my lip, I counted to ten in my head, the proper amount of time for faking consideration. "Nah, I've got a little work to do for the party."

"That was exactly ten seconds." He bent to brush a kiss to my lips, lingering with his mouth an inch from mine. "You need some new material; I taught you that trick."

I was about to mention that the proper length of time for a peck on the lips was one second—according to *Beckett's Rules To Live By*.

And he'd just spent a good four seconds with his mouth pressed to mine. But that would only start a debate. Most likely he would want to provide a demonstration. I wasn't going down that road. I'd only kissed Beckett a handful of times in the past few months. Really kissed him. I wasn't sure if I did it to keep him with me, a vague promise for a future that would never be. Really, I wanted to see if I could breathe life into the corpse of our relationship. It'd be so much easier if I could love him the way I used to.

"You better go." I patted his chest. "I'm so proud of you, Becks."

The new album was a masterpiece. And tomorrow night everyone was going to know it. I kept my back to him when he walked away.

Pausing at the door, he said quietly, "I love you."

My chest constricted at the sincerity in his tone. Six months and our roles had reversed. "Love you too."

I waited until I heard his car door slam to shuffle to the refrigerator. Pulling out the bottle of chardonnay, I frowned at the thin sheet of metal covering the cork. Life was simpler when my wine came with a top that screwed off. Spotting the box in the corner labeled "Stuff," I sank to my knees in search of a corkscrew.

As I dug through the mishmash of items, a pair of yellow eyes caught my attention. I plucked the card from the box, my thumb tracing the Nite Owl Pub logo. Grabbing the elusive corkscrew, I stood on shaky legs and then released the card. It fluttered to the top of the heap of junk, the yellow eyes staring up at me.

I gave the box a good kick, and the container skittered across the hardwood. Snatching the bottle of wine from the counter, I headed out the back door and onto the beach, leaving all thoughts of Chase Noble where they belonged. In the past.

Passing one of the bonfires dotting the landscape, I trudged along the water's edge to avoid the raucous game of football taking place a few yards away.

"Want a beer, honey?" one of the shirtless hunks called out.

I resisted the urge to look over my shoulder and see whether he was actually speaking to me. I was never insecure about my looks until I moved to California. At home, in the land of sanity, the few extra pounds I carried in my hips and the laugh lines around my mouth were sexy. Out here? A standing appointment for Botox and a plastic surgeon on speed dial were all the rage to wipe away such imperfections.

"No, thanks." I lifted my hand and dropped it just as quickly when I realized I was waiving a half-empty wine bottle. Which may have been the reason the guy was proffering an invitation.

Pathetic, drunk girl walking on the beach. Yeah … I was a catch. I bet the hunk could smell the desperation from a hundred paces.

I shivered as the tide crept in, soaking me to mid-calf. Stupid California and its stupid weather. It was hot enough downtown this afternoon to fry an egg on my head. But in my little corner of heaven, the temperature plummeted as soon as the sun dipped below the horizon. The climate was as schizophrenic as the people.

Pulling out my phone, I glanced at the time and seriously considered calling Beckett. But that would be awkward.

What would I say?

Please come find me. I'm drunk on the beach, and I lost my house.

Not the way to go. It would only cement his theory that I had no business living out here alone. A battle I was fighting on the daily. Since I realized this afternoon I was unwittingly aiding Beckett's cause by turning my place into our place, I needed to tread lightly, or I'd end up with a roommate. And at some point, I'd like to get laid.

I giggled at the thought. Drunk and horny. Not a good combo. Drunk and horny led to rash decisions of the Chase Noble variety.

Get out of my head.

I glanced at the rows of houses cupping the shore. They weren't the custom two-story homes with elaborate decks that lined the beach two miles north. I knew I was headed in the right direction.

Finally.

When I'd first ventured out this evening, I'd taken a detour after I'd spotted a small patch of trees in one of the more palatial enclaves a mile or so up the shore from my bungalow. I missed trees. And grass. Staking out a spot under a palm, I'd finished most of my wine and didn't get back to the beach until the sun had set. Hopelessly lost, I'd wandered the same three-mile stretch of beach for the last two hours trying to find my house.

The tension floated away as I approached the familiar sign warning of high tides and the danger of swimming without a partner.

No worries there.

The Pacific Ocean was beautiful, with its sparkling blue water and frothy waves. But like the people, I found this particular ocean cold and foreboding. The Gulf of Mexico was inviting. I could venture into the warm, still water without falling off the edge of the world. That's what I felt here; like I was at the end of the world, and if I wandered too far into the frigid deep, I'd be lost forever.

I took another sip of the wine. Then another.

Spotting the rickety steps attached to the back of my cottage, I trudged up the small dune, my feet sinking into the unforgiving sand. My legs wobbled from the exertion as I climbed the stairs. Four steps from the top I lost my footing, falling to my knees.

"Fuck!" The ear-piercing shriek escaped into the night air, full of all the frustration that bubbled inside me.

My chin fell to my chest as hot tears stung my eyes. I had everything I wanted, the freedom and the success, and it wasn't enough.

More time.

I just needed more time to adjust.

Panic seized me when the wood planks on the deck creaked. And then a beat-up pair of Doc Martens appeared in front of me. I knew those boots. And even in my drunken haze, I recognized the scent drifting to my nose.

My mouth dropped open when Chase extended his hand. "Let me help you, baby."

Inwardly I balked at the request, even as my palm slid into his.

Knees weak from the contact, I dropped the bottle clutched in my other hand, and the glass landed with a thud and then rolled down the steps.

Chase's arm slid around my waist, and I was off my feet, pressed against him. "Careful."

I blinked up at him. His lips were right there. So close I could lean in and ...

Coming back to myself, I scrambled to the top of the deck. Our gazes now level, I scowled. "What are you doing here? How did you know where I live?"

A stupider question never left my lips. His brother was my client. My best friend was his business partner.

"Never mind," I said, defeat coloring my tone. Not because he was here, but because I wanted him to be here. "Thanks for the hand."

Stumbling to the door, I pressed my shoulder against the wood and pushed, nearly falling over the threshold.

Fucking perfect.

The rickety steps protested Chase's weight when he walked away. It was that easy. Tell him to leave, and he was gone.

More wine.

I stumbled to the counter and grabbed the hated merlot. My fingers froze around the neck of the bottle when Chase's voice sounded from the door.

"Judging from this bottle," he held up the wine that I'd dropped, inspecting the contents, "you might not need anymore."

"Well, that's none of your concern now, is it?" A smug smile lifted my lips as I poured the crimson liquid into Beckett's old glass. "This is California, not Texas. They have laws against stalking, so you better *get*."

The southern belle warred with the angry drunk bitch in my head as I leaned against the edge of the counter and glared at him. He looked too damn good, this man. And he brought feelings to the surface I'd suppressed for months.

"Technically, you're the one who's stalking me." He grinned that cocky grin. "Since I've owned a house on this beach for five years."

I nearly choked on my next sip of wine. "W-what?"

Before I could process the information, Chase stepped inside. "I had to see you, baby. I want to explain. If you let me ... I ..."

Brazened by the wine, I snorted a very unlady-like laugh while he fought to find the words.

"This should be good." I lifted my goblet to him. "Can I pour you a glass? You'll probably need it to wash down your bullshit excuses."

He gazed at the glass in my hand, then up to my face. "I don't drink."

Another snort tickled my throat. "Since when?"

My mouth dropped open to protest when he took tentative steps toward me. But I couldn't find the will.

Stopping a foot from where I stood, he released a staggered breath. "Since I got out of rehab."

Chapter 40

CHASE

*T*he goblet slipped from Taryn's hand, shattering against the hardwood. Wine spread at her feet and bits of lead crystal scattered along the floor.

"Don't move." I looked around at the boxes. "Do you have any paper towels? Or a dish cloth?"

Since my little confession left her speechless, I was on my own. Pulling open a container marked "Kitchen," I sifted through the clutter, turning in horror when she screeched.

Balanced on one leg, she gripped the edge of the counter while a steady drip of blood slid from her foot, splattering the puddle of wine.

"Baby, I told you not to move." I slipped my arms under her knees and then lifted her up, the glass crunching under my boots as I extricated her from the mess. "Where's your bathroom?"

"Ouch." She squirmed to get a view of her injury and then looked up at me. "I think I stepped on glass."

Heading toward the dim light in the hallway, I held her tighter. "You did. We need to see how bad it is."

From the amount of wine she'd consumed, Taryn probably didn't feel it. But having her in my arms?

Shit.

"Put me down," she protested.

Even as she said it, she burrowed closer to my chest, so I ignored her rambling. It's not like she could walk, I reasoned. I drug my feet as I crossed the room, just to prolong the contact.

Pathetic.

"Do you have a first aid kit?" I asked.

"I think so." She blinked up at me, then frowned. "It's in a box somewhere."

Sweeping the toiletries from the counter, I eased her onto the granite. "I'll find it." I took her ankle and gently maneuvered her foot over the sink. "Are you in pain?"

A small amount of blood dripped onto my hand, and she gasped, squirming to get free of my hold.

"Baby ..." Sliding my hand up her leg, I inched my way in front of her. "It looks worse than it is. I don't think you need stitches." Noting the panic in her big blue eyes, I fed her the first bullshit line that popped into my head. "Your blood is thinner here. It's the dry heat or something."

She narrowed her gaze skeptically. "You're full of shit," she blurted, her bottom lip pouting in the most adorable way. "I think you're full of shit."

My common sense left the building, the same way it did the first day we met.

"Probably," I said as I pressed a kiss to her mouth. The bitter wine mixed with her sweet taste in the best way.

"You're trying to distract me," she breathed, resting her palms on my chest.

"Is it working?"

"Uh-huh."

Only the prospect of an infection from the gash on her foot tore me from her lips. That and the fact that she was probably drunk, and I didn't want to give her another reason to hate me. I hadn't gotten a chance to explain all the reasons she shouldn't hate me for my last lapse in judgment.

"Let me fix you up." I stroked her hair. "Where are your tweezers?"

Confusion lit her blue irises. "Uh ... in that box. If I have any. I get waxed."

She turned beet red at the admission, since we both knew that her eyebrows weren't the only place that received that particular treatment. After six months with no sex and no release beyond Taryn's image behind my lids when I stroked myself in the shower, my mind immediately went *there*.

Much to my embarrassment, my dick decided this was the perfect time to acknowledge Taryn's presence.

"Let me just find those ... um ... tweezers." As I crouched to open the container, I discreetly adjusted my erection. I needn't have bothered. The minute I saw the stash of men's razors and the other obviously male toiletries, all the wind left my sails.

Flinging the deodorant and aftershave on the travertine, a stick of Degree for Men slid across the floor, landing right below her.

"T-that's not mine," she stammered.

No shit.

"I didn't think it was." I grabbed a first aid kit, a bottle of alcohol, and the elusive tweezers. "Unless you've developed a wicked perspiration problem."

Her eyes widened, zeroing in on the rubbing alcohol in my hand. Considering my ardor had cooled dramatically, I debated letting her squirm. But that look on her face. God ... she was terrified.

"The alcohol is to sterilize these." I held up the tweezers.

Relief flooded her face. "Oh."

I washed my hands before pouring alcohol over my fingers and the little pink tweezers. "You ready?"

Swallowing hard, she nodded.

I gave her a small smile as I set up the makeshift triage supplies on a towel. The wine was still playing havoc with her emotions. The fear morphed into something else, some thought wicked enough to hood her eyes as she stared at me.

"I'm going to try not to hurt you." Dropping to my knees, I took her ankle without breaking our gaze. "Don't move. If it gets too bad—scream. Or grab my hair. I'll stop."

Grab my hair? If she did that, she wouldn't be thinking about the pain in her foot. With my head between her legs, the only thing she'd need to worry about was banging her skull against the mirror when I sent her into orbit.

But that's not what I wanted. That was easy. I could find that in Austin. I wanted her. Sweet Taryn.

I touched the inflamed skin, and she flinched, gripping the lip of the counter.

"Baby, this is lead crystal." Making small talk to distract her, I provided her with some useful knowledge. "The pieces aren't that small, but they are sharp. I should be able to get them."

"You went to rehab?"

Whoa, whiplash.

Blowing out a breath, I steadied my hand and gently extracted the first piece of glass. "Yeah." Examining the shard like it was a map to the lost city of gold, I avoided her gaze and released the glass into the sink. The pebble clanked against the porcelain on its path to the drain.

"When?" She narrowed her gaze. "I haven't seen you in six months."

"Six months and thirteen days," I said quietly.

"That's how long you've been clean?" She crossed her arms over her chest in a manner I'm sure she thought was menacing. If she weren't drunk, she could do the math. Or maybe it wasn't that important to her.

"Nope." Looking up, I rubbed my thumb in circles on her instep. "That's how long it's been since I've seen you. Six months and thirteen days."

Giving her the exact number of days might freak her out, but I knew them. Missing Taryn became my vocation after I got out of rehab. She was more addictive than Oxy, I'd realized. It took all my newly acquired willpower to stay away until I completed aftercare.

I went back to work on her foot, allowing her to lead the conversation. I'd tell her anything she wanted to know, but I wasn't volunteering. This shit was heavy enough, and she'd obviously moved on. Or more likely, she'd taken Beckett back. Guilt settled heavy on my shoulders for any part I'd played in that. But that was why I was here, wasn't it? Step number nine in the recovery process—make amends to those you've hurt.

Taryn broke the silence. "Is Laurel here with you?" The question took me aback, and the tweezers slipped, causing me to go a little deeper than I expected. "Ouch! Damn it, Chase!"

In case I didn't get the picture when she howled, Taryn grabbed my hair for good measure.

"Shit, I'm sorry." I rubbed the outside of her thigh soothingly. "There are only a couple more pieces."

"Answer my question," she snapped. "Is your girlfriend here with you?"

My girlfriend?

The depth of my lie hit me in the chest. Taryn believed I chose Laurel, when all I wanted her to believe was that I'd cheated. That I was an asshole. Like Beckett.

Mistaking my introspection as an affirmation, Taryn wiggled to the end of the counter. "Get out!" She was poised to jump, regardless of the injury. I guess the pain of hearing whatever she thought I'd say was worse. "Out!" She pointed at the door, steely determination flashing in her blue eyes.

God, I missed those eyes.

Sliding my palms up her thighs to hold her in place, I locked our gazes. "I haven't seen Laurel since the day before you left my loft." I slid my arms to her back while I stayed on my knees. Appropriate, since I was begging her to believe me. To forgive me. "She's not my girlfriend, baby. She never was."

Taryn blinked at me impassively. "That's right, you don't do girlfriends." Her lips tilted into a bitter smile. "I guess Laurel wanted more. Maybe she wasn't such a 'fun girl' after all, huh?"

I weighed my options. In this case, discretion was definitely not the better part of valor. I needed Taryn to understand.

"Laurel's an addict, like me. She's in rehab now, thanks to Logan." I rubbed small circles on her lower back to calm her. Or myself. "I left you at the river that day because she was fucked up. But I never even kissed her."

Confusion clouded Taryn's features as she cocked her head. "I don't ... you said ..." She licked her lips, and my gaze drifted to her mouth. Anything to avoid the hurt in her eyes. "Why would you say that?"

My chest constricted, stealing my air so I could keep the ugly truth bottled inside.

You're as sick as your secrets.

The mantra played in a loop in the back of my head, spurring me on.

"Because I wanted you gone. And I knew that was the way to do it."

I delivered the harsh truth with as much sensitivity as I could muster given the circumstances. But it didn't help. Tears spilled onto her cheeks in a rush, shredding me.

"You could have just told me to leave," she said. "I wouldn't have, like, stalked you or anything."

The notion was so absurd I laughed. "I should be so lucky." I caught a fallen tear, rubbing it between my fingers as I looked down. "When you came ... after that thing with my dad ... and you comforted me, without knowing what happened. I knew a part of you trusted me." I shook my head ruefully. "And I didn't deserve it. I couldn't let you see—"

"See what?"

"Me." Falling back on my haunches, a shuddering breath escaped. "All of me. The train had left the station, and I didn't want to drag you along for the ride."

The truth dawned on Taryn's beautiful face like a ray of sun piercing the fog. "You were doing drugs when we were together?" Her eyes widened, panic rippling from the pupils. "What drugs do you do? How long have you been doing them?"

She barraged me with so many questions, I covered her hand to stop the flow so I wouldn't miss one.

"I started doing drugs when I was a kid, but I'd been clean for over ten years. I went to rehab when I was eighteen." I smiled. "And, no, I wasn't doing drugs when I was with you. But I was drinking too much. Not really my thing, but ..."

My words trailed off as I battled with the inner voice urging me not to make excuses. Anything could become my thing. And Taryn needed to know that. In the silence her thumb caressed mine. I wasn't sure she was aware, so I stayed still so she wouldn't stop.

There was healing in Taryn's touch, a quiet contentment I'd only known with drugs. I'd felt that peace when we were together, but it scared me, giving so much control to another person.

"What is your thing, Chase?"

With the moment of truth upon me, I needed a distraction, so I took her foot. "Oxy. Sometimes coke. A little speed." I examined the dried blood and then picked up the tweezers, shooting her a small smile. "I'm a poly, baby. So it depends on what I can get my hands on."

Her brow furrowed as she appraised me. "Who's Polly?"

I took the opportunity to extract the last piece of glass. She barely shuddered.

"Not who." I sighed. "Poly means polydrug user. If I can swallow it, snort it, smoke it—" I tried not to flinch, "—or shoot it, I'm in. I used to do heroin. But not for a long time. I ... I didn't use any needles this time."

Unfazed by the confession, she tipped her chin. "How many times have you relapsed?"

"After my first stint in rehab? Just the once." I got up, then shook the cramp out of my leg on my way to the sink. I felt her eyes on me as I cleaned her wound. Applying gentle pressure, I smiled when she didn't stir. "How's that feel?"

Since she was unresponsive, I massaged her instep and waited. I'd stay as long as she let me.

"It's good," she finally said. "Just sore. Are you going to ... cover it? I hate the sight of blood."

"It's not bleeding anymore. But I'll stick a Band-Aid on it. Just make sure you change it every day."

She surveyed her foot skeptically. "I ... I hate bandages," she stammered. "I almost passed out every time they would come to the room to change Tori's dressings after the accident. All those open wounds." Her eyes widened. "How open is it?"

"It's just a cut." I opened the Band-Aid while she looked anywhere but at me. She jerked when I brushed my lips to the inflamed skin. "Just a kiss to make it better." I'd never felt so exposed. I quickly dressed the gash with ointment and pressed the adhesive in place, then stepped back.

"If it bothers you that much, have Beckett change it for you tomorrow," I said as I gathered the supplies. "It might bleed a little if you're walking on it."

"Yeah, no." She snorted. "Beckett won't be helping me."

I shrugged as I placed the antiseptic under the sink. "Okay."

"We're not together, you know."

My focus shifted to all of the little items Beckett had strewn around her space. "Okay."

Easing herself onto the floor, she hopped on one foot. "You don't believe me?"

"Course I do." I rose to my full height and looked down at her. "Y'all are just friends. That's the tag line, right?"

Maybe they weren't together, but Beckett was here. Providing her comfort, even if it was only physical. My fingers curled into fists at my sides to keep from doing something stupid. Like kissing her. Or stripping her. Or kissing her before I stripped her.

She rolled her eyes, releasing a chuff of air as she hobbled toward the bedroom. When she grabbed the side of the tub for support, I swooped in and pulled her to my side to take the weight off her foot.

She looked up, chin quivering. "Beckett is my friend." She sniffed. "The only person who's been here for me since I moved. But there's nothing between us." She laughed without humor, her shoulder sagging. "Nothing but you, that is."

"What do you mean?"

"I told you a long time ago, Chase, I'm not a friends with benefits kind of girl." She looked away as if it was a bad thing. "I can't use one body to replace another. Beckett and I ... we don't ... we're not together like that."

"Do you think about me, baby?"

Say yes. Please, say yes.

"Yes."

She looked pained at the admission, but all I heard was "yes." Cupping her cheek, I pressed a tentative kiss to her lips. Her mouth fell open, maybe to protest, but I dove in before she had the chance, seeking her velvety tongue.

She deepened the kiss, wrapping her arms around my neck. Breathless, she pulled away, her hand on the hem of her T-shirt.

I caught her wrist. "Not so fast." Scooping her up, I pulled her leg to my hip. "I want to undress you."

"I just didn't want to get sand in my sheets," she said, looking up at me as I walked us toward the bed. "It's like living in a tent on the Guadeloupe. There's sand everywhere."

I could live with her in a tent on the Guadeloupe. Or my beach house. Her loft. "Everywhere?"

"Uh-hum." Her lips brushed my neck.

As I eased her to her feet, I took her T-shirt along for the ride, slipping it over her head. Soft, creamy flesh spilled from the cups of her plain white bra.

Her arms flew to her chest to cover the tattered lace. "I ... um ... I didn't expect ..."

Pulling her against me, I smiled down at her while I fumbled with the two small hooks at her back. "This is the sexiest bra I've ever seen."

A smirk lifted her lips as I slid the cotton straps down her shoulders. "Nice try."

Her arms were still crossed over her chest, though I'm not sure she was aware, so I sank to the side of the bed to unlace my boots. "Totally true." Sliding my hands to her hips, I pulled her between my legs. "Of course, I've never gone six months without sex." I popped the button on her loose cutoffs. "Since I started having sex, that is."

"Six months?" she squeaked.

I tugged the little shorts over her hips. "Six months and thirteen days."

"I don't understand," she said, confusion creasing her brow. "You didn't ..."

"Couldn't," I corrected as I cupped her breast, circling her taut nipple with the pad of my thumb. "There's a difference."

"Why?" She eyed me with concern as I eased her onto the rumpled sheet. "Is that one of your restrictions?" Are you not supposed to ... you know ...?"

I chuckled as I settled on top of her. "No." I brushed a kiss to her parted lips. "I'm not that kind of addict."

The statement was as much the truth as it was a lie. I wasn't a sex addict, but I craved Taryn with an intensity that matched any I'd ever felt. It scared me so bad, I actually talked to my counselor about it. Embarrassing as fuck.

"Then why?"

I pressed my forehead to hers, apprehension knotting my insides. "Because I love you." The words escaped the prison where I'd kept them locked away. "And using someone else when it's you I'm thinking of, well, that's not healthy."

Tears gathered in her eyes, but not the joyous ones I'd hoped for. "I don't know what you want from me—"

I pushed the hair out of her face to look into her eyes. "I didn't say it for you to say it back." I smiled despite my disappointment at her reaction. "I said it because it's the truth, and I own it. Even if you don't feel the same right now, it doesn't change how I feel. I just want a chance, baby. We can start over, and I can prove—"

"No, we can't." She squeezed her eyes shut tight. "You live in Austin. Your business is in Austin." Her face crumbled. "I live here now. My company is here. I'm not going back."

I rolled off her, the force of the blow stealing my breath. Scooting to the head of the bed, I regrouped and then pulled her into my arms. "That's what planes are for." Wiping her tears, I finally gave up when there were too many to wick away. "We don't have to think about all of this today. We'll take it slow."

Before I could finish, she was shaking her head furiously, determination tightening her jaw.

"It doesn't work," she croaked. "Long distance relationships, they don't work. Separations ... they don't work. I can't even think about doing that again."

Again ...

I welded my back teeth together to steady my tone. "You wouldn't be doing anything again. Because we've never even tried." My attention turned to the infinity tattoo on her finger. The broken promise from the asshat she still allowed to wander freely in her life. "I'm not Beckett. Don't compare us."

"No, you're not." She narrowed her eyes. "Beckett would never go six months without speaking to me. He would never check himself into rehab without telling me. And he would never let me believe he slept with someone if he didn't."

All of that was probably true. But the fact she refused to see all the things he did do? Yeah, that was more than I could take.

"Beckett doesn't have to lie to you about sleeping with other women, Taryn." It took effort, but I softened my tone. "He only has to worry about begging forgiveness after the fact."

"That's why I'm not with him anymore," she said softly. "We're just friends."

I glanced over all the items in the room that bore his fingerprint. The guitar in the corner. The T-shirt thrown haphazardly over the arm of the sofa.

"Friends?" Tipping her chin gently with my thumb, I searched her eyes. "Like we were friends?"

"No." She swallowed hard. "You and I were never friends."

Her blue irises frosted, and she slid off my lap. She didn't retreat, though. She knelt at my side, determined to finish this. So I obliged.

"What are we then?" I caressed her thigh, drawn to her silky skin even now.

Tears streaked her face. "I don't know."

I nodded. Because I didn't know either. Taryn didn't want me ... want us ... so there was nothing left to say. Pain shot through my fingertips, still brushing her thigh. I pulled away reflexively, but she stopped me, her palm pressing against my chest. I shuddered when she climbed on top of me, molding her legs to my sides. Her moist heat warmed me through my jeans. Though I knew I shouldn't, that it was the worst idea in the history of ideas, I rolled her over.

Pinning her to the mattress, I lowered my mouth to hers, stopping just short of soft lips. "Is this what you want, Sweet Taryn?"

She nodded.

This wasn't good for me. I'd spent months sewing the gash back together after the monster ripped open my insides. "Okay, baby." The fragile stitches pulled tight as I lowered my forehead to hers. "Okay."

Shoving to my feet, I glanced at her stricken face. "I'm not going anywhere."

Yet.

I dug the condom from my wallet and tossed it on the bed. She watched me undress, then lifted her hips so I could slide her panties off.

"Chase ...?"

I kissed her stomach as I hitched her leg over my shoulder and settled between her thighs. "Yes?"

"I ... I want you." Tears glistened in her eyes. "I really ... I do ... I want ..."

I prayed she'd stop and let this be what it was. A sweet goodbye. "I can see that." I kissed her thigh. "What else do you want?" I found her pulsing center and my tongue darted out to trace her swollen nub. "This?"

She moaned, so I slid two fingers inside her sweet pussy and pumped slowly. I coaxed her to the edge, teasing her with my tongue until she writhed in pleasure. Gripping my cock to relieve some of the pent-up tension when she shattered, I continued the relentless assault on her clit, even as her legs quaked.

"Oh, God ... no more ... I ... I can't."

I turned my hand to give her a different angle. "One more time, baby."

Even if she willed her brain to leave me behind, her body would remember. When she broke again, I tore myself away and kissed my way to her mouth.

"I'm sorry ... I'm sorry that I can't ..." she stammered, the conflict in her eyes strangling any thoughts she wanted to convey. "That we can't ..."

I brushed a kiss to her lips. "Just hold me, baby."

Tears trailed into her hair as she wrapped her arms around me. I whispered her name as I pushed inside her warmth, setting a slow rhythm that would last and last.

My mind wandered to places it shouldn't. Tomorrows that we'd never have.

Riding out another wave of pleasure, her head thrashed from side to side as she mumbled softly. "Love me ... Chase ... please ... love me ..."

The ache inside spread through my limbs. "I do."

Her eyes fluttered open. "You do what?"

I smiled. "It doesn't matter."

Anguished by her hidden thoughts, buried so deep she couldn't even acknowledge them, I pressed my mouth to hers, thrusting deeper. To the end of her. The end of us.

When I finally let go, spiraling down to meet her, there was no regret. The love was stronger, by far. And that's what I'd carry with me.

Chapter 41

TARYN

I cupped the steaming mug of coffee in both hands, my teeth chattering as I stared out at the waves crashing against the shore. Chase's note stuck out from under my iPad, the edges fluttering in the morning breeze.

Sweet Taryn,

I'm heading back to Austin. Have a good time at your party. You deserve it. I hope you find everything you're looking for in your new life.

Love,

Chase

If not for the hastily scrawled message and the pain in my foot, I could almost believe the whole thing was a dream. But the ache in my chest, expanding and contracting with every breath I took? Yeah, that was real.

The back door creaked open, and I twisted around, my lips frozen in a smile that slid right off my face when Beckett walked toward me, a blanket tucked under his arm and a look of discontent coating his features.

"It's freezing, babe." Draping the coverlet over my shoulders, he took a seat beside me on the chaise lounge. "What are you doing out here without a robe?"

His gaze shifted to Chase's note. Prying the letter from its hiding place, his brow furrowed.

"Unfuckingbelievable." He released a short, irritated breath. "He was here?"

Unable to meet his gaze, I stared at the shore and nodded.

Please don't ask ... please don't ask ...

"Did you sleep with him, T-Rex?"

Throwing in my pet name was a nice touch.

"Yes."

I waited for the fallout, but there was none. Instead, he pulled me to him and whispered, "Why?"

There was too much hurt in his voice, so I took the easy way out, buying some time. "Why what?"

"Why him?"

"It's not a competition, Becks."

Resting his chin on my shoulder, he gazed at the ocean, caressing my stomach over the fabric of my T-shirt. "I love you, Taryn. So help me, I do." Pausing for a moment, he continued in a deep, sorrowful tone. "We were happy once, remember? Won't you at least try?"

Morning sun danced off his thick, dark locks. And he looked seventeen. Or Eighteen. Twenty-four. Beckett would always look that age to me, I realized. Time stood still after the accident when he started seeking the company of other women. I didn't want to know that Beckett. But he was in there. The older version.

I tucked a strand of his long hair behind his ear. "You've got a couple of grays popping out."

"Nobody stays young forever." Gaze fixed on the water, his smile turned bitter. "Except ..."

Rhenn and Paige. Forever twenty-four.

"Yeah, I know."

Reflexes took over, and I pulled away. I didn't want to go there. To the place where the wounds were so deep, so raw, if you grazed them they would bleed.

Beckett scooted to the head of the lounger. "So why did you let him ..." Jaw clenched, he shook his head. "I've been waiting for you."

"I didn't ask you to wait."

"You didn't need to."

I wrapped the blanket around my shoulders to ward off the chill that swirled between us. "Have you forgotten how long I waited? I asked. "Years. I've been waiting for you since ..."

We could run from it, but we always ended up in the same spot. That moment in time that everything changed. The tiny fissure I felt that day became a chasm we couldn't breach.

"It wasn't all me, T-Rex." Anger flashed in his eyes as he took a step into our past. "You booked the first tour. I asked you to go."

"You know I had to stay with Tori."

"I know that. But I was hurting too." He looked down at his clasped hands. "I needed you."

"Yeah, I could tell."

He shuddered, the verbal blow rocking him in his seat. "I made a mistake."

"Once is a mistake, Beckett. I could forgive one mistake." I sighed. "But after that—"

"It was easier after the first time," he admitted. "Everybody knew. Hell, you knew. And you forgave me." I didn't fail to notice a tiny bit of blame in his eyes. And I accepted it willingly. He was right. I'd prolonged the agony. "I never made you a promise I didn't try to keep," he said.

Tears stung the back of my eyes, but I willed them away. "Don't you see? You're asking me to do it again. And nothing has changed, not really."

He pulled me forward, his fingers digging into my arms. "But it has. After Maddy ..." He closed his eyes as her name slipped over his tongue. "After she moved in, I realized it was you I wanted. It was always you."

He was telling the truth. Finally. It didn't change anything. But it was nice to know the depth of his feelings for me.

"I believe you." I smiled softly. "And I love you. I really do. But I'm not in love with you."

He pressed his forehead to mine, his cobalt eyes etched with pain. "Can't I love you enough for the both of us?"

"I tried that. It doesn't work."

He gripped the back of my hair, and for a second I thought he would kiss me. Instead, he asked, "But you're in love with Chase, aren't you?"

Yes. "It's not that simple."

"He explained things, though, right? Y'all talked?"

I cocked my head. Beckett knew something. Maybe he knew everything. Maybe it was only me that lived in the dark, blind to everyone's faults.

"Talk is overrated," I said dully, recalling Chase's face the day he said that very thing to me in his loft. "It doesn't change things."

Beckett ripped a hand through his hair. "Not everyone is fucked up like me, T-Rex."

"I didn't say that."

"If I thought there was a chance in hell for us, I'd kick Noble's ass and take what's mine." He blew out a resigned breath. "But you're not mine anymore, are you?"

"I'll always be yours." My brow furrowed at the admission. "But not in that way."

He pulled me to him, stroking my back as I laid my head on his chest. "I guess that'll have to be enough."

His heart beat steadily against my ear providing the assurance no words could ever convey. What we had, it was real. So real, it evolved. Like our matching tattoos, there was no end for Beckett and me. We just completed the circle and wound up where we started. As friends.

Friends at least ...

I took a deep breath as I looked out the black tinted windows.

Two searchlights pierced the haze of smog, beckoning the army of limos snaking the winding driveway to Mac's Beverly Hill's mansion.

I glanced at Beckett, thrumming his fingers on his bobbing leg. "Nervous?"

He shook his head. "I just want to get this shit over with."

A stab of guilt shot through me.

The launch party was meant to be the crowning jewel in the band's history. A shining moment. But since I'd insisted on recutting most of the tracks on the album, and we came in six months behind schedule, a dark cloud hung over the event.

Mac, the head of the label, insisted on using his personal home for the venue, and I capitulated in the interest of diplomacy.

As the exhaust fumes penetrated the cabin, choking me in my seat, I questioned my decision.

"I'm sorry, Becks." I sighed. "I know this is all kinds of messed up. But we need Metro's support. If I snubbed Mac's invitation, we'd—"

"Stop apologizing, babe." He took my hand, entwining our fingers. "It's not your fault. Metro's not pissed because of the delay. They're pissed because we're leaving. That's on Tori." His lip curled inadvertently. "And Noble."

I nodded, marveling at Beckett's loyalty. He obviously had reservations about leaving Metro and signing with Phoenix Souls, the fledgling label Tori formed with Chase. But he did it. And that was just the tip of the iceberg. All of the Big Three were jumping ship, following their leader, though it was yet to be announced in the press.

"Chase is a brilliant musician," I begrudgingly admitted, caressing my thumb over his to soften the blow. "You won't regret it. I've heard some of the rough cuts he produced on the Caged project. They're awesome."

Beckett ran an agitated hand over his scalp. "I said I'd give it a try," he grumbled. "For Tori. But if Noble starts—"

"He won't." I tried for a smile, but failed miserably. "What unites you is greater than what divides you."

Me. I was the divisor. And since I wasn't in a relationship with Chase or Beckett, they'd work things out for the greater good.

"Here we go," Beckett said as the limo ground to a halt.

As his manager, I waited for Beckett to forge ahead, claim the spotlight he so richly deserved. But like a hundred other times, as he stepped onto the curb, he reached for me. I slid my hand into his without hesitation. For tonight at least, I'd play my role.

Beckett's girl.

The flashbulbs popped as he pulled me onto the red carpet. "Smile pretty," he whispered, brushing a kiss to my temple. "You look beautiful."

Becks, Taryn over here ...

Taryn turn this way.

Beckett ... where's Maddy?

A small tremor shook Beckett's body, but the smile remained. "Fucking moron," he grumbled, dropping his hand to the small of my back to guide me to the door.

My steps faltered when I spotted Tori waiting at the end of the red carpet, her face an inscrutable mask.

Beckett nudged me gently as we approached. "Play nice, T-Rex."

I shifted my gaze to Dylan, rooted to his spot beside Tori. I'm sure he'd issued a similar order. Tori's lips curved into a smile, and six months of stilted conversations and awkward silence evaporated. Reaching for each other, we collided, arms wrapped in a tight embrace.

"I missed you," she breathed.

I blinked hard as tears threatened to reduce my smoky eye makeup to sludge. "Me too, Belle."

I pulled away, and then Beckett slipped an arm around my shoulder, smiling softly at Tori.

"Let's rock this fucker," he said, pulling me to his side. "One more for the road."

Chapter 42

CHASE

I looked up from the makeshift desk in the deconstructed loft when Tori stepped off the elevator. Her heels clicked insistently against the subfloor as she stomped toward me.

Retrofit the elevator so crazy people can't enter at will.

I jotted the idea on the punch out list of items to be completed before we opened our doors. Considering the studio was one level above where I slept, the notion entered my mind more than once. But seeing Tori standing twelve feet from me with murder in her amber eyes solidified it.

"Come on in, Tori." I sighed, throwing my pen on the blueprints. "No, the 'by appointment only' sign downstairs is not for everyone."

Her eyes flitted to Cameron and Logan, stretched out on the couch in the corner, working through some lyrics.

"I assumed knocking was perfunctory," she replied, her lip curling. "I didn't expect you'd be getting busy with some chick in the studio since you fucked my best friend less than a week ago."

Two sets of boots hit the ground simultaneously. I hadn't bothered to tell the guys about my epic fail with Taryn, but Tori had no problem putting me on blast.

I went back to the plans. "I guess you and Taryn are on speaking terms again," I said. "Good to know."

Closing the gap between us, Tori tapped her foot impatiently to get my attention.

"Is there something else?" I muttered. "Something business related?"

"Are you going to call her?" she persisted. "Or was that just another hit and run?"

Tamping down my fury, I met her gaze. "That's not what happened."

She dropped into a dust-covered folding chair. "Enlighten me, then."

Clasping her hands, she rested them on her lap. Her amber eyes pleaded, despite her confident posture.

"Ask Taryn," I said.

"I'm asking you," she responded through clenched teeth. "I heard the CliffsNotes version from Beckett at the launch party. You know, the one you didn't attend."

"Shouldn't you be worried about your own love life, Grayson?" Logan chimed in. "Where's your six-foot shadow, by the way. In your purse?" He pushed to his feet. "No ... that space is reserved for his balls."

"If you mean Dylan, he's six three," she retorted. "And if he hears you talking about his balls, he'll kick your ass."

Logan's eyes danced with amusement as he stalked across the room. "That's cute, but ... no. Your boy isn't getting anywhere near my junk." He puffed out his chest. "And I'm six four, so there's no way he's an inch shorter than me."

She raked him over with an annoyed glare. "I'm happy for you, jackass. Now go back and play with your friend. I'm talking to Chase."

Logan slid a hip onto the far side of my desk, grinning. "You kiss your sister with that mouth?"

"With tongue," she growled. "Now shut the hell up and let the grown-ups talk."

Logan's mouth fell open and snapped closed just as quickly. I'd never seen him speechless.

A satisfied smirk curved Tori's lips, then she turned her white-hot gaze to me. "Well?" she demanded. "Are you going to tell me?"

"Just drop it, Tori," I said wearily.

Cameron meandered over, staking a spot next to Logan while Tori took a calming breath. "Is this about your problem, Chase?"

I had several problems. The construction project that was moving at a snail's pace. The show my brother roped me into at Austin City Limits—in four fucking days, no less. Taryn's radio silence. And, oh yeah, I was a drug addict.

I actually smiled when I realized that was the least of my worries.

"What problem would that be?" I asked coolly.

"Are you on drugs, Chase?" she asked

"Hey!" Cameron snarled, his lip curling over his teeth like a junk-yard dog. "You don't know what the fuck you're talking about!"

Reclining in my seat, I steepled my fingers. "Is that what Taryn told you?"

"Fuck no," she said with a wave of her hand. "I knew about the drugs a long time ago. I don't go into business with someone without doing a complete background check. What I'm asking is if you're on drugs *now*."

If I were on drugs now, I wouldn't be at my fucking desk, pouring over blueprints for the studio. "You're clueless, Tori."

She cocked her head and continued like she didn't hear me. "It has to be drugs, because you're not fucking stupid." The smirk was back. "Or, are you?"

"Tori ..." Cameron warned.

I'm sure this little ploy worked with most. But I wasn't about to get pissed and give her any information. "Say what you've got to say. I'm busy."

She shrugged. "If you'd sleep with Taryn and then just leave her in California, with Beckett, you're either high or dumb as a box of rocks."

Images of Taryn and Beckett popped into my mind. They weren't sexual, which was worse. I pictured Taryn making Beckett breakfast in her terry cloth robe. I pictured Beckett bringing her lunch while she worked at her desk. When the little slide show morphed into him feeding her that lunch, I closed my eyes and banished the wretched thought.

"I didn't leave her, Tori. I ..."

Left her.

Yeah, she told me she wasn't ready, but usually that would only strengthen my resolve. The truth? I couldn't sit around, eating my heart out, waiting for Taryn to decide if we were worth the trouble. It would hurt too much, and there was only one way to dull that kind of pain. Sadly, the price was too high. Any other price? I'd gladly pay ... with interest.

"If you didn't leave her, then you must have been hiding under a table at the launch party," Tori said sarcastically. "You can check the blogs for a blow by blow. There are plenty of pictures of Taryn on the red carpet. With Beckett."

Logan and Cameron stared at their boots. I wasn't sure whether to thank them or throttle them for sparing me the details.

"She's free to date anyone she wants." My hand shook slightly as I picked up the pen. "Just like me."

"You asshole!" Tori jumped to her feet. "It was a hit and run."

Spinning on her heel, she stomped toward the elevator.

"It wasn't," I called after her. "I told her how I felt." *I love you ...* "She didn't ... she said she couldn't do the long-distance thing." When her footsteps went silent, I glanced over my shoulder. "I tried, Tori."

Her face crumbled. "Well, you didn't try hard enough."

As I took in Tori's defeated posture, I thought about the picture on her desk at Twin Souls. It was a school play or something. Tori was hogging the spotlight, standing between Taryn and Paige Dawson with a huge toothless grin. But she held their hands so tight, her knuckles were white. Now Paige was gone, and she had to live without Taryn as well.

I smiled sadly. "I can't exactly bring her back here by force."

Tori's face contorted with greater anguish. "Why?"

"Because it's her time to shine. She won't go back to Beckett." *God, don't let her go back to Beckett.* "She's putting value on herself for once. I guess we don't fit into that world right now."

Coming back to herself, Tori tugged the bottom of her blouse with determination. "I don't accept that," she said stubbornly. "Taryn is going to be here in a couple of days. I'll talk to her, since you seem to be content with the status quo."

I wasn't. But there was nothing I could do.

Exasperated, I went back to my work. "You can't order her, Tori. She's not a blue-plate special."

"I guess we'll have to see about that."

The industrial elevator clanged shut, and I took a peek at Logan, frozen in his spot, staring after her. He'd met his match in Tori Grayson.

The two of them together could probably rule their little portion of the world. Or blow it apart entirely.

Chapter 43

TARYN

S weat dripped from my brow as I lugged my suitcase down the hallway. While most people went gaga over the California weather—if one more person told me it was a "dry heat" I was seriously going to smack someone—I loved the humidity here. From Beckett's whining and groaning, he didn't share my opinion.

Cursing, he threw open the door to my loft. "It's hot as balls in here," he grumbled as he adjusted the thermostat. "The air conditioning isn't even on. T-Rex, did you hear me? The air isn't ..."

His focus shifted to an ornate planter on the breakfast bar. Star-shaped blooms in varying shades of blue tilted toward the window. I'd never seen flowers so beautiful.

"Who are they from?" he asked.

Standing behind me, his chest brushed my back as I gingerly plucked the note from under a gray stone. Gazing at Chase's familiar scrawl, I turned the rock over in my palm, my thumb tracing the jagged edges.

Taryn,

I picked up this stone at the Guadeloupe on the float trip. I almost chucked it back in the river. On the surface, it looked like every other stone—plain, gray, and jagged. Like me. But the other side was smooth and beautiful, with little veins of color. Like you. So I kept it. I had it with me when I went to rehab. I thought I needed it, that little piece of stone that reminded me of you. But I don't. Because you're in my head. You'll always be in my head. In a place where you'll never be lost. And just so you don't think that I'm an ass for giving you a rock, the flowers are Blue Amaryllis. They're all the colors of your beautiful eyes. They grow best in over forty percent humidity, but they can adapt. Just like you. Take them back to California and transplant them. They will thrive. That is what I want for you, Sweet Taryn. I want you to thrive. But if you ever, ever, get lost, I'll be here. Because I love you. That's the truth, and I own it.

Chase.

I sank onto the barstool, tears streaming down my face. Beckett reached for me, but stopped abruptly. "Let me get the bags upstairs," he said thickly as he ambled to the luggage we'd abandoned by the door. "Then I'll get out of here and let you unpack."

I glanced at his Travel Pro suitcase, still in the foyer, then back to him as he trudged up the stairs. "Where are you going?"

He stopped at the landing and gave me a smile. "My place, babe."

When he disappeared inside my bedroom, the tether that had bound us since childhood tugged in my chest, but it didn't break, as I feared it would when he finally accepted the truth. I took a cautious breath, almost surprised when air filled my lungs.

I'd quit my job. Moved to California. Reinvented myself. But the new life I'd been afraid to embrace hadn't really begun until this moment.

I buried my face in my worn terrycloth robe. I'd left the little pink wrap in Austin because I mistakenly believed the ratty and frayed piece of home didn't fit my needs anymore. How wrong I was.

A knock at the front door echoed through the loft. Damn it. I checked the time as another knock rang out. No way the realtor was this early.

"Coming!"

Checking the peephole, my pulse galloped.

Tori jolted when I pulled the door open. "Hey, Belle. What are you doing here?"

And why didn't you use your key?

"I wanted to see you ... but ..." She cleared her throat, her focus shifting from my robe to the stairs. "If you've got company, I can come back."

I snorted. "Company?"

She bit her lip, shifting her weight to the other foot. "Yeah. I should have called, I guess."

"Since when do you call?" I pulled her across the threshold. "What is it?" I flopped on the couch, then arranged my hair in a messy bun. She didn't move an inch from the square of travertine in front of the door. "You look weird."

"I ..." She eased into the overstuffed chair. "I wanted to talk to you."

Fingers locked in her lap, she looked around uncomfortably. My gaze traveled from the dark circles under her eyes to the faded slash at her throat where they'd inserted the trach tube, and beyond to what I couldn't see. The mazes of scars hidden beneath her clothes, many of which barely missed vital organs.

Panic gripped me as I shot from the couch, squeezing in next to her on the chair. "What's the matter?" Inadvertently my hand traveled up her arm, squeezing gently as I went, like my mother used to do when I fell off my bike. But I'd been to enough doctors with Tori to know the bulk of her injuries couldn't be seen or felt. "Tell me right now," I demanded.

"I'm fine." She observed me with curiosity and a creased brow. "There's nothing, like, physically wrong with me."

"Oh, thank God." I melted into the cushions, pulling her back with me. "You scared me, Belle."

"N-no, it's nothing like that." A little of the defiant edge returned to her tone, and I was grateful to hear it. "I'm just ... I ..." She sat up, then scooted to the edge of the cushion. "I just miss you, Taryn. A lot."

Her revelation didn't surprise me. I felt it last week in the desperate way she hugged me.

When she finally met my gaze, my eyes darted around.

"What?" she asked, genuinely perplexed.

"I'm just waiting for the chill to reach us," I whispered conspiratorially.

"Huh?"

"Tori Grayson, admitting a frailty? I think Hell just froze over, and I left all my winter clothes in LA."

She punched me in the arm, her bony fingers sure to leave a bruise.

"Ouch," I yelped, rubbing the tender spot. "Bitch."

"That's what you get for laughing at me." She pouted. "It's not funny." She dropped her head into her hands. "Things are really fucked, Taryn."

I edged closer, propping my chin on her shoulder. "What things?"

"Stacia for one."

She gave me a sidelong glance, rolling her eyes when my lips inadvertently tilted in a smile. "What did the anti-Christ do this time?"

"She thinks she knows every damn thing." Her despair momentarily gave way to irritation. "She's messing with the boys' schedules and pissing everyone off."

"Hm." I sat back, contemplating. Giving Tori advice was hit or miss under the best circumstances. "Have you told her to stop?"

Another eye roll. "No, because I have no backbone and I'm just fine with it." She threw herself against the cushions. "Of course I told her to stop."

Her distress prompted my response, though I wasn't sure if my motives were pure. "Why don't you ... you know, fire her?"

"I would, but I can't do it by myself!"

My brows shot to my hairline. "Of course you can. Just follow my system and—"

"You don't understand." Genuine fear clouded her gaze. "There are other things. Metro is really pissed. They're threatening legal action."

I snorted. "No way Mac would sue you, Belle."

She worried her bottom lip. "He would, and he is."

Anger stiffened my spine. "I had those contracts drawn myself. Any of the Big Three are only committed to one release at a time. If they want to change labels, they can. Period."

"That's not stopping Mac's legal department from threatening us with—" Her brow furrowed as she pulled a crumbled two-page letter from her bag. "Inducement, fraud, and breach of fidu ... fiduc ..."

"Fiduciary interest." I finished her sentence, bitterness rising in my throat.

"Yeah, that." Tori tossed the letter on the cushion, glaring at the papers with so much fury I half expected the pages to turn to ash.

"It's bullshit," I mumbled. "It's a scare tactic."

"It's working."

My stomach sank as I scanned the verbiage in Mac's instrument of betrayal. It was a good old-fashioned shakedown. The lawyers knew Twin Souls would exhaust time and resources fighting the bogus claims, so they expected a compromise. Digital rights ... or possibly a percentage of the catalog.

Not. Going. To. Happen.

I took Tori's hand. "I'll talk to our ... *your* ... lawyers," I said. "I know the chinks in Metro's armor. And I'll use Ayers Public Relations to launch a media assault. Mac will rue the day he started down this path." I laughed dryly. "I'll take out a full-page ad in every industry magazine, letting everyone know the greedy fuck is trying to strong arm the talent. Mac will have artists jumping ship left and right." My voice rose as I formulated the plan. "And then ... I'll talk to every new artist that breaks on the Billboard Chart or makes a ripple on iTunes or Spotify. I'll ... I'll give them free public relations for a year to keep them from signing with Metro."

Tori threw her arms around me. "That's why I need you, Taryn." I forgot how freakishly strong she was until my ribs threatened to crack beneath her embrace. "Please ... I want you to come back to Twin Souls."

"Tori ... I can't ..."

She scrambled to free a manila folder from her tote. "No, no! I don't want you to work for me. I want—" A hopeful smile curved her mouth as she shoved the file at me. "I want you to be my partner."

"We were partners. We were always partners."

Shaking her head, she extracted a two-page contract with her lawyer's inscription on the header. "I know. But I want it to be legal."

I took the papers from her shaking hand and then laid them aside. "I just opened a business in California. Ayer's PR is a real company, Belle. With a roster full of clients." I sighed. "I can't just drop that."

"I don't want you to." Panic crept into her tone. "We can add Ayers Public Relations to Twin Souls. We can change the name."

"That wouldn't be smart." I gave her hand a loving squeeze. "You're branded."

Her shoulders sagged. "I know I haven't made the best decisions, but branded?" She winced. "I'm not that bad, am I?"

She waited for my confirmation, and I chuckled. Then she scowled, and I laughed even harder.

"It's not funny, Taryn."

"What's funny is that you managed to graduate with a degree in business." I bit my lip to keep from dissolving into another fit when her scowl deepened. "You're not branded, dumb ass. Twin Souls is a brand. A much bigger brand than Ayers PR."

Her frown turned sheepish. "Whatever. I don't care about that. I just want you to come back. Fifty-fifty."

I paused, the next wave of laughter catching in my throat. "No, Belle," I said emphatically. "Twin Souls is your company. Yours and Rhenn's."

"Rhenn's dead." She fused her lips and looked down, her chest rising and falling like she was trying to catch her breath. Her brutal honesty stole my air as well. When she finally lifted her gaze, tears brimmed in her eyes. "Twin Souls ... the name ... it wasn't for Rhenn," she said softly. "It was for you. Mostly. You're my Twin Soul. You're who I have left. The one person alive I trust above anyone else."

She'd proved it in a million different ways, but Tori needed control. And I always let her have that. Mostly because there were so many things that happened that she couldn't control.

I pulled her close like I used to, and she let me. "You know I love you, right? But maybe it isn't a good idea for us to work together." She stiffened. "Not because I don't want to," I quickly amended, stroking her hair to soften the blow. "But I've been so worried that maybe I'd do the wrong thing—hurt the company inadvertently—that I started to second guess myself. I have to have the freedom to make mistakes without dragging you down."

She pulled away and gripped my shoulders, her amber eyes pleading. "That's what I'm trying to say. Even if we drive this bus off a cliff, I know in my heart that you have the best intentions. So it won't matter."

I raised a brow. "So, you're saying we're Thelma and Louise?"

"More like Jack and Rose." She sniffed. "You jump, I jump."

"Comparing our partnership to the Titanic?" I hissed a breath. "Let's keep that to ourselves. I don't think our clients would see the humor."

"Our clients?" Her voice rose a notch with excitement. "Does that mean ...?"

"No." I cringed when her face fell. "But how about this: I'll help you work out this little difficulty with Metro. As a consultant. We'll table the idea of a partnership for now. And we'll see how it goes."

She hugged me tightly, forehead pressed to my shoulder. "Okay."

"But," I continued. "I'm staying in California. No matter what, I have to service my new clients."

The kinder, gentler Tori was still fierce and singularly focused on achieving her goals. So I wasn't surprised when she sank against the cushion, eyeing me intently.

She tapped her lips absently with her index finger. "Your three biggest clients are here, right? Four, if you include Caged."

"That's true," I conceded. "But I'm trying to diversify. That's why I'm in town. I've got a few meetings set up with some music groups performing at Austin City Limits."

She perked up, a wide-open smile lifting her lips. "Are you going to the Caged show?"

"No. Um, Elise really needs some ... you know ... experience with the clients. So ... yeah. She's going in my place."

My reasons for pawning my client off on my new partner sounded fine in theory. But under Tori's scrutiny, the lame ass excuse didn't hold water.

"All right," I grumbled. "I admit it. I don't want to run into Chase."

"I understand." Empathy, not recrimination swam in her eyes. "I was just hoping you'd go with me."

"You're *going?*"

Austin City Limits, one of the premiere rock music festivals in the country, was hardly a place where Tori could blend into the crowd. Not to mention, several of the local bands would likely be doing Damaged covers.

"I'm trying to turn over a new leaf," she said. I followed her gaze to the documents on the table. And I had to smile. It wasn't the first contract Tori and I ever entered into. In the first grade, Paige, Tori and me all signed a pact, in purple crayon, vowing to be best friends "forever and a day."

"Promise me you'll consider it," she said softly. "The offer, I mean."

"I will." Reluctantly, I pushed to my feet. "I've got a meeting I have to get ready for. Maybe we can meet for dinner?"

She brightened. "Sure. Do you want to go out, or ...?"

With the influx of tourists in town for Austin City Limits, Sixth Street was packed.

"Let me see if I can get us a table somewhere private. If not, I'll pick up some barbecue and meet you at your place."

She hugged me and then headed out the door.

A half hour later, I greeted my realtor, a tight smile firmly in place. She ushered in the couple that I'd met yesterday afternoon. We took a seat at the dining room table. While the couple went on and on about the views and the "perfect" place for their couch, I concentrated on the paperwork in front of me, holding back the tears blurring the small print.

"Any questions?" the realtor asked, handing me a pen.

I shook my head and then quietly signed away the rights to the first home I'd ever had.

Chapter 44

CHASE

My leg bobbed uncontrollably as the cheers from the crowd filtered to the green room. "You okay, bro?" Cameron asked, looking me over with concern.

I wasn't really sure of anything except the knot in my stomach and the lump in my throat, but I played it off well. "Worry about your own show. You've got a tough act to follow."

He laughed. "I'm going to go find Logan and make sure he's not stuck in a closet somewhere with ..." He scratched his head. "Who knows?"

Distracted, I thumbed through my sheet music. "Yeah, see you out there."

In an hour. I glanced at the clock above Cameron's head. One hour and I'd be in front of the largest crowd of my career. Playing Austin City Limits was a dream come true for most. It just wasn't my dream. Once it was my father's. Now it was my brother's.

But never mine.

That's what rehab and six months of therapy will get you. A whole lot of self-awareness. I loved music. Loved the feel of the crowd. And hated just about everything else associated with the business.

I only hoped that once the studio opened, Cameron would stop trying to provide a "safe environment" for me to exercise my talent. The kid went to a few therapy sessions, and now he thought he was Dr. Fucking Phil. He'd been badgering me to help him with arrangements. Dragging me to band practice to "sit in." And then he went and surprised me with an invitation to perform as Caged's opener at the festival.

I get it. My life was a dichotomy. Living above the bar, but not working in the bar.

Really, it was just convenience. A way to stay on top of the construction project. But there was no use trying to convince my brother. And just because I was in recovery didn't mean I needed to leave Sixth. I could live anywhere, but that little strip of asphalt was the only place I felt truly at home.

"Knock knock," came a voice.

And when I turned, Tori hovered at the door. She stepped inside, and my eyes widened.

"Hey ... Tori ...?" Intellectually, I knew it was my business partner. She was in there. Behind heavy eye makeup, tousled black hair ... and the outfit. Ripped jeans, riding low enough to send any man under forty, hell fifty, into cardiac arrest, knee-high boots, and a shirt that hit her just below ... *don't look at her tits.* I locked our gazes and kept my eyes north of her neck. "You look ... um ... good. What are you doing here?"

And why do you look like you just stepped off the set of an MTV video shoot?

I was hoping the answer to the first question would give me some insight into the second. She walked into the dressing room, sidling to the catering table to peruse the items.

"Same as everyone else," she said casually as she loaded a couple of appetizers on a paper plate. "Just catching some shows. Mingling."

"Alone?" Logan's gruff voice sounded from the door.

She paused, then walked to a folding chair and took a seat. "Not that it's any of your business. But, no."

He grabbed a beer from the bucket. "I'm guessing Dylan's

around?" He eyed her with a feral gaze as he took a slow pull from his bottle.

"Nope." She nibbled on a cheese stick. "Leveraged is doing some interviews at Twin Souls for the press junket."

Logan's arm fell to his side, spilling beer onto the floor. "So who's the lucky guy?" He didn't even try to hide the edge in his voice.

She rose, then sauntered toward the plastic trash bin to deposit her plate. Fluffing her hair in the mirror, she met his gaze in the reflection.

"I'd say by your reaction, every guy here." She chuckled. "You're a jackass, Logan. But you're good for a girl's ego."

The frost in his eyes didn't thaw. "Glad to be of service." He did a slow sweep of her body, starting at the back of her head and ending at the spiked heels on her boots. "But you really shouldn't be walking around like that, sweetheart."

"If you think I look good, you should see my friend." After a beat, she shifted her focus to Logan. "You're not really her type though, Cage."

Logan took her comment as a challenge. "I'm every woman's type, *Grayson*."

She stared at him for a long moment, then shrugged. "I guess I'm not every woman then." Smiling, she brushed her hands on her jeans. "Anyway, I just wanted to wish you luck, Chase."

"Thanks," I nodded, glancing at the clock for the hundredth time. "Are you sticking around for the show?"

"Wouldn't miss it," she said

"Blink and you might. I'm only doing a half set. Six songs."

"Maybe I'll see you after," she chirped. "You never know." She slid past Logan, who hadn't taken his eyes off her. "See y'all."

Logan whipped his head to me. "What was that about? Are you two ...?"

Closing my eyes, I shook my head. "You were there last week, right? When she stormed in and accused me of the hit-and-run on her best friend?"

Logan started to grumble, but I tuned him out. I had fifteen minutes to get my shit together. The nerves fluttering in my belly were not only uncomfortable, but disconcerting. I'd been on a stage before I could walk. The size of the crowd didn't matter. You couldn't see shit when you were under the lights. Which is why I never understood stage fright. You were alone up there.

Hands clammy, I recalled the half-ass pep talks my old man used to offer. It didn't help. My chest hadn't felt this tight since, well, since I barged into Taryn's beach house. But that didn't count.

I glanced at the beer in Logan's hand. And I cursed inwardly. My counselor told me that my mind would always go there. It always had. Even when I was clean, I had dirty thoughts. The difference was, now I admitted to them.

"I gotta make a call," I said as I shot to my feet.

Locking myself in the bathroom, I pulled the tattered piece of paper from my wallet. And then I called my sponsor.

Chapter 45

TARYN

I huddled in my seat near the stage, cursing my best friend's existence. A group of guys passed as they trudged by, slowing their pace to give me the once-over. I smiled tightly as I discreetly pulled on the neck of my low-cut blouse. Low cut was a nice way of saying there was nothing but skin between my neck and my navel.

Why did you let her talk you into this?

Not only did she wear me down at dinner the other night, convincing me to accompany her to the concert, but when I arrived at the lake house to get ready, she vetoed my skinny jeans and simple black button-down blouse. If I was truly serious about giving Austin a last hurrah, she'd quipped, I might as well go out in style.

Her style. Her old style, at least, judging by the amount of skin I had on display. She paired the barely there blouse with a short mini that made me glad I waxed. Yeah, it was that short.

I was about to dive under the seat when Tori teetered up, a big smile on her face and two plastic cups in hand.

"Where have you been?" I hissed, grabbing the extra-large frozen margarita.

She plopped into the seat next to me. "Long line at the concession stand." She took a drink, then smacked her lips. I gulped the frozen concoction like I hadn't had any liquid in days. "Chill out, T-Rex. You're going to get a ..."

"Ouch ... fuck!" I pressed my palm to my forehead.

"... brain freeze."

With my eyes screwed shut, I couldn't see her smile. But I heard it in her voice.

I gave her a sidelong glance while I continued to rub my forehead. "I'm plenty chilly, thanks to your fashion advice."

She settled into the chair, hooking the heel of her boot on the back of the seat in front of her. "Relax, you look hot."

Honestly, *she* looked hot. I'd seen the jeans before, ripped to show skin in all the right places. But she paired them with a tight shirt that showed a nice expanse of midriff. And the boots. God, I hadn't seen them in years. Black suede with four-inch heels.

Surprisingly, Tori wasn't getting the usual amount of "Belle Grayson" attention. She looked like every other twenty-something-year-old fan tonight.

I glanced over my shoulder, giving the bodyguard I'd hired on the down low a small smile. At Tori's insistence, we'd kept our plans for tonight completely secret. But I didn't want to end up on the wrong side of a mob, or something worse, if things got real. Don't get me wrong, this little adventure was fun. But she was her, and I was me, it was our band about to take the stage, and we were trying to blend in like tourists.

Tori sipped her drink, looking down her nose at her phone when Dylan's name lit the screen. She hit ignore, then fixed her gaze on the stage.

"Why didn't you tell Dylan where we were going?"

She shrugged. "He's with Beckett. Didn't want either of them to hulk out and ruin our fun."

Hiding my skepticism, I stared into my drink. "We're at the Caged show. You don't think they're going to find out?"

Another shrug. "You'll be on a plane in the morning. And Dylan

...." She blew out a breath. "He won't say anything. He might get angry, but he won't show it."

I wondered if that's the reason she never let their relationship blossom. Tori liked to fight. She preferred to win. But she never minded the battle. And her and Rhenn? God, they could battle.

The crowd milled around while we sipped our drinks in relative peace and companionable silence. It'd been years since I'd attended an event like this from the audience side. It was ... thrilling.

Tucked in a corner to the right of the stage, our seats provided an optimal view. To my surprise, we were basically alone. Nobody around us. This was an open-air concert, so any seat was a premium.

I finished the margarita, a buzz tingling through me. "Wonder where everyone is?"

"These are industry seats. I called in a favor. I want to experience the show, not fight off a mob."

Suddenly, someone appeared at our side, holding two drinks. I gaped as Tori reached past me, handing the dude a twenty in exchange for the beverages. "What?" She cocked a brow. "I got mad skills, or did you forget?"

She chuckled to herself as a single spot hit the stage. I whipped my head to Tori, smiling around her straw.

"How ...?" I croaked, as I turned my attention to the black Fender propped against the stool.

If she answered, I didn't hear. The crowd jumped to their feet, stomping, and clapping. And then he was there. Chase. Striding to his guitar, that victory grin on his face. And I couldn't think at all.

Chapter 46

CHASE

$\mathcal{M}$y fingers slid across the frets, my sweaty palm gripping the neck of the Fender. The crowd settled enough to hear my voice in the earpiece. As I prepared for the last song, I glanced down at the set list taped to my guitar.

Sweet Taryn.

Appropriate, since she was every song. And every lyric. Everything I'd ever wanted.

Adjusting the mic, I raised a hand and then waited for the applause to fade to a dull roar. "Hope y'all enjoyed the warm up. Before we get on to the main event ..." The crowd cheered and I glanced to the wings where Caged waited to take the stage. For all my resistance, I was grateful to my brother for this moment. Maybe the kid actually learned something in those therapy sessions. Something about me that even I didn't know.

"I'd like to play a song for someone special. This song is called "Blue-Eyed Summer.""

My fingers glided through the chords as I began to sing.

"Can you take my broken soul? Were you sent to make me whole?

Take me, baby, make me your own. Don't believe what you can't be shown.

Thoughts they scatter, twisting and turning. Blue eyed summer's got me burning.

Always in my head, every song I sing.

Tied me up and tied me down, hanging on a string.

Thoughts they scatter, twisting turning. Blue eyed baby, you've got me burning."

My eyes fluttered open as the last lyric floated to the rafters. It took me a minute to process the tiny flickers of light glowing in the abyss beyond the stage as faceless strangers held their lighters and cell phones to the sky. The roar that followed nearly cracked me in half. I was right. The song I'd written for the girl with the sad blue eyes was my best. Soft, but with a hard edge. Like us.

I wobbled to my feet, then waved. Even if I had another song to play I wouldn't. And I knew in that instant, I'd never be here again, on stage. And I was fine with it. At peace, finally.

Slinging the Fender behind my back, I strode toward Cameron with a wide smile. He wrapped me in a hug the minute I stepped behind the curtain. Not a bro hug ... well, technically it was, since he was my brother. But this embrace was much more. He held on as I let go ... of everything. Jealousy I'd never known I carried. Resentment. All of it.

"Fuck ... that was awesome," he croaked as he pulled away.

I wasn't going to give him shit for the tears that glistened in his eyes. Hell, I was misty myself.

"Like I said, you better bring your 'A' game tonight."

I patted Logan, Sean, and Christian on the back, stepping outside the circle before things got any heavier. The announcer's voice echoed in the deserted maze as I made my way back to the tent serving as a green room.

Rounding the corner, my steps faltered. Considering my history with drugs, I thought for a moment that maybe it was all in my head. A flashback. Because there was no way that Taryn was six feet in front of me, tears streaking her face. There was no way she was running toward me on impossibly high heels. And there was no way her lips were pressed against mine.

I buried my hand in her hair, grasping the strands tightly. "You're here." My forehead rested against hers, but I'd yet to open my eyes for fear she'd disappear. I just stood there, breathing in her rain shower scent. "Why?"

Shut the fuck up, you moron.

It didn't matter why. It didn't matter how long. Nothing mattered.

She brushed my lips again, and I groaned. Loudly. Her mouth curved into a smile. "I didn't know you were going to be performing. Tori brought me and ..."

I looked down at her chest, rising and falling as her breath evened. "If she's responsible for this outfit," I kissed her neck, "thank her for me. Then burn it." I nuzzled her ear. "But keep the shoes."

Music spilled into the hallway along with the roar of the crowd. I had so many questions. But I couldn't ask them here. "Are you ..." I cleared my throat. "Can we go somewhere? Back to your loft?" Her forehead creased, so I tightened my grip reflexively. "Just to talk."

"It's not that." She tipped her chin. "I sublet my loft. It's a mess."

Pain shot through me, but I kept my composure. "Okay. How about my place, or we could go get something to eat somewhere?"

"Your place is fine."

Desire filled her stormy eyes. But we'd always had that. I pushed aside the knowledge that nothing had changed. In fact, this was worse. She'd subleased her place, solidified her plans.

But this time, I'd fight. I was up for the fight. All I needed was a chance, and a little sliver of light under the door she'd closed in her heart so I could edge my way inside.

"Is that so?" I slid my hand to the curve of her ass. "What do you have in mind, baby?"

"You and me in your bed." She entwined our fingers. "Naked." A slow smile crossed my face as she led me to the exit. "Except for the shoes. I'll keep those on."

Cursing, I slid my mouth from Taryn's as I tried to find the light switch in the narrow stairwell. The single bulb illuminated the space, and she came into focus. Tousled hair, swollen lips, and her blouse askew, the neckline hanging off one shoulder. I thought I'd done a pretty good job holding off on the car ride over. I guess I was wrong.

She pulled off her shoes, then scurried up the steps with me in hot pursuit. "I thought you were going to keep those on," I growled, snaking an arm around her waist as I pulled her back against my chest, walking us toward the bed.

She tugged on the zipper of her skirt, and it fell to the floor. "Don't worry, I'll put them back on. I never knew you had a thing for heels."

"I've got a thing for you." I spun her around, then yanked the blouse—and I used the term loosely, since it barely covered her tits— over her head. "Fuck, baby, I ..." *Love you.* "... Missed you."

I tipped her onto her back, and she landed on the mattress. Locking our gaze, she slid her black lace thong over her hips.

"Show me," she breathed, her knees falling open.

I shed my clothes like they were burning my skin while she removed her bra. Dropping to my knees in front of the bed, I looped my arms around her legs. I dragged my tongue up her inner thigh, then placed a kiss on her swollen nub. Her hips shot off the bed.

"Chase?" Her fingers slid across my scalp.

"Hmm?" She tugged my hair gently, so I looked up.

I was ready for some type of disclaimer.

This is only for one night. This doesn't change anything. Can you drive me to the airport when we're finished?

That last one was a little far-fetched. Still, I went there.

Reluctantly, I climbed onto the bed. We met in the middle, facing each other.

"I don't know if this can work," she said softly, her fingertips grazing my cheek. "It's probably a bad idea."

Coppery blood trickled from the inside of my lip as I bit down to keep from running her over with my rebuttal.

She pressed a kiss to my mouth. "I love you, Chase." A wary smile curved her lips.

"Then why ..."

The "why" was evident. Betting on me probably made Beckett look like a sure thing.

"Because I'm scared." She cringed. "I believe that you love me ... now. But ..."

I'd just spent months training myself to live in the now. Now was all we had. It was a rule I had to live by. I blew out a breath, then chuckled. Because I was never good at following the rules.

"Tomorrow's not promised, baby. It's a gift." Her back stiffened, so I pulled her close. "If you want me to wrap it up in a bow and give it to you ... I will. All my tomorrows." I took her hand, pressing her palm to my heart. "You own me. But there's nothing I can say to convince you. So, let's just let it happen. Let me prove it to you. Please ... just let me."

Her mouth crashed into mine with such force our teeth clanked. "I love you," she murmured between kisses.

I rolled on my back, pulling her on top of me. "Say it again."

"I—"

"No." She fused her lips together, and I smiled. "Say it when I'm inside you."

The lamp on the nightstand crashed to the floor as I jerked open the drawer. I grabbed at whatever was in the compartment, frantically searching through the mess for a condom. Taryn laughed, and reached all the way to the back, pulling out a foil strip. "Looking for these?"

"Yeah ..." I gave her a sheepish grin. "You might want to blow the dust off the package. They've been in there for a while."

She tore the wrapper with her teeth, then slid down my body. A grin lifted her lips.

I was ready to explode as it is. If she wrapped her mouth around my cock, I might ...

Fuck. I cursed, sliding my hand into her hair. She damn near swallowed me. My free hand gripped the comforter as I tried to think of anything but the tightening in my balls and her head bobbing beneath my hand. She moaned, and a jolt of electricity shot to my spine. I clenched every fucking muscle in my body to keep from giving in. "Baby ... come here," I bit out. "Now."

She slid up, and we were nose-to-nose, her chestnut hair curtaining our faces.

"Say it now, Taryn." Her sweet pussy beckoned, and I couldn't hold back any longer.

"I love you ..." She sank on top of me. "I love you so much."

I grasped her hips, holding her still. "I love you."

She smiled a smile I'd never seen, and then her eyes fluttered closed. When I finally began to move, I slid a hand into her hair and pulled her flush against my chest. And I knew right then, I'd follow wherever she led. I was lost and I was found and I was complete. And for the first time in my life, totally at peace.

Chapter 47

TARYN

*D*rawn to the sound of rain on the window, I snuck out of bed and shuffled to the wall of glass. Sixth Street was still alive, and I smiled at the people running to take cover from the sudden shower.

Resting my forehead against the glass, my lids fluttered closed.

After the initial euphoria of our reunion wore off, Chase and I had spent hours talking, and my mind was brimming with thoughts about our future.

Chase's addiction didn't scare me. Not being scared about Chase's addiction ... that's what scared me.

Was I fooling myself? Blind like always.

"*No,*" came the voice in my head. And my heart stuttered. My mind hadn't conjured Paige's voice in so long.

"Are you sure?" I whispered.

Peels of laughter tinkled in my head, lighting the dark place where her memory would always live. "*No.*"

A tear slid down my cheek. "A lot of help you are."

"*Are you happy?*"

I nodded. Because I was. For the first time, maybe.

"*Well, there you go ...*" More laughter, and then ... nothing.

My eyes popped open when Chase's arms banded around my waist. "What's so funny, baby?"

I slanted my gaze to his. "Huh?"

He dropped a kiss to my forehead. "You're laughing. What's so funny?"

Shifting my focus back to the window, I searched the feathery wisps of gray for an answer. And then I saw them—two perfect stars, illumining a small patch of clear sky.

Tears gathered, the good kind, and I melted against him. "I'm just happy."

Finally.

"I love you, Taryn," he whispered as he nuzzled my hair. "Come back to bed and let me show you."

I pressed my fingertips to the glass, warmed by the yellow glow from those two little stars. And then I took Chase's hand, and let our future begin.

EPILOGUE

TARYN

FOUR MONTHS LATER

*P*ropping the phone between my shoulder and my ear, I pulled the plate of leftover spaghetti from the microwave.

"Where have you been?" I hissed a breath as I walked to the couch, jumbling the hot plate. "I've been trying to get a hold of you for hours."

Chase and I had taken the art of phone contact to a new level. I spent half the day with my Bluetooth attached, his voice humming in my ear. Sometimes we even fell asleep like that.

"I had some business to attend to, woman," he teased. "Why, did something interesting happen in the last five hours?"

"No." I sulked, twining some noodles on my fork. "I just ..."

Miss you. God, I was pathetic. We'd just seen each other four days ago when he flew out to see me.

"Yeah, I know, baby," he said softly. "I miss you too."

"I wasn't going to say that," I lied.

He chuckled, glossing right over my attempt at deception. "So you don't miss me?"

"Of course I miss you." I tried my best to infuse some cheer into my tone. "You sound like you're driving."

"Yep, on my way home."

My heart stuttered when I thought of him gliding down Sixth Street. I looked out the window at the dusky sky. The horizon glowed orange and pink, the last rays of sun casting an opal shimmer off the water.

"It's already dark there," I said quietly. "But the sun is still hanging on out here. You should see it." My voice trembled with emotion. "It's beautiful."

"Baby, if you're so miserable, why don't you just come home?"

A tear slid down my cheek. "I will. Just not yet. With Metro forging ahead with their bogus ass lawsuit, I've got to be available for depositions."

"You can't do that from Austin?"

I could. But there were logistical details to take into consideration. Closing the office here. My lease on the bungalow. Finding a new counselor. That was a big one. I'd finally taken steps to deal with the grief and the guilt over the accident. Over Paige.

And then there was the fact that I had no place to live in Austin.

"It's not that easy to pick up and leave at the drop of a hat," I said glumly.

"I guess you're right."

Silence stretched, the burden of our distance weighing me down. I shifted my gaze to my Blue Amaryllis tucked in a corner by the window, her petals reaching toward the sun. Always reaching. With or without Chase, I would be fine. I was fine. I just missed him. So much it hurt.

My appetite gone, I dumped the food in the sink. "How was your day?" I forced a smile, even though he couldn't see it. "Any new plans to take over the world?"

"Not today. Just looking forward to stretching out with a plate of barbecue."

I groaned as the limp noodles slid into the garbage disposal. "Franklin's?"

He laughed. "What else?"

"So. Not. Fair." I sighed again. "On that note, I'm going to take a shower and leave you to your food orgy. I'll call you in a little while." I paused for a moment, listening to his soft breath in my ear. "I love you."

"Not as much as I love you."

We could do this for ten minutes, go back and forth. But tonight, I couldn't handle it. I hit end on the call, then plugged the phone into the charger.

The pipes in the old house rattled as I set the water for my shower. Steam rose, tickling my nose with the scent of Chase's body wash as I poured a liberal amount onto my sponge. It was a manly scent, not suitable at all for me. But I used it anyway. Along with his shampoo.

Yeah, I'd officially taken the turn into crazy town.

Panic rose in my throat when the front door slammed. I know I set the alarm. Leaving the water to run, I reached for a towel, securing it around my body.

Cupboards opened and closed. Then drawers. Someone was definitely here. Fuck. I was being robbed. Frantically I looked around for my phone. *No!* It was in the dining room.

Tiptoeing into the bedroom, I grabbed the guitar Chase kept beside the bed and then slipped into the hallway, leaving puddles of water in my wake.

I swallowed hard as a huge shadow sprawled over the hardwood.

Holding the guitar over my head with both hands, I shot into the living room. "Stop right there!"

Chase turned to me, amusement coating his features. "You hungry, baby? I brought barbecue."

His grin evaporated when the guitar crashed to the floor and I reached for the wall to steady myself. "What the hell?" Spots danced in front of my eyes as I clutched my chest. I couldn't take a full breath to save my life.

Chase was in front of me in a flash, holding my soapy body

against his chest. "Easy, baby." He captured my chin, tilting my face to his. "It's just me." He brushed a kiss to my lips. "Just me."

"I thought ... you said ..." I pressed my palm to his chest. He was here. Really here. "You said you were going home."

"I am home, baby." He rested his forehead against mine. "Anywhere you are. That's home."

Chase made a second pass at my towel when I reached for another rib. I slapped his hand.

"Eating here," I growled, fingers dripping with barbecue sauce.

He gripped my chair, dragging it next to his. Soft lips brushed my ear. "I'd like to eat too." He reached under the terrycloth. "God, I love the way you smell." He inhaled sharply, then tipped back, confusion lining his brow. "Usually. Tonight you smell like—" he took another deep breath. "—me."

Color rose in my cheeks. "I ran out of body wash, so I used yours."

From the grin on his mug, he saw right through me.

"Sure you did. You just like smelling like me." Heat flooded my stomach as his fingers danced along my inner thigh. Clenching my legs, I trapped his hand.

"Knew it." He nipped my shoulder and then moved north.

Abandoning the rib, I dropped my head back to give him greater access. "I'm full of barbecue sauce."

I groaned as his teeth scored the sensitive flesh on my neck.

And then he licked a bit of sauce from the corner of my mouth. "Umm ... mesquite."

Scooping me off the chair, he strolled toward the bedroom. As he undressed, I scooted to the head of the bed. He looked at me quizzically as he eased to my side. "What is it, baby?"

Time, that's what. There was never enough. "When do you go back to Austin?"

Rolling on his back, he tucked his arm behind his head. "Depends."

I curled into his side. "On what?"

"On you." He stroked my thigh. "How long is it going to take you to wrap things up around here?"

"I don't know." I peered up at him. "A couple of months, maybe."

"A couple of months it is then."

I sat up. "Chase, you can't—"

"I can—" Entwining our fingers, he pressed a kiss to the back of my hand. "And I did. There are three suitcases in the trunk of the rental car."

"What about the studio?" Averting his gaze, he blew out a breath. The longer he stayed silent, the more my stomach knotted. "Chase, what is it?"

"Metro served me with an injunction." Closing his eyes, he shook his head. "I want to rip Mac's fucking head off and skull fuck the son of a bitch."

I blanched at the visual. "What are you going to do?"

He caressed his thumb over mine. "The question is: what are we going to do?"

"We?"

"We're partners, baby." He sighed. "Or we will be as soon as you sign the paperwork with Twin Souls." Clouds gathered in his eyes. "Tori and I were talking. Maybe it's not the best time to fold Ayers PR into the mix."

"Why?"

"Because talent is you're only business. If Mac's people seize your accounts ..."

"He can do that?" My thoughts hopscotched straight over Ayers PR to Twin Souls. "What about Tori?"

Cupping my cheek, he smoothed the tension lines around my mouth. "Tori's got millions in the reserve account. There's nothing legally in place to keep her from moving that money, but she needs your signature to do it."

I blinked. "I don't ... I haven't even signed the partnership agreement yet."

We'd been trying to hammer out the details for two weeks, Tori's attorney and mine. She drove a hard bargain, that girl. I abandoned the lawyer four days ago and just called her. When she wouldn't relent, I signed the letter of intent granting me a fifty percent stake in Twin Souls.

Chase smiled thoughtfully and said, "Because the reserve account is in your name as well." He brushed his thumb over my lips to silence me when I went to speak. "It's always been like that, baby. I saw the account months ago when Tori and I set up the joint venture for the studio."

I sank back. "Oh ..."

"Anyway," Chase continued, "I've got some land; it's worth about twice what's in the reserve account. I'm going to sell it to y'all for half of what it's worth. You'll form an LLC to protect it, just you and Tori. Even if the market takes a shit, you'll be covered with that kind of equity."

I shook my head. "I can't ... you can't do that." Emotion clogged my throat. "I won't let you."

He laughed. "I love you, baby, but you don't 'let me' do anything." Pulling me to him, he pressed a kiss to my lips. "I'm doing it because I want to. For you. Tori's protected. The Damaged music catalog is her sole property except for the small annuity she set up for Miles."

"But I have money coming in," I insisted. "The Big Three. I've got an exclusive on the PR." Chase inhaled slowly, and I sat up. "There's something you're not telling me."

"Mac enjoined them in the action, all of them. Breach of contract. Fiduciary interest. Promissory Estoppel. All of it."

My eyes widened. "What about The Phoenix Group?"

"The Phoenix Group is worth about four hundred million dollars, baby. And growing. Sure, I've got a huge chunk of change invested in the studio, but Metro can't do shit to keep me from developing land." He shrugged. "Mac can't touch me."

I sank against him. I don't know which was harder to absorb, my boyfriend's astronomical wealth or my possible demise.

"Listen." He rolled over, trapping me underneath him. "I won't let anything happen to you. You'll have plenty of money to weather this."

I tried to shake my head, but he held my chin. "Not my money ... yours. Trust me, baby." His brow creased. "You do trust me, don't you? There are fail-safes. If anything ever happened ..." He swallowed hard. "With me. The Phoenix Group and all the holdings are protected."

Grimacing, I squeezed my eyes shut. I couldn't think about anything happening to Chase. "Don't ever say that to me." Tears spilled from the corners of my eyes. "Nothing is going to happen to you. I couldn't ... that couldn't happen. Not again."

"I wasn't talking about dying, baby." He tucked a strand of hair behind my ear, a sad smile lifting his lips. "You're fucking amazing, you know that?" Shaking his head, he looked away. "So fucking amazing."

And then it dawned on me. Chase was talking about his addiction. Even though I'd attended family sessions at the local NA chapter like he'd asked, my mind rarely went there. Chase was so strong. So capable. Of course, I didn't see him at his worst. He made sure of it.

"So everything is going to be all right?" My voice was thin, reedy, to my own ears. I cleared my throat. "And you're going to stay here until ..."

He kissed me again. Soft, sweet, and chaste. "Until."

I hated to ask him for anything else. I was in the negative category as it was. "Can you do me a favor?"

Distracted, he sprinkled kisses on my collarbone. "Anything."

"If a loft becomes available at Bluebonnet Towers can you ... I don't know ..." My cheeks heated. "Put me at the top of the list."

"Why?" He murmured. "What's wrong with your loft? Do you need more space?"

I pushed him backward to look into his eyes. "My loft was subletted. I don't have a loft anymore. I told you that."

Another laugh. I was getting tired of being kept out of the joke.

"Your loft is safe and sound," he said, his lips curving into his signature victory smile. "And waiting for you."

"How ...?"

"Do we have to talk about this now?" Gritting my teeth, I nodded, even as he circled my nipple with his thumb, bringing it to a painful peak. "Okay, then," he grumbled. "Legally, you can't lease your loft without my, er, The Phoenix Group's, approval." He smiled innocently. "I didn't approve."

I wiggled out from under him. "What are you talking about? I signed paperwork. Paid a realtor." My eyes widened. "That couple ... I made an agreement."

"That couple is one floor up. In a bigger loft." He cocked a brow. "For the same lease amount. I even gave them an additional two-year option at the same rate to sweeten the pot." He entwined our fingers, pulling our joined hands over my head. "Happy?"

Deliriously. Unrepentantly. Unabashedly.

There were more adjectives I could use. Three wasn't enough. Three thousand didn't come close. But Chase's mouth was on mine, his tongue sliding between my lips. And when he pushed me into the mattress, I melted beneath the weight of his love. But I didn't disappear. Chase wasn't the sun, and I didn't live in his reflection, fearful that one day the music would stop. Because we made the music, he and I.

One note at a time.

JAYNE SAID:

I hope you enjoyed *Lost For You.*

As always when I write a story, I try to draw on real life to enrich the characters. In this book, Taryn spent quite a bit of time coming to terms with the death of her best friend, Paige. That part of the plot hit very close to home for me, as I lost my childhood best friend when I was twenty in an unspeakable tragedy.

Her loss is something I've never completely gotten over. And while I'm no longer mired in grief, I still think about Bonnie everyday, and her unfinished life. And maybe that's how it's supposed to be. A lesson I was supposed to learn.

Life is precious. And sometimes short. Bitter and sweet and everything in between. And as Chase so eloquently put it, "a gift."

Thank you for reading. See you next time. :)

ACKNOWLEDGMENTS

Jeff—My twin soul. *Words and music, baby*.
Matthew and Victoria— You are everything to me.
Bonnie Marie—Always in my thoughts. I love you.
Patricia— For all that you do and all that you are.

And finally—to all the readers—*thank you*.

ABOUT THE AUTHOR

Jayne Frost, author of the Sixth Street Bands Romance Series, grew up in California with a dream of moving to Seattle to become a rock star. When the grunge thing didn't work out (she never even made it to the Washington border) Jayne set her sights on Austin, Texas. After quickly becoming immersed in the Sixth Street Music scene...and discovering she couldn't actually sing, Jayne decided to do the next best thing—write kick ass romances about hot rockstars and the women that steal their hearts.

Want to join the tour and become a Jayne Frost VIP?
Sign up for the **Sixth Street Heat Newsletter**
http://bit.ly/2fS3xiQ
to receive exclusive members only content, swag, giveaway
opportunities, and all the latest news.

ALSO BY JAYNE FROST

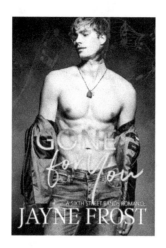

Gone For You —Sixth Street Bands #1

Fall With Me—Sixth Street Bands #2

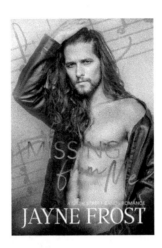

Missing From Me— Sixth Street Bands #3